Pel and the perfect partner

Chief Inspector Evariste Clovis Désiré Pel was missing. Kidnapped? Held for ransom? To be traded for the release of prisoners? Murdered? To Inspector Daniel Darcy, Pel's deputy, all these possibilities were appalling. Brave and still calm, panic button on hold, Madame Pel was also beginning to worry.

At the Hôtel de Police nothing extraordinary was afoot, just the usual five million cases of drunk and disorderly, swindles, theft, rape and violence.

But the next day, the press reported the escape of 'The Poltergeist' from the high security prison of Fresnes. Two hundred thousand police all over France were on major alert. And locally, in beautiful Burgundy, things began to hot up: a daring midnight robbery from the gun room of wealthy Baron de Charnet's château, and a collection of diamonds stolen from a high street jeweller's safe.

Miraculously, Madame Pel had received a phone call: her husband was alive.

Assisted by two new recruits to his investigating team – a stately Arab and a luscious lady biker and university student of criminology – the newly restored Pel not only nails the country's most dangerous criminal but reveals the mystery of his strange disappearance. Juliet Hebden's wondrous assumption of her father Mark's mantle is manifested in this her second Inspector Pel novel. Inventive, humorous and affectionate, it is a delight from start to finish.

PEL AND THE PERFECT PARTNER

Juliet Hebden

Constable · London

First published in Great Britain 1994
by Constable & Company Ltd
3 The Lanchesters, 162 Fulham Palace Road
London W6 9ER
Copyright © 1994 by Juliet Hebden
The right of Juliet Hebden to be identified
as the author of this work has been asserted
by her in accordance with the Copyright,
Designs and Patents Act 1988
ISBN 0 09 473310 4
Set in Palatino 10 pt by
The Electronic Book Factory, Fife
Printed and bound in Great Britain by
Hartholls Limited, Bodmin, Cornwall.

A CIP catalogue record for this book
is available from the British Library

1

Pel was missing. Kidnapped? To be held for ransom or traded for the release of prisoners? Murdered? It was an appalling idea but Inspector Daniel Darcy had to consider the possibilities.

Darcy, for once, hadn't been dragged from the bed of a passionate girlfriend. He'd been sitting in his own flat gritting his newly mended brilliant white teeth and trying to be faithful to Kate. But with the girl he loved living so far away he was finding it hard. When Madame Pel's phone call roused him from his nail biting, he was only too pleased to leap from his chair and gallop to her side like the knight in shining armour he liked to think he was.

As he arrived in front of Pel's house Madame opened the door with an elegant but worried frown on her face.

'Daniel!' she exclaimed, obviously relieved to see him. 'I'm sorry to trouble you so late, but I'm beginning to worry.'

Darcy crossed the threshold and installed himself in the *salon*, noticing as he passed the kitchen door that their housekeeper, Madame Routy, a dragon in disguise, was crashing her casseroles about in an ear-shattering way. Pel would have been pleased to have so successfully upset the evening of his old enemy from his bachelor days.

Madame Pel smiled bravely as she sat opposite Inspector Darcy. She had always had a soft spot for him and his sparkling Disney smile, as it was he who had finally persuaded her that Pel, his senior officer, was not such a bad catch after all, and all the faltering courtship needed was time and patience – that and a great deal of tender loving care. He'd been right and, although Pel wouldn't have given himself house room, his wife curiously loved him dearly. She was therefore always pleased to see Darcy's handsome face, particularly now his broken teeth, once demolished by a rifle butt, had been reinstated, as white and shining as before.

Madame Routy, the housekeeper, ceased throwing pots and pans about in the kitchen to provide them with a tray of coffee. Leaving it noisily on the small table in front of the sofa, she left the room wringing her hands as she clumped across the *carrelage* in what Darcy could have sworn were hob-nailed boots.

'He rang early this afternoon,' Madame Pel said, as she poured Darcy his coffee. 'I had come home early to finish some paperwork. Pel, bless him, for once had remembered our wedding anniversary and rang to say he had booked a table at Le Relais St Armand for eight o'clock. It's in the Avenue Maréchal Foch, and where we first met. I was really quite surprised, and very touched,' she added. 'He's a dear man, but police work comes before everything. It was the first time he'd remembered our anniversary.'

Darcy sipped his coffee silently, knowing it had been thanks to Annie Saxe, the only female member of Pel's team and a very necessary addition. She had noted all the team's birthdays and anniversaries in a diary, and reminded them gently as anything that concerned each member arose. Thus, for once, wives and children stopped complaining that the police force was manned by selfish and unromantic people. It was a small thing, but a bright idea, much appreciated by the over-worked and sometimes regrettably forgetful men of the force.

'When he didn't arrive, I assumed that, as usual, something had cropped up at work and he would arrive a little later. I rang the Hôtel de Police at ten o'clock, however, and they told me they hadn't seen him since six, which was when he passed the desk clerk on his way out. The desk clerk remembered clearly, because Pel was cheerful and actually managed to wish him a good evening. Usually,' she said, her eyes twinkling as she thought of her husband, 'apparently, Pel scowls and makes his departure like a prisoner escaping from jail.' She took a dainty sip of her coffee before rising to fetch the brandy bottle and two glasses. Without asking she poured two good measures for herself and Darcy. 'Darcy,' she said confidentially, almost

6

in a whisper, 'it's not like him. He can be bloody-minded, we all know that, and I know I come second to his work, but he's always careful to let me know if he's likely to be late. Always. This time not even the duty officer rang with a message. Now that it's past midnight I'm worried.' She took a gulp at her brandy and shivered slightly as she swallowed. 'Very worried.'

Darcy had to admit it was odd. He was well used to Pel creating fireworks one way or another: the whole of Burgundy was well acquainted with his ability to put the fear of God into policemen and villains alike. He was also well known for the clouds of blue smoke that enveloped him constantly from the million packets of Gauloises he was forced to smoke every day through stress and pressure of work, but disappearing acts were something completely new, and very out of character. Crossing to the phone he frowned heavily. As he gave his instructions to a colleague at the Hôtel de Police he realised he too was worried.

Putting the receiver back in its cradle, he was still frowning. 'I think, madame, that may bring results. We should know shortly if he's anywhere on our patch. You never know,' he added cheerfully, for her sake, 'he may have been witness to something bizarre and has stayed while statements are taken.'

'Or been involved in an accident himself,' she replied. It had not gone unnoticed that Darcy had asked for a search to be made at the local hospitals as well as the gendarmeries in the area. Everyone, particularly his wife, knew Pel's reputation as a driver. When there was no one else on the roads Pel managed quite well behind the steering wheel of his car. But usually he arrived at his destination perspiring freely, having escaped collision at least once by the skin of his teeth. Even with their brand new Citroën, which Madame had delicately forced Pel to buy, he still left a trail of motorists in his wake mouthing expletives and shaking their fists. In the old days he'd said it was because the car was too old and didn't respond quickly enough; now it was because the car was too new and had too many gadgets to be controllable. For all his efforts, but mainly because he always had too many things on his mind, Pel was a bad driver.

As Darcy went back to sit beside his boss's wife, his mind was on the cases they were involved in, searching for a reason for his Patron's sudden disappearance.

'As far as I know,' he said eventually, 'there was nothing extraordinary on the books at the moment, just the usual five million cases of drunk and disorderly, swindles, theft, rape and general violence. We have a series of robberies that are becoming an embarrassment to the crime-fighting statistics, an illegal immigrant problem that's surprising us all, and the eternal drugs problem coming from the coast into our area. We're working away slowly and surely at them all but it'll take time before we crack any of them. Nothing really extraordinary at all for once.'

Madame smiled. She knew only too well the work load under which they operated. 'No,' she agreed, 'he seemed quite calm at the moment. For Pel, that is.'

When Darcy's colleague phoned back he had nothing to report. Pel was nowhere to be found; he must therefore be presumed missing.

'I think we should make it official,' Darcy suggested as he rose to leave.

'You don't think it's too soon?' Madame was not wishing to panic, although she could feel it stirring in the pit of her stomach. 'There could be a very simple explanation.'

Darcy looked at her. 'Do you really think so?' he asked gently. 'Chief Inspector Pel is not a man who moves about in mysterious or secretive ways. When he does something, even drink a beer in the Bar Transvaal, he is noticed. I think I should act now, or at least first thing in the morning when I've discussed it with the Chief – he obviously should be the one to make the decision.' He flashed his film star smile at her. 'And when your husband rockets through the door at the Hôtel de Police first thing tomorrow morning, as if nothing unusual has happened, I shall take great pleasure in ticking him off for being so inconsiderate.' He was trying to make light of something that he sensed was very serious.

Madame felt the same, but had no wish to put her anxiety into words. Instead, she quietly closed her front door on Darcy's retreating shadow and went to calm Madame Routy in the kitchen, who had by this time successfully broken half a dozen glasses in her excited state of true French nerves.

Turning the ignition key in his car, Darcy frowned. He had a nasty feeling that Pel wouldn't turn up the following morning in his usual bad mood at all.

<h1 style="text-align:center">2</h1>

The following morning, as Darcy had suspected, Pel didn't appear in his usual bad mood. He was obliged to inform the Chief of his disappearance. The Chief was a large man who had been a boxing champion in his youth; this gave him the appearance of a friendly buffalo only just under control. On hearing the news of Pel's absence he leapt from his chair, upsetting half a dozen filing trays that had been sitting innocently on the edge of his desk.

As they crouched on the floor to recover the spilled papers, Darcy reiterated the events that had led to his conclusion that Pel had been abducted or worse.

'What the hell was he working on?' the Chief bellowed.

'Nothing special. You've seen the case book yourself.'

'But we've got to find the little bugger, he's the lynch pin in this department. It'll fall to pieces without him. He can be a prize pain in the backside, but my God, he's a necessary one.'

The Chief had summed up Chief Inspector Evariste Clovis Désiré Pel in a few words. Darcy was inclined to agree with the Chief's summing up. Pel was a difficult man to work for, particularly when he treated you to one of his blood-curdling scowls. In fact, Darcy was convinced that his boss had practised his famous scowl in front of a mirror for years before releasing it on the world in general, particularly on whimpering criminals or complaining young policemen. But for all his bad moods and well-used scowls, he was a fair man, scrupulously fair, and there was a surprising feeling of affection for him amongst his team members: affection and respect. The choking clouds of cigarette smoke insinuating their way round his office door would be sorely missed without Pel in residence. The joke about police-issue gas-masks when called for a meeting with him would no longer be funny, no longer be cracked. His intense intelligent bespectacled face, topped by thinning hair that lay across his head like wet seaweed on a rock, would be missed. He was a dynamic little man with a brain that whirred like an old computer that slowly but surely came up with the right answer. He was a damned good detective and they knew it.

Having retrieved most of his files from the floor, the Chief threw them haphazardly on to his desk without a second glance. 'Contact the stations, the airports, the autoroute pay kiosks,' he said. 'Contact the taxis, the buses, the tramps that lurk about the city at night. The prostitutes, the pimps, the villains – in fact anyone and everyone you can think of who may have been on the streets between six and midnight last night.'

'The entire 146,703 inhabitants, in fact,' Darcy said, 'not to mention the other couple of hundred thousand who come into the city to work from surrounding villages and towns, and who would normally be leaving again between six o'clock and eight.'

The Chief stared at him coldly. 'I mean precisely that,' he said, 'and I want it done quietly. The press are not to hear of Pel's disappearance. If they get hold of the story the city's criminals will hang out the flags and have a fête day. If they know Pel's no longer on his patch there'll be no stopping them.'

The Chief was exaggerating, but he had a point. Darcy turned to leave the office.

'By the way,' the Chief called him back, 'it has been reported in today's nationals that the Poltergeist escaped from the high security prison at Fresnes yesterday evening. All hell has broken loose in and around Paris and the 200,000 police and gendarmes all over la République Française have been instructed to be on their toes. That includes us. The Poltergeist is considered a dangerous man and he must be recovered. Apparently, he is believed to be still in France – perhaps you can camouflage your questions about Pel by supposedly investigating the Poltergeist's escape.'

As Darcy left the office, he sighed; even the pretence of making inquiries about an escaped prisoner wouldn't hide their questions about Pel for long. However, with the journalists tied up with such a good scoop, it was possible he could at least keep it out of the newspapers for a while. Although he wasn't sure – a local story was always the best sort of story for local newspapers. He was going to have to be cunning to get the local journalists to co-operate.

Outside the office door Darcy stopped. The thoughts that occupied his mind like an unwelcome mother-in-law had brought him blindly down the corridor to ask advice from his boss. He was standing outside Pel's door. But there were no wisps of blue smoke curling out through the keyhole. The room was empty and fog-free. This time Darcy had to make the decision alone. As second-in-command of the department he was now responsible for its running. He was perfectly capable; that was why Pel had chosen him and why he'd been promoted. Darcy trusted Pel's judgement; he knew he was capable of taking over. He'd done it on the few occasions that Madame Pel had kindly bullied her husband into taking a holiday. Darcy was a good detective, Pel had said so himself, although at the time it had been a rather back-handed compliment, but he'd said it all the same. Briefly he wondered when Pel would finally surface to terrorise them all again. If he surfaced. He had to face the possibility that he might not come back at all. Life without Pel would be very peaceful, but it would be dull! The idea disturbed Darcy more than he liked to admit.

However, the show must go on, and doing what he suspected Pel would have done, he called the two senior officers of his team to his office.

Newly married Nosjean was the first to arrive, looking as if he'd crawled out of a dog's basket – a scruffy dog's basket. His usual youthful shining face, which made him look like the young Napoleon on the bridge at Lodi, was tending to be frayed at the edges since he'd returned from his honeymoon a few weeks previously.

'How's married life?' Darcy asked as Nosjean fell into a chair on the other side of his desk.

11

'The *voyage de noces* after the wedding was great. All I had to do was lie under a palm tree all day and recuperate my strength for the following night, but a riotous sex life and being a policeman don't go together. I'm finding it exhausting. How do you do it?'

'I don't any more,' Darcy said seriously, 'but when I did,' he went on, grinning, 'I must admit it took a bit of practice. The more you do it the better you get.'

'A question of training, then, I suppose.' Nosjean sighed. 'Perhaps I'll get used to it before they cart me off to a convalescence centre. At the moment I feel as if I'm approaching the *troisième age* before I've even made it to middle age.'

Nosjean's voice trailed off as de Troq' slid through the door without making a sound. The aristocratic member of their team, though claiming to be impoverished, the Baron Charles Victor de Troquereau de Tournay-Turenne, was impeccably dressed and he managed to make his presence felt without saying a word. Looking younger than his age, he had surprised a number of villains and policemen by his efficiency and cool-headed application to his job. Both he and Nosjean could be relied on to behave with discretion.

However, Darcy wasn't sure how to break the news to them. Lighting a cigarette, he inhaled deeply and decided there was only one way.

'Pel's disappeared,' he said simply. The reaction was as expected. Even de Troq' slipped momentarily from his ice-cool perch and dramatically raised an eyebrow. 'But no one's to know,' Darcy went on quickly before the questions started. 'So far the duty sergeant last night has his suspicions, but I managed to nobble him when I arrived. The Chief knows, of course, but he has asked for silence, at least until we know a bit more about it. Madame Pel fortunately isn't the panicking type and has reassured me that their housekeeper has been metaphorically bound and gagged for the time being, she's not letting the old girl out of her sight. I'd rather you told no one else, even here at the Hôtel de Police – especially Misset,' he added as an afterthought.

'As if we'd tell Misset anything,' commented Nosjean.

Misset was the weak link in their team, and while nothing

had ever been proved it was suspected that he occasionally leaked snippets of information to the press for a bit of pocket money.

'For the moment,' Darcy continued, 'we are to make our inquiries as quietly as possible, under cover of the escape of the Poltergeist, though God knows it'll still be difficult. We'll slice the city into four sectors and spend the day digging into the dark corners. Take one section each with Didier Darras for the fourth. He grew up next door to Pel, before he married and moved – he's always been very fond of the Old Man and can be trusted to keep his mouth shut. We'll keep the whole thing on a low profile and hope the press don't find out.'

'Hope won't keep them from finding out,' de Troq' pointed out. 'Five minutes after we ask the first question, they'll guess exactly what we're up to.'

'They mustn't!' Darcy snapped, but he knew de Troq' was right. When the two detectives had gone, and young Darras had been startled by the news and briefed as to what was expected of him, Darcy took his life in his hands and telephoned Sarrazin, the freelance reporter who was always the first on the scene of a crime.

'Nice of you to call.' The journalist was surprised that a police officer should contact him. Usually it was he who hassled for stories at the Hôtel de Police. 'What can I do for you?'

'It's more what you can't do,' Darcy said. 'Come in and see me and I'll explain.'

Sarrazin, his curiosity always too strong for his own good, was sitting in Darcy's office waiting for an explanation almost before Darcy had had time to put the phone down. The reporter was looking smug at being the only newspaperman present for what he hoped would be an important announcement. Darcy's announcement wiped the satisfied grin from his face in a matter of seconds.

'Merde,' he said very quietly. 'But why the hell are you telling me? Surely you don't want it generally known that your ace crime fighter has finally gone up in his own puff of smoke?'

'That's just the problem. I called you in to put you in the picture because you're bound to hear rumours, but I must ask you to do nothing. Could you keep the story under wraps for, say, forty-eight hours? We need a little time before the grapevine takes over and the news breaks. I know Pel isn't exactly your hero,' he went on hurriedly, 'but we need him. We've got to act quickly and get him back as soon as possible.'

'If he's not dead.'

Sarrazin had a nerve-racking way of saying things either verbally or in print that other people barely dared think.

'Let's cross that bridge if we come to it,' Darcy replied, not wanting to discuss the possibility.

Sarrazin was silent for a moment. When he spoke, Darcy was surprised by what he said.

'No, you're right, Pel's never been my hero, but at least he's honest. I've always trusted him, and given different circumstances I could possibly even like the old sod. So I'll keep my mouth shut together with everyone else's as far as I can. On one condition,' he added, smiling.

'That you can have the story first whatever happens,' Darcy finished the sentence for him.

'Precisely.'

The day's inquiries, however, brought only frustration and frayed tempers. The April showers that had been forecast had again turned into sleeting stinging rain that fell like slithers of glass from the heavens to shatter on the pavements, drenching anyone foolish enough to be outside in a matter of seconds. The four policemen, not foolish by any means, but braving the downpour in the course of duty, arrived back at the Hôtel de Police that evening, tired and soaked to the bone. They had nothing to report, just blank faces and shaking heads. Pel had not been seen.

It was a gloomy meeting they held in the Chief's office that evening. At long last it had stopped raining, but the heavy black clouds brought a depressing darkness into the office, forcing them to switch on the electric lights when normally it wouldn't have been necessary. There was still a constant and irritatingly monotonous tap as the gutters overflowed and dripped on to the windowsills.

Although the Chief wasn't wet through like the four men

14

standing in his office, he was wearing an expression more morose than any of them. He sighed and went to the cupboard for the private brandy bottle which he kept for emergencies.

'So,' he said, serving each of them, 'nothing at all. That's a good start, and we haven't even had a ransom demand or the usual lunatics claiming responsibility – but that, I suppose, is because they don't know about it.' He scratched the top of his head as he eased his bulk into a chair. 'What about Madame Pel?'

'I've spoken to her briefly,' Darcy replied. 'Like us, she's keeping the panic button on hold, but I'm not sure how long she can keep it up. She's under considerable strain.'

'Tomorrow,' the Chief said quietly. 'We'll give it until tomorrow at midday, then I think I'll have to call in the powers that be for a national if not international search – although God knows I don't want to; it'll be hell on earth with interference from all directions. Yes,' he said, trying to convince himself the decision was correct, 'we'll give it until tomorrow at midday.'

3

Darcy was roused from his slumbers and lusty dreams of his English girlfriend by an urgent phone call. There had been another daring robbery, this time at one of the local châteaux. As he unwillingly dragged himself from between the sheets, he decided that being the boss could easily make him as grumpy as Pel. He'd had only four hours' sleep and it felt like less. The burden of responsibility, he realised, was what one longed for without considering the consequences. No wonder Pel had bags under his spectacles.

The April showers were still saturating the countryside. Standing on the massive stone doorstep of the château, Darcy stared out gloomily through the sheeting rain which turned the dawn into a thick grey soup. The gargoyles high on the stonework dribbled large cold drops down the back of his neck. If hats had suited him, he would have been wearing one; as it was, his neatly cut black hair was so plastered to his head by the rain it looked as if it had been painted on.

The château looked ominous in its dank and dripping setting. It was a massive square construction with towers at each corner, poking like sharpened black pencils into the wet sky. He'd met de Troq' and the men from Fingerprints at the bottom of the wide stone steps and they'd arrived in a group at the studded front door that was large enough to drive a couple of tanks through. Being the senior officer, Darcy had the privilege of ringing the bell, or rather of swinging on a heavy brass knob that reminded him more of a lavatory pull, hanging as it was by the side of the door from a stout metal chain. He stood back to wait. Finally a shuffling was heard from inside as, someone in carpet slippers approached, then the scraping of bolts being released before the door was finally heaved open a mere crack. To the slit between the doors Darcy presented his identity card with the red, white and blue stripe of the Police Judiciaire de la République de France, explaining why he and the men behind him were there. The door swung open to reveal a painfully thin man, possibly six foot tall when upright, but who stooped to greet them. The butler, Darcy thought to himself. De Troq', however, stepped forward, did his infuriating clicking of the heels and presented himself with his full title, turning to Darcy at last and introducing him, Darcy was pleased to see, as the man in charge, though why he did all this pantomime nonsense to impress a butler he couldn't understand. He soon did. It was the Baron de Charnet standing before them with bowed head, shuffling about in his bedroom slippers. Having been recognised, he brightened visibly and shook de Troq's hand warmly. He shook Darcy's hand too and nodded at the Fingerprint men waiting patiently in the unrelenting downpour behind them.

At last they were allowed to enter. Stamping their feet on the flagstone floor as they did so, they came face to face with an upright and fully dressed butler who looked as if he had a nasty smell under his nose. At the Baron's slight wave of the hand he stepped forward to take their dripping coats. To a man they declined. Inside the château walls, as was often the case in these old stone places, it was bitterly cold; whereas outside

16

the wind had been a background noise to the drumming of the rain, inside it had knives in it, whistling down the huge dark corridors like a ghost looking for someone to haunt.

"'Spect you want to see the scene of the crime?' the Baron asked casually as he struggled to shut the huge door against the howling gale outside. Darcy caught the strong smell of stale garlic on his breath. Cold and first thing in the morning it was repulsive. He stepped back a pace before nodding and allowing de Troq' to take the lead behind the retreating Baron. The butler faded away as the Baron de Charnet led them down a series of chilly passages inhabited by rusty suits of armour and sad-looking heads of wild animals obviously shot by the Baron's ancestors over the preceding centuries. It was a morbid old place full of family history and damp. Darcy pulled his coat collar tighter round his neck and hoped he wouldn't suffer from rheumatism because of his dowsing and the draughts. Horrified, he realised he was behaving like Le Vieux and fretting about his health. Perhaps being a hypochondriac went with promotion – Pel was the most experienced hypochondriac he'd ever met. He glanced across at de Troq' who was walking beside him. He looked perfectly at home, but then he would, damn him. Eventually they descended a winding and slippery stone staircase into the cellars.

'In here,' the Baron announced in a gust of bad breath, opening a small, thick oak door. It was the gun room, well stocked with an impressive display of shining arms, smelling of metal and musty cellars. 'They only took the best,' the Baron announced, sadly pointing at three empty places, one on the racks, two on a velvet-covered shelf. 'Got a collection, you see, quite my pride and joy, and the devils took my prize pieces.'

De Troq' seemed impervious to the foul-smelling words that the Baron emitted, and while the Fingerprints team went to work on the racks, the door handles and the rest of the armoury, he endeavoured to get a full description of the three pieces that were missing.

'My pride and joy,' the Baron repeated, 'that one.' He pointed to the empty space in the gun rack. 'A Hercule, 40 calibre, 10 mm hunting gun. Beautiful piece. Grandpapa shot wild boar with it. Paid nearly a thousand francs for it before the war.'

17

'1939-45?' Darcy asked.

Baron de Charnet looked mortified. 'No, young man, the Great War, 1914-18, so you can imagine what it's worth now. Irreplaceable,' he said, shaking his head sadly. 'Irreplaceable.'

'Easy to identify, though?'

'Know it a mile off. Only one like it, don't you know – hand-engraved for Grandpapa.'

'Easy to sell?'

'To the right person, no problem at all. Mind you, he'd have to have the money. That sort of thing is searched for by collectors all over the world.'

'And the other two missing pieces?' Darcy indicated the velvet-covered shelf.

The Baron sighed. 'A Gaulois, *pistolet de poche*, tiny little thing, one of a pair, real *bijoux*, only weighed 250 grammes, but still lethal for all its smallness. 13 centimetres long, including the barrel, of course.'

'Of course.'

'6 centimetres wide and just $1^1/2$ centimetres thick. Bullets were 8 mm calibre. A semi-automatic. Little beauty it was. The wife carried it everywhere she went during the war.'

'1914-18 war?' Darcy asked tiredly.

'Good God, we're not that ancient. No, of course not, when the bloody Boche occupied us, 1939-45. They were a rotten bunch, good thing we had a decent escape route for the Brits and Yanks, or anyone else that needed it for that matter. Didn't do it all alone of course, me and a Jewish chap that got out just in time, nice bloke called Blanc . . .' His voice drifted away with his memories.

De Troq' had finished scribbling in his notebook and looked up with sympathy at the bereft Baron. 'And the third missing piece?' he asked quietly.

'An American revolver, Smith and Wesson, de luxe model. Could kill a man at 120 metres. My pa brought it back with him from his travels just after the war.'

Everyone resisted the temptation to ask which war.

'Who knew about your collection and its value?'

'Everyone for miles around, and further I suppose. Used to

18

lend them for exhibitions from time to time, even been to Paris with 'em. I'll never see them again now.'

'We might find them.'

'Not a chance. Whoever took them knew what they were looking for and already had a buyer. I've read about that sort of thing in the papers.' It seemed that the bad-breath Baron was on the verge of tears. Darcy took a step towards him, ready to ask another question, and was met by another blast of stale garlic. 'Might as well give up now, no point in collecting without my masterpieces. Although there was another Gaulois somewhere about – as I say, one of a pair. Haven't seen it in years, have to ask the wife . . .'

Having retreated a couple of paces, Darcy asked his question, 'When did you discover they were missing?'

''Bout an hour ago, I suppose.'

'In the middle of the night.'

'Couldn't sleep – getting old, don't you know. Can't deprive my wife of her beauty sleep.' He laughed; it came out as a strangled cackle. 'Gawd, she needs it, not so young herself now.' He paused to consider his joke. 'So I wandered about a bit, but it's still bloody cold at this time of year, so I came down here. Got a little fan heater, see.' He turned and showed them a small electric heater sitting in front of an ancient moth-eaten armchair alongside which was a small table sporting a half-full bottle of equally ancient brandy. There was no glass. Either the Baron had removed it for washing, which Darcy doubted, or he had swigged the beautiful old brandy from the dusty bottle.

'Came in here to warm myself up, have a tot of internal central heating and look at my collection. Quite perfect. Peaceful and warm.'

'Do you know how the intruders got in, sir?'

'Haven't the vaguest idea, so many bloody doors in this place, sometimes get lost myself, and damn it I was born here. Often got lost as a lad. I just sat down and shouted until my governess found me. Took all day once – gave me a stiff clout round the ear for my trouble, too.'

'Perhaps we could ask your butler?'

'Certainly, yes, good idea, he was born here too. Over the stables as a matter of fact, he's the only one left of the old staff.

19

Got a woman who comes in to cook and things, my wife doesn't know how to, you see.'

'We'd better have her name.'

'What – the wife's?'

'No, sir,' Darcy said patiently, 'the cook's, together with anyone else who works here.'

'Got a gardener,' the Baron said doubtfully. 'Don't know what he does though, the grounds are in a terrible state. Not like when I was a young man, can't get good staff any more. Anyway, enough of all that. If you don't need me any more I'll be off to bed. Feeling a bit drowsy now, after all the excitement.'

The Baron ambled off, mumbling about his sad loss, to be replaced by the butler who materialised noiselessly in the doorway.

Darcy understood why he had a permanent sneer on his face now; having the Baron Bad Breath as an employer was enough to make the oldest and most faithful of staff feel ill. He answered their questions cheerfully enough, however, saying that although he couldn't be sure that all the doors were bolted – there were two outside doors in that part of the cellar alone – he had made his tour of the main ones, and he himself had heard nothing, but as his bedroom was about three kilometres to the west of where they stood, high up in one of the towers, that was hardly surprising. The Baron and Baroness would have heard nothing either; they were three kilometres down the corridors in the other direction.

'So we'll just have to rely on fingerprints and luck', Darcy said to de Troq' as they left the château.

Later that morning Darcy set Sergeant Brochard to work on locating arms collectors and dealers, and informed the rest of the team of all recent events – that is, all except one.

'So keep your ears and eyes open,' Darcy added. 'I'd like to get them back for the old boy. It's probably the only thing of value he had left.'

'Don't you believe it,' de Troq' said. 'The Baron de Charnet is worth a fortune. He also collects carpets, paintings and

Ming china, not to mention the antique furniture in every room.'

'And they took the only things that are easy to carry,' Darcy thought out loud, 'so it looks as if we're after one man, not a band of thugs.' He looked up at de Troq". 'Is he insured?'

'No. I checked with the butler this morning – no insurance company would touch the place without having grilles, locks and alarm systems attached to every window and door in the place. The Baron refused, not because of the cost, but because of the upheaval. He likes to feel master of his castle.'

'And his garlic.'

'He eats it raw, one clove morning, noon and night, *bon pour la santé*, so he says.'

'God help the Baroness.' Darcy laughed and turned his mind to the next file on his desk. 'What about the escaped Poltergeist – not that we're expecting him to turn up on our patch, but have we extra men watching at the airport, at the entrances and exits of the motorways, at the stations and so on and so forth? As we're not far from the Swiss border here, it might be wise to be alert. It'll take a lot of extra manpower, but Pujol and Rigal can go out on this one. I know they're new to us, but all they've got to do is keep their eyes and ears open. While they're about it they can check the legality of any non-French that they come across: the *douanes* in Paris are bleating about immigrants arriving in the capital from the coast, probably via us. It seems reasonable, straight up the motorway from Marseille. However, don't let them waste too much time on it – it's not really our problem. They asked for co-operation, not full-scale investigation. Make that clear. Those two are so thick personally I wouldn't trust them with a book of parking tickets.'

'They had excellent references,' de Troq' pointed out.

'Not from me.'

The meeting over, Darcy's men began leaving the building to start their investigations. Mercifully, it had stopped raining temporarily and miraculously the sun was shining hard and hot, making the pavements steam and forcing open many of the city's shutters that had remained closed against the foul weather for months. It was as if the city was waking up to the spring after a long winter's slumber.

Nothing so romantic was in Darcy's mind as he made his way to the Chief's office. He was sitting behind his desk looking like a bull about to have a nervous breakdown.

'Any news, Darcy?'

Darcy knew at once, he meant Pel. 'No, nothing. I went to see his wife on my way in this morning, but she's heard nothing either – except for the housekeeper, that is, who spends all day washing and polishing frantically and has so far broken nearly all the ornaments in the house.'

'Poor Madame, she must be worried sick.'

'As we all are. Shall I let Sarrazin release the story to the papers and see what that brings in?'

'It'll bring in all the weirdos and cranks in the city, claiming it's them who have him, or murdered him and chopped him up for breakfast, plus numerous ransom demands, plus a soaring rise in crime. To be honest, Darcy, I'm not sure. If we don't let the story go into the papers it'll be hiding something that is fact, we can't do that, but if we do let the story out it could just open the floodgates to problems that may cloud the way to ever finding out what's happened. If the little bugger was here with us, I think he'd let it stew for a while.'

At that moment the decision was taken out of their hands. The door burst open and Sarrazin stumbled in, closely followed by the red-haired and equally red-faced Annie Saxe.

'I'm sorry, Chief,' she gasped.' I told him you were in conference with Inspector Darcy, but that made him all the more insistent.'

'Darcy,' the journalist said, 'tell this charming girl, who I give high marks for rugger tackles, to get the hell out of here. I've got to talk to you.'

Seeing that Annie was about to do grievous bodily harm, Darcy waved her away.

'Okay, what's it all about?'

'You sure there's nobody listening?' the reluctant journalist said, looking over his shoulder like a novice in a cheap spy film.

'Sure,' the Chief sighed. 'Now for God's sake *accouche*.'

'It's about Pel.'

Both the Chief and Darcy jumped to attention.

'What about him?'

'I had a phone call half an hour ago. I don't know who it was, the voice was very distorted, as if through a badly connected microphone, but it said quite clearly, "Tell Darcy not to do anything. I'll be in touch later with instructions.'

'Is that all?'

'The voice asked me If I'd understood the message, to which I said I had, then the line went dead.'

'And you think it was a message from Pel? Why?'

'There's only one person tricky enough who'd think of ringing me, in the event he couldn't telephone the Hôtel de Police for fear of being traced, or giving the game away, and that's Pel.'

'You may be right.' Darcy turned to Sarrazin. 'I think le Vieux trusts you, Sarrazin. It must have been him. Who else would know you'd come barging in with a ridiculous message like that?'

'Can I print the story now?'

'No.' The Chief was adamant. 'You're going to have to keep all this to yourself for a while longer. If that message was indeed from Pel, and we have to assume for the moment it was, he asks us to do nothing, so that's what we'll do. You included,' he added firmly.

'But what if it's a hoax?'

'Only five members of the police force plus you know he's disappeared, except of course his own wife and housekeeper, and I'm sure none of us made that phone call.'

'But if it's a play for time?'

'That's a possibility,' the Chief acknowledged, 'but for the moment we'll have to risk it. Until midday tomorrow, that is. If we have no further news by then you can print the story and there'll be hell to pay all over Burgundy until we find Chief Inspector Pel.' He sighed, unhappy with the situation and the decision he'd been forced to take. 'Now, the pair of you get out of my office and let me do some work.'

'Just before I go, Chief, if I can't print the Pel story, how about a bit of inside information on the Poltergeist story?'

The Chief sighed. 'We don't know any more than what you can read in your own newspaper, or see on the television.'

'Yes, but what is your department doing?'

'The same as every other Hôtel de Police all over France – we've got men at the airport, on the autoroute pay kiosks, at the stations – '

Before he could finish, Sarrazin cut in. 'Great, local police on red alert for escaped prisoner.'

'That's not what I said.'

'Yes, it is, almost.'

'I shouldn't have said anything, I know you of old.'

'Rubbish, what difference will it make? Do you honestly think a chap as clever as the Poltergeist, who can make himself disappear into his own reflection, is going to try and leave the country now? Either he's long gone, or he'll wait until you're not looking.'

'You'd make a good policeman,' Darcy said honestly, having had exactly the same thought that morning.

'That's why I'm a good journalist,' Sarrazin replied smugly. 'I'll give you until tomorrow at noon on the Pel story. After that I'm going to print.'

If there was no news by noon the following day both the Chief and Darcy knew that Sarrazin's story, whatever he said, would make little difference. In their experience it was the first forty-eight hours that counted; after that, hope began evaporating, but neither of them wanted to admit it.

Darcy wasn't sure he agreed with the Chief's decision to keep Pel's disappearance under wraps for another twenty-four hours, but Madame Pel took it very calmly when he told her at midday.

'I'm sure he has his reasons,' she said. 'The Chief knows Pel well, and I must confess I do find it very strange that no ransom has been demanded – nor,' she added quietly, 'a body found.'

The sound of breaking china echoed from the nearby kitchen. 'But please, Daniel, beg the Chief to do something dramatic tomorrow. Staying at home with Madame Routy in her state of nerves is driving us both round the bend. I daren't go out of the house for a moment, for fear she'll telephone her sister, or her aunt, or some other relation, and blurt it all out. And if

I have to stay cooped up with her alone much longer you may just have to arrest me for attempted murder.'

During the afternoon, Nosjean appeared in Darcy's office followed by a very attractive young woman with startlingly green eyes and long auburn hair. She was carrying a shiny black crash helmet, a satchel full of papers and an extremely charming smile.

'Cécile Ortille,' Nosjean introduced her, 'student of criminology at the University. She's on an exchange from the Sorbonne and has asked permission to sit behind the scenes of the Hôtel de Police to see how this side of the law works.'

She shifted the cumbersome crash helmet into her left hand and came forward to give Darcy the full benefit of her smile and, he noticed, the rest of her, which went in and out in all the right places. It made him wish he wasn't trying to be faithful to his own girlfriend. She looked very like a young Charlotte Rampling, and although the days when Nosjean fell in love with any girl who looked remotely like Charlotte Rampling were over, now that he was a married man, it was quite obvious Nosjean had seen the similarity and, like Darcy, was trying hard not to enjoy the view.

'I can't see that it'd do any harm,' Darcy said, quickly, determined not to be distracted. 'Yes, you can sit in if you like, but I suggest not in the Sergeants' Room – you'll give Misset heart failure.' He turned to Nosjean. 'The typing pool isn't going to be very interesting, so how about the front desk, out of sight behind the switchboard?' He turned back to look at Cécile. 'At least there you'll see all the comings and goings and not be in anyone's way. If there's anything in particular you want to ask, I'm sure Nosjean here will be delighted to help.'

'I'm afraid I already have a question,' she said, still smiling. 'Could I put my bike in the courtyard behind this building? It's a brand new Kawasaki and I don't want someone to steal it.'

Darcy told Nosjean to have a word with the duty officer and to let her in with the motor bike. Nosjean, however, wasn't so sure he wanted to be responsible for such a luscious lady biker, particularly with his new young bride, Mijo, waiting for him at home every evening. In his bachelor days it would have been different. In his bachelor days, Darcy had been unattached too,

25

and he would have had to fight him for her, and most likely would have lost. He thought perhaps he'd have a word with de Troq'. Though his junior in rank, he always knew exactly how to cope with every situation. Nosjean was sure he'd be more than pleased to take over the duty.

Cécile Ortille was surprised to be passed from one detective to another. Usually all she had to do was smile her Charlotte Rampling smile and she got exactly what she wanted. She couldn't help feeling that policemen were after all a race apart. However, she allowed herself to be hidden behind the switchboard and promised to behave.

The news of Cécile's arrival travelled fast and the men found an excuse to stroll past the switchboard to feast their eyes on their stunning student of criminology. On his way down, Debray, the department's computer expert, put his head round the door of Darcy's office. Knowing what Debray was like, Darcy was expecting the usual incomprehensible announcement delivered in computer code, which would render the entire team speechless. He was however, surprised.

'The gap left by Lage's retirement has been filled,' he said. 'His replacement is arriving tomorrow.' Darcy looked up and waited for the rest; he knew by the expression on Debray's face there was more to come.

'And?' he said.

'And he's called Cherif Mohamed Kader Camel.'

'An Arab?'

'Yes. Will you tell the Patron, or may I have the pleasure?'

Darcy had to do a bit of quick thinking – Debray still knew nothing of Pel's disappearance. 'Neither. He's not in at the moment, but I'll let him know as soon as he arrives.' He grinned unwillingly at his colleague. 'God, that's just what the Old Man needs to stir up his ulcers – an Arab on his team. He's about as racist as they come. Me too, considering it was an Arab who rearranged my teeth – that little episode cost me a fortune at the dentist.'

'Just what I thought,' Debray said, grinning back.

4

Late that night Pel's wife tried urgently to contact Darcy. Finding only Misset on duty, and knowing his reputation as a bungler, she left no message and, pouring herself a small night-cap, she went to sit patiently by the telephone.

As Madame Pel sipped her drink in the warmth of her own comfortable home, Darcy was standing once again in the pouring rain. Floods had been forecast all over France, which for the end of April was incredible, but he could well believe it. He felt well flooded himself – his shoes were overflowing, his collar was distinctly soggy and there were moments when he felt the need to attach windscreen wipers to his eyeballs. Sometimes police work was depressing. Not only that, he felt sure he had a cold coming on. Darcy shook himself: Pel was creeping into his soul again. Even when he was missing he made his presence felt. Haunted, and he didn't have any evidence of his death. Darcy sincerely hoped he wasn't being haunted by Pel, it was worse than working with him. Pretty soon he'd find himself complaining of stomach ulcers and not being able to give up smoking. Smoking in this downpour, he thought, would be a feat of genius, but I bet the Patron would manage it.

He brought his mind back to business. A jewellery store in rue de la Liberté had been broken into and its alarm was wailing like an air-raid siren. One of his men was endeavouring to find the control box and switch it off before the Fingerprint boys and the rest of his team went in. As they entered the shop the owner arrived in a state of panic. He ran into the shop and fussed over the individual displays.

'That's odd,' he said at last, 'nothing seems to be missing.'

'Do you often have false alarms?'

'Never before.'

Bardolle came through from the back of the shop. 'We've found the point of entry,' he announced in his foghorn voice. 'The lavatory window,' he went on, 'though God knows how they got in through there, it's tiny. I certainly couldn't get through there.'

That didn't surprise Darcy in the least: Bardolle was built like a carthorse and had fists like sacks of coal.

Darcy turned to the owner. 'Are you sure there is nothing missing?'

The man nodded his head. 'Nothing. All the collections are complete – and, as you can see, there are plenty on show. I just don't understand it.' He shook his head.

'Have you got a safe?' If nothing was missing from the shop then it occurred to Darcy it had to be missing elsewhere. Jewellery shops weren't broken into simply for fun.

'Of course, but that's burglar-proof. I had it verified only a few weeks ago.'

'Perhaps we could have a look all the same,' Darcy said patiently. 'In my experience no safe is burglar-proof.'

'Oh, but this one is, and for good reason – I have the new collection of diamond rings locked away. Spring being the season . . .' He broke off with a look of panic on his face and, sprinting round the back of the main counter, disappeared into a small back room, where he sighed with relief.

'There, you see,' he said pointing at the safe door. 'Still locked.'

'Would you open it, please,' Darcy asked, 'just to make sure.'

The proprietor did as he was told. As he opened the small safe door his hands flew to his face. 'Oh, they couldn't have!' he cried.

Apparently they had.

The safe was bare, as if a large vacuum cleaner had been attached to the door and sucked the entire contents out. Only half a dozen velvet-clad trays were left. Someone had spring-cleaned the safe.

'Every single diamond gone!' the poor man cried. 'The collection was worth millions of francs!'

28

Darcy interrupted him. 'Would the collection be easy to sell, monsieur?'

'Oh, no! It was most exclusive, most distinctive. I ordered it myself from the dealers in Paris.'

A voice belonging to one of the new boys, yet to make an impression on anyone, made Darcy realise he wasn't as dim as he looked behind his schoolboy glasses and thick wet lips.

'Impossible to sell perhaps as it was, but they could easily break the pieces up and simply sell the stones,' Pujol said ominously.

This brought new cries of distress from the owner. 'Oh, they wouldn't!'

'Unfortunately, monsieur,' Darcy added, 'that's probably what they are doing right now. I presume you were well insured?'

Dawn was breaking as Darcy opened the door to his flat. The phone was ringing. His inclination was to let it ring. For the second time in two days he'd had very little sleep. Usually he infuriated Pel by arriving at the Hôtel de Police a few hours later looking like Prince Charming, while Pel looked like something the cat had dragged in, but with the extra burden of responsibility Darcy was beginning to realise why Pel felt permanently frayed at the edges.

He lifted the receiver, however, and was glad his call of duty was stronger than his personal feelings.

'I've spoken to Pel!' Madame was almost delirious with happiness. 'He telephoned late last night to say he was safe and we're not to worry.'

'Is that all?'

'Yes.' She paused, not insensitive to Darcy's dull, heavy reply. 'Is something wrong, Daniel?'

Darcy hauled himself together. 'I'm sorry, madame, I'm delighted Pel's all right. Truly I am, but I've just come in and am rather tired.'

'Forgive me for disturbing you, but I thought it was important.'

'Please don't apologise. Tell me,' he said, making the effort

29

to step back into his efficient policeman role, 'what did your husband say, exactly?'

'Simply that I wasn't to worry, he was safe and in no danger. I was to tell you not to press the panic button yet.'

Darcy sat in his bath reviewing the situation. Two major robberies to add to the list, and a disappearing boss, who was in no danger. Well, that was something. One thing was certain, he couldn't wallow in his suds all morning. The Chief must be told.

It was almost midday when he finally appeared in the Chief's office. Sitting in the chair opposite him was Pel, his spectacles pushed up on to his forehead; as usual he was puffing frantically on a cigarette as if his life depended on it.

'You're late,' he said casually to Darcy before dissolving into a coughing fit that turned his face purple.

'So are you,' Darcy retorted, 'two days late. Where the hell have you been?'

'Nice to be loved and missed. Didn't realise it had been so long.' Pel tried one of his rare smiles and succeeded in making himself look like something out of a horror film. Darcy was used to him and ignored it. 'I went on a little trip,' Pel went on, letting the smile subside into non-existence, 'to see a celebrity. I was invited for the rest of the week, but decided I couldn't bear to live without you all, and declined the invitation.'

'Have you seen your wife? She was worried sick. And prepare yourself for a large bill for new crockery and glass – Madame Routy's nerves have caused extensive breakages in your kitchen.'

'I thought she was looking sheepish when I arrived,' Pel said, 'and now I know why I drank coffee out of the best china and not my usual bowl. Yes,' he said to Darcy, 'I have seen my wife, although regrettably only briefly.'

'Did you wish her a belated happy anniversary?' Darcy asked, quietly determined to make Pel pay, if only slightly, for his nonchalance.

It worked. 'Holy Mother of God! Get Annie Saxe in here! She

must send off the biggest bouquet of flowers she can find in the city.'

The Chief, who had been openly enjoying the short exchange between the two men, now brought it to a close and told Darcy to sit down and calm down. Having allowed Pel to give his instructions to the young red-headed policewoman, he leant forward on to his desk and spoke to Darcy.

'We've got something quite extraordinary on our plates to cope with,' he said seriously. 'Pel will explain fully himself. He has quite a story to tell you.'

5

Because of Pel's temporary, though unpublicised, disappearance, the usual morning meeting of senior officers at the Hôtel de Police took place that afternoon. The Chief also decided, this time, to be present. Pel, smiling to himself at his wife's appreciation of the lorry-load of roses she had received, sat contentedly behind his desk puffing on his thousandth cigarette that day without any feelings of guilt at all. After his abduction and release, not to mention, he thought, all that had gone on in between, he deserved to be forgiven his weakness at being unable to give up, though he knew the struggle must begin again very soon if he wasn't to expire from lung cancer, bronchitis, asthma, heart failure or any other of the diseases related to smoking that were lurking ready to pounce on the unprepared Pel – who still managed, in spite of his delirium over his health, to keep going longer than anyone else. Smoking was a constant worry to him, and every time he took a fresh cigarette he tried in vain to avert his eyes from the ominous warning on the packet that he was sure was there specifically for his own personal harassment and fear. Behind this worry was the added one that, although in his professional life he was businesslike and successful, his willpower seemed non-existent when it came to giving up. It baffled him. But for the time being, reinstated in his rightful place as Chief Inspector of the Police

Judiciaire de la République de France, he inhaled deeply and pushed his concern for his health temporarily out of sight.

His men were assembling themselves in front of him, mostly unaware that he had been absent. The most they'd noticed was that for a couple of days life had been surprisingly peaceful and they assumed Pel had been either out or behind locked doors considering a case so important it required all his powers of concentration, which in the event wasn't so far from the truth, although Pel had been very far from the Hôtel de Police – how far, unfortunately, he didn't know. Now, however, seeing the sickly smile sitting lopsidedly on his face, they all knew the amnesty was over and trouble was brewing. Leaves would be cancelled and policemen's wives would begin to wonder where the hell their husbands had got to.

The Chief sat to Pel's right, trying to make himself comfortable in a chair that was too small, and Darcy to his left, the only other man in the room who knew exactly what had happened to Pel. In front of the desk were Nosjean, newly scrubbed and looking better for a good night's sleep, de Troq', slight and elegant as ever, plus Misset, their weak link, with his brain in neutral, sporting a pair of dark glasses that he felt made him look rather devilish. His good looks were fading rapidly and, having been a bit of a womaniser in his youth, he took unkindly to the growing lines on his face and the growing number of children in his family. His wife was not the pretty young thing she had once been and had the unfortunate habit of asking her mother to stay for long periods, making life at home no longer bad, but plain unbearable. For that reason, and only that reason, Misset had stopped complaining about extra duties, as long as they didn't involve too much leg work, and preferred to remain at work. The rest of the team, tired of his old jokes and his constant gossip about the typists, preferred him at home.

Brochard, the farmer's son, sat quietly waiting for the worst, next to his flatmate, Debray, who balanced on his knees a collection of files with data print-out and information from their computers which only he could understand. To Pel it was like looking at a file written in Chinese. Bardolle, their very own Hulk, with a chest six foot wide and a foghorn voice which after much pleading from Pel he had learnt finally to keep under control, at least in front of him, stood beside Debray. Didier Darras, a young and keen cop, Pel's protégé, encouraged out of school, through police training college, right into Pel's team, stood beside Annie Saxe. Since her startling arrival, which had earned her the nickname the Lion of Belfort, the town she came from, she had settled down well and was appreciated by her male colleagues not only for her femininity, which she managed to hang on to even when she was swinging her fist, but also for her intelligence which was considerable. At long last, instead of tearing down the corridors at a hundred miles an hour, colliding frequently with whoever dared to step into her tracks, she had slowed to half-revs and was only in collision a dozen times a day. Lurking in the shadows were the two new boys of the team, Pujol and Rigal; they'd rapidly learnt to keep out of everyone's way and only speak when spoken to, particularly if Pel was around.

The Chief, giving up on his chair, pulled himself to his feet. 'Apart from the cases you are already working on,' he said slowly, 'we now have two more complicated matters to attend to.'

The Chief signalled to Pel to continue. He snapped his glasses down from his forehead on to his nose and squinted through the blue Gauloise smoke at the congregation before him.

'De Troq', you're in charge of our two new robberies. This series of break-ins is beginning to give us a bad reputation and I want it stopped. Take one of the new boys, Pujol or Rigal, to do the initial inquiries.' He looked across at the two young men, who were trying to make themselves invisible in the corner. 'They might learn something,' he added. 'Find the common denominator. These have been very daring and well-planned robberies, there must be a connection. Let me know when you've discovered what it is.' Pel paused to consider. 'If you need him, I would suggest Darras as a back-up man – he's got good young eyesight and a distinctly overactive brain.'

Pel let his crushing compliment sink in, knowing it would have the desired effect. Didier Darras would report anything and everything. It would probably be of no use at all, but just in case, it was exactly what they wanted. He stubbed out his cigarette and without noticing was lighting another as he called for half-time.

'I think perhaps we could all do with a drink. I rarely have the chance of buying my round, so perhaps this is the opportunity. How about a beer?' The Chief looked at Pel as if he were mad.

'Do you want me to go?' Annie Saxe was already half out of the door.

'No, Annie, you gallop around enough, in fact I'm surprised you haven't worn your legs down to the knees yet. Perhaps Misset would be gallant enough to go – as he's one of the world's remaining gentlemen, I'm sure he would be glad to save you the trouble.'

The Chief no longer thought Pel was mad. He understood now what he was up to: getting rid of Misset long enough to discuss the more confidential part of the meeting. Juggling a dozen open bottles of beer across the road from the Bar Transvaal would keep him busy for quite some time.

As Misset disappeared, Pel rose and came round to the front of his desk to perch on its edge. 'You've all heard of the Poltergeist?' he asked. His men nodded. Since the daring escape from Fresnes prison the national papers had carried the story as headline news. 'The Poltergeist was arrested on the Champs-Elysées in broad daylight after five years of being chased across France, and although he pleaded not guilty, protesting loudly that he was innocent, he was finally sent down for drug-smuggling on such a scale it made everyone else's attempts look like Puss in Boots . The other charges against him, such as murder, gun running, extortion and blackmail, had to be dropped as there was not enough evidence against him, but the general feeling was that thirteen years in a high security prison would teach him a lesson and put a stop to the disastrous flow of drugs all over the country. Strangely, it seems to have only caused a hiccup in trading and now the authorities are faced with tracing his replacement. If there is one. It has been suggested that the Poltergeist has been controlling his operations from prison for the last two years, even while he was shouting his innocence, and now he is away and free to continue as before. The Special Police are puzzled; they have raided all the hideouts they knew of, mostly mansions

34

with magnificent gardens. Police stations and gendarmeries across France search continually for clues as to where he is. He left no trace. Disappeared into thin air, just like a ghost at dawn, which is why, I suppose, he's earned the nickname of Poltergeist. The word, I'm told, is of German origin – as he is. He escaped from the Nazis and helped many more follow him. Poltergeist means noisy, mischievous spirit, in other words a phantom that likes to have fun. We thought his fun had been stopped, but apparently he's back in business.'

Pel paused to let it all sink in, and to prepare them for his next statement which he hoped would make them all jump.

'I was his guest for the last forty-eight hours.'

Pel watched for wide eyes and open mouths. He wasn't disappointed.

'However, he didn't look like any of the photos we have on record – which is hardly surprising, we all know he's a master of disguise – but it was him all right. Unfortunately, as I'd been blindfolded, taken first by car, then by plane, then by car again, I couldn't even hazard a guess as to where I was. They could have driven and then flown me round and round in circles and landed me in the same spot from where we took off, although I think not: however, I don't know. Which is exactly what they wanted, but for the moment that's not important.'

There was a clattering in the corridor outside as Misset fought with his bottles of beer. Finally appearing, puffing and out of breath from the stairs, he began handing them round.

'Good man!' Pel smiled, offering him a crisp hundred franc note. 'Off you go for the final instalment.'

As Misset lumbered out, Annie Saxe tried to close the door quietly behind him and Pel winced as the glass rattled in its frame.

'What is important is his granddaughter,' he continued. 'She's disappeared and he wants her found. The Poltergeist still has one or two faithfuls working for him but unfortunately all they found were vague rumours that she was keeping bad company and a trail that went suddenly cold. Personally, I don't give a damn what's happened to the girl, she's probably following in her grandfather's footsteps and setting up her own band of rogues and law breakers. But, and it's a big but,

35

she may be in trouble and, as has been pointed out to me perfectly plainly, she is a French citizen and as such is entitled to protection from harassment, abduction, violence and so on. The Poltergeist believes her to be in danger or held against her will. It is apparently very out of character that she hasn't been to see him or at least contacted him. Apparently, and to quote, "she's a good girl". How many times have we heard that of daughters who have got themselves into trouble one way or another? So I'm not taking that statement very seriously. When the rumours of her keeping bad company started he became extremely scared. After all, he knows all about bad company and the consequences – he's bad company himself. She has now been officially reported missing, to me. I was chosen because of my reputation for being, and I quote, an obstinate little bugger.' Pel paused, glaring at his men, daring them to snigger, but only the Chief allowed himself a partial smile. 'And, more importantly, because they think she may be in our area.' Pel paused again, but this time to light another cigarette. He drew on it so deeply that the men directly in front of him half expected his socks to burst into flames. 'We are obliged', he went on at last, having coughed happily until his eyes bulged, 'to take her disappearance seriously. If her grandfather's enemies, and he's got a few nasty ones, have got their hands on her, she could be in danger. He is willing to give himself up the moment she is returned safely to his loving grandfatherly arms, so he says.' Pel sniffed. He could say a lot with a sniff, and it was quite obvious he didn't believe in villians' promises.

'Therefore,' Pel continued, 'I want every possibility covered. I was given a photo of the girl taken three years ago and copies are being made. Don't leave without one. She was at law school in Paris, would you believe – whether she was studying law with a view to becoming a bona fide lawyer or in order to bend it, is debatable, but someone had better start there. I'd like you to handle this, Nosjean. Take Annie, you may need a woman to ask the more delicate questions about this girl's comings and goings, but keep her under control – you know what she's like. And while you're in Paris find the most expensive defence lawyer in the city. You know, the one who's always appearing

36

on de Chavanne's talk programme. Ask him if anyone has approached him to deal with the Poltergeist's appeal. It's my guess the Poltergeist has something more up his sleeve than simply finding his granddaughter while he's at liberty.

'I want the background of this girl, where she was at school, what she's done since, who her friends were, the men in her life, where she was seen last. The lot, and it's all got to be followed up. Interviews with anyone who had anything to do with her. Between the Poltergeist's granddaughter and the robberies we're going to be busy. Most of it will be tramping the streets, asking the same questions over and over again, and making out written reports. Boring, but an essential part of police work. I shall be going through every report you make, so for God's sake make them succinct, short but accurate.'

Someone was trying to kick the door in. Turning the handle, Annie revealed a puffing and red-faced Misset. From the time it had taken him to do the second trip, it was obvious that he had stopped for a quick one. He was expecting the usual brisk ticking off from his boss for wasting precious time and was ready with an excuse, but was surprised by a very unusual cheerful greeting. 'Ah, Misset, just in time,' Pel said. 'Well done. Now you can all take your beers and get to work. Misset, you have a special assignment. I want all, and I mean all, paper cuttings on the entire life of the Poltergeist.' Misset looked blank, his brain was still in neutral. Pel sighed and patiently explained. 'The prisoner who escaped from Fresnes by helicopter. The one the whole country, except you it seems, is on the alert to trace and rearrest.' Light was dawning at last. Misset nodded his fading good looks. 'We've been ordered', Pel went on, 'to make our own dossier on the man. So you're going to do it. I want you to get inside the story and come up with where he might be hiding.'

It could have been worse, Misset thought; at least he'd be able to sit down most of the time. He'd have to go to the library to look up old copies of newspapers and magazines. The library was warm and out of the rain and, he thought happily, librarians were often attractive young women. It certainly could have been worse. Misset began to feel almost enthusiastic about the next few days' work. He had no idea he had been disposed of neatly and efficiently so he wouldn't hinder other inquiries, or get on Pel's nerves, which was inevitable and best avoided for both of them.

Pel watched his men leave, satisfied that they would be thorough and efficient, satisfied also that Misset would be kept out of trouble for a while. He knew he'd make his investigation last as long as possible, and was for once quite happy to let him. As he rose to leave the conference room himself the phone rang, and as he was the only one there he saw no alternative but to answer. He heard a girl's voice that he didn't recognise.

'Chief Inspector Pel?'

Pel agreed that was who he was and found he was being put through to an hysterical woman.

'There should be a law against it,' she shrieked.

'Perhaps there is, madame,' Pel said calmly. 'Against what?'

'Poisoning pussy cats.'

Pel stared in disbelief at the phone in his hand. 'I beg your pardon?' he said.

'Poisoning pussy cats,' the woman repeated, sounding as if she were about to burst into tears. 'It's absolutely disgusting. I put food out for them every day, poor little things, and it's good food, not the cheap stuff. Buy it specially I do, I know what they like, not just your cut-price tins of mush, oh no, not for my poor little dears, they get the best, and I feed them two or three times a day, whenever they ask, sometimes I open three or four packets in a day, well, they don't always like the flavour, so I have to open another, but I always find out what it is that they want, of course their favourite is fresh salmon, I buy an extra piece on Fridays when the fishman calls. My husband has a piece, I have a piece, and I buy an extra couple of pieces for the kitties, don't tell my husband though, he'd . . .'

Pel was staring in disbelief at the unintelligible flow of drivel, then his patience snapped and he clasped his hand over the phone while shouting loudly enough to make the windows rattle.

Darcy poked his head round the door. 'Sir?'

'Get this put through to some fool, any fool that likes cats,' Pel bellowed, 'and fire whoever's manning the telephone.'

* * *

38

Sarrazin had been as good as his word: there hadn't been even a hint of Pel's disappearance in any of the newspapers. Time was up, however, and he was now hammering at Darcy's office door expecting satisfaction, and a scoop.

At first he was disappointed.

'Pel's back,' Darcy told him, 'safe and unharmed.'

'Where the hell was he, then? Seeing his mistress?' Sarrazin wanted a story, any story.

'The Chief Inspector was away on business, not pleasure, and in any event he's a married man.'

'That doesn't stop most people having a bit on the side.'

'A happily married man,' Darcy added firmly.

Sarrazin flopped into a spare chair, 'Look, mate, you asked me to hold off while you sorted out your problems and found out what had happened to your super-sleuth. I did – I kept my side of the bargain, and believe me I was tempted not to. Now it's time for you to keep your side. You promised me the story – for God's sake, let me have it. I don't want to have to guess and make ambiguous remarks about his whereabouts, and police secrecy, broken promises and so on. And don't worry – I know my job well enough not to be caught on a libel charge.'

Darcy grinned unexpectedly. 'Keep your hair on, Sarrazin. Your co-operation was much appreciated. Even the great man himself appreciated it.'

'Wonders will never cease. Where was he, then – having a character change for the benefit of Burgundy?'

'And', Darcy continued unabashed, 'he told me to prepare this statement for you. He dictated most of it himself.' He pushed forward three neatly typed sheets of paper. 'By the way, it's an exclusive. On his instructions the story was kept for you alone.'

The newspaperman snatched up the statement and bolted for the door, shouting as he went, 'I told you he wasn't such a bad old sod, didn't I?'

Rain poured from the black clouds above in an unrelenting torrent on to Pel's men as they left the building to start their inquiries. The pavements were glistening and deserted, the shutters firmly shut against the new barrage of storms. Pel turned from the window of his office where he'd been standing thinking and smoking, and pressed the intercom on his desk.

As Darcy appeared, he was sitting pen in hand hoping for inspiration that was slow in coming. 'You sent for me, Patron?' Darcy sat quietly opposite his boss and waited.

Pel looked up at the polished good looks of his colleague. 'Interrogate me,' he said.

Darcy raised his eyebrows.

'For the love of God, jog my memory. I've been racking my brain to remember the little details that count, and I've come up with less than the usual dim witness. Fire some questions at me. I've got so much whirring about in my brain, I must put that part in order. They were damn clever, I didn't see a thing, and have no idea where I was taken, but there must be something that I saw, or heard, that'll tell us where the devil the Poltergeist has his hideout. I want him found,' he stared at Darcy viciously, 'before we find his granddaughter and he disappears into his own shadow again, because he will. I don't believe for a minute that he'll surrender himself when she's found.'

'Right.' Darcy wasn't surprised by his boss's reaction; he was of the same opinion himself. 'Let's forget your journey for the time being,' he suggested. 'As you pointed out yourself, they could have taken you round and round in circles to give the impression of distance while in fact you may have landed exactly where you took off. I have, however, sent Pujol to all the airfields to see if he can trace the plane that took you. All flights have to be logged, so with a bit of luck we'll find it.'

'Question the farmers as well, the ones that do their crop spraying from the air. There can't be that many with private aircraft at their disposal within an hour's radius of the city, and it wasn't longer than that that I was in the car.'

'Already under way. Pujol's going to be busy.'

'Good man.' Pel was satisfied Darcy's brain was in top gear and working as usual. 'Now get on with the interrogation.'

'When you arrived at your destination, you got out of the car – was it night or day?'

'I was blindfolded.'

'Even with a blindfold you would have some impression of light or dark,' Darcy insisted.

'It was raining,' Pel said obstinately.

'When you went into the house and the blindfold was removed, were the lights on or off?'

'On.'

'Curtains and shutters?'

'Closed.'

'Noises outside? Birds, tractors, cars? City noises, village noises, country noises?'

'Rain.'

'Inside, what could you hear there?'

'The fire crackling in the fireplace, and the rain bucketing down outside.'

'Let's forget the rain, shall we? It's no good trying to find out where it was raining because it's been raining almost solidly all over France for the last three weeks.' Darcy was being patient, but Pel was, as he'd pointed out, being as bad as most dim witnesses who just about managed to notice the man running away had two arms and two legs, and the car he jumped into had four wheels.

'How many men were in the house to greet you?'

'How should I know, there could have been dozens hidden in the cellars.'

'Patron!'

'The driver, with hat and coat collar pulled up to hide his face; second man, pointing gun at me from back seat, hat, collar, glasses, beard, possibly false. Me. Out of car, into house, all drenched. Three of us dripping on to the flagstone floor. In house, my host, you know who, showed me to a neat and tidy bedroom, offered a tray of food and drink, briefly discussed the weather and buggered off to bed. One other man, your age, your height, clean and tidy, not dripping, dry. Didn't get a good look at him, he clung to the shadows. The two other drippers left, so I was alone with you know who, except of course for this type who remained virtually out of sight – I got the impression that he was an extra because I was there. He sat outside my bedroom all night and spent most of the day lurking by the front door. My

41

host did all the talking, served the wine, heated up our food and put it on the table. He even did the washing up!'

'While you dried, I presume?'

Pel glared at him.

'It all sounds very cosy,' Darcy grinned.

Pel glared more ferociously. 'I suffered terribly.'

Darcy sighed. 'Tell me about the house, the architecture, the furnishings,' he suggested.

'It looked like a hunter's lodge,' Pel said brightly. 'There were a number of rifles on a rack in one corner, a couple of stuffed hares, a wild boar's head over the fireplace, and one of a stag. The furniture was old, not antique, good solid country stuff.'

'What did you eat and drink?' Darcy decided to try another tack, hoping for some indication from regional dishes or wine.

'We ate *boeuf bourguignon*, which was ready prepared, and we drank a superb Nuits-Saint-Georges.'

'They knew you were coming.' Darcy allowed himself a smile – they were good regional products but from their own beloved Burgundy, and available anywhere in France, probably the world. 'Did they never draw the curtains or open the shutters?'

'Yes, during the first day, the afternoon. It was after we had eaten. The air was becoming stale with Gauloises and pipe smoke – the Poltergeist smokes a pipe, you know – and he drew back the curtains and opened the windows. The shutters were opened a crack to let in some air.'

'But you arrived in the dark, the lights were on, so that must have been the day after?'

'Well, of course it was,' Pel snapped. 'I'd been to bed, got up again, eaten breakfast and demolished a packet of cigarettes before the Poltergeist emerged. Later there was lunch, and later still a light supper of cold meats and a salad. We slept and the whole thing was repeated the following day. But when I came down that morning the window was still open, and the shutters just a crack. There was a thin ray of sunshine coming through it, together with a sweet smell. A flowery smell, one I know – I've smelt it in someone's garden. It made me think of my wife.'

'Roses?'

42

'Not so sweet, but quite strong all the same, sort of like a perfume.' Pel thought for a moment. 'God knows', he said. 'I don't. Leave the smells for the moment and try something else.'

After another half-hour, the only other thing they had established was that Pel had not been near the coast: at no time had he heard a seagull, a boat hooting, or waves breaking in the distance. So that narrowed it down to the whole of the rest of France, if he hadn't been taken out of the country, a great step forward in finding the location.

Shortly after Darcy left, Pel remembered something that had happened in the plane on the return journey. He remembered it well because it put the fear of God into him and left him in a muck sweat and ready to say his prayers. Darcy wasn't in his office so he burst into the Sergeants' Room hoping to find him there and tripped over a crash helmet. Arms flailing like a windmill he finally came to a stop facing the attractive criminology student.

'What the hell was that? And who the hell are you?'

Darcy turned from Annie Saxe's desk, where they were studying a map of France. 'Let me introduce you to Cécile Ortille, Patron. She's a student from the University doing a thesis on crime and punishment.'

Pel extended his hand. 'What's she doing in the Sergeants' Room?' he demanded, still looking at Darcy.

'Less harm to your nerves than on the switchboard.' Darcy grinned.

'It was you that put through the cat call?' Pel stared at the girl as if she'd just dropped through the ceiling armed to the teeth and ready to attack him.

Cécile flashed her green eyes, smiled her best smile and opened her mouth to apologise.

'Annie,' Pel said quietly, 'now that you seem to have yourself under control, you'd make me a very happy man by keeping this under control.' He indicated the silenced Cécile, turned on his heel and left, shouting from the corridor for Darcy to follow.

'The plane lurched,' he said as they arrived back in his office. 'I thought we were about to drop from the sky at any minute, but it was just an air pocket.'

'That means mountains,' Darcy said. 'It's not much to go

on, but it's better than nothing. We might just strike gold eventually.'

'Eventually will probably be too late,' Pel growled.

Darcy shrugged. 'Doing our best, Patron, doing our best.'

The following morning, gasping over his first delicious cigarette that made him feel like a dying man while he was smoking it, but slightly better by the time he stubbed it out, Pel was surprised to find the previous day's reports handed to him by Cécile Ortille. She didn't smile, and backed out of the office looking as if she expected him to bite her.

Momentarily Pel felt guilty and decided he must be pleasanter to the poor child, then forgetting immediately he turned his attention to the pile of reports.

The first was from de Troq' on the recent robberies. He read it through and put it to one side, knowing de Troq' to be an efficient and imaginative policeman: he could leave him to work on his own for the time being. He turned to the next file, a report on the Poltergeist's granddaughter. The first page was a summary.

Her name in bold capitals headed the sheet of paper: LEBON, LAURA. Next to it were her place and date of birth, then her parents' names, Fontes, Michel and Lebon, Christianne, and the family's last known address. Pel noted that Lebon had never been one of the many names the Poltergeist had used. He was on record as Blanc, Gaillard, Marchal, Tisserand and Vaissier, but never Lebon.

The girl's history, however, started at the age of twelve when she was sent by her grandfather to a private school at Lugano in French Switzerland. In brackets he read that the girl's parents had been killed in a car accident when she was eight; she had been in the grandfather's care ever since, but no record could be found of her until the age of twelve. So now they knew why they were so attached to each other: she was the only surviving relative of the Poltergeist. The girl had been bright and although she went eventually to a very expensive finishing school, still in Switzerland, she dropped out during the second term and came back to France, appearing on the register of a Parisian *lycée* a couple of weeks later. She worked hard, recovered the time lost and succeeded in getting a good baccalaureate. The following September she started her degree in history. Eighteen months later she changed her degree course and moved over to the law school. As she was such a good student the University Proviseur gave permission for the change. His comments were, Pel read, noted on page 25.

He wondered if the Proviseur had had any idea who Mademoiselle Lebon's grandfather was and what a catastrophe it could be if she was ever called to the bar. Pel considered the possibility with horror.

However, that was not the imminent problem for the moment and, noting there was no more in the summary, he started leafing through the weighty document to find the Proviseur's comments. A single sheet of paper floated from the middle of the report, landing gracefully on the desk in front of him. Pel started reading the paper, feeling as he did his blood coming to the boil and all his resolutions about being pleasanter dissolving in fury. It was a report about Clavell, a small hamlet of few houses, where a woman had reported a case of cat poisoning.

As he was about to throw the crumpled report into his waste-paper basket something at the back of his mind made him unroll it and look again.

Clavell, he knew that name. He'd visited it on a case with Didier Darras. He began to remember more clearly: that's where the party was when Annie Saxe disguised herself as a photographer.

He buzzed through to the Sergeants' Room, praying it wouldn't be Cécile that answered. Pretty girls were fine by him – for looking at, not for working with. For that, they were nothing but a nuisance and a distraction to his men.

When Annie answered he breathed a sigh of relief and asked her about Clavell.

'Yes, Patron,' she said immediately, 'that's where our old friend Vlaxi lived before he took off just before you made the arrests over the satellite case.* He's never been seen since, not

* (see *Pel picks up the pieces*)

45

that we could prove a thing, but the house does still belong to him although no one's been near it for ages.'

'You've been checking?' Pel sounded surprised.

'Yes, Patron. I noticed the report Rigal was typing and out of curiosity telephoned the Mairie to find out if there'd been a change of ownership. There wasn't, so I then phoned the distributing post office who deliver to that address and was lucky enough to be able to speak to the postman himself. No one's been seen in the house for nearly a year.'

God bless all redheads with brains, Pel thought happily. At least there was one young woman he could rely on to be alert.

He might just find the time to visit the mad cat-woman at Clavell and have a poke about in Vlaxi's direction. It was a long time ago but he still wanted that one behind bars. You never knew what might turn up if you tried hard enough.

What did eventually turn up in the quiet little hamlet of Clavell was a surprise even to Pel.

6

Pel needed time to think; perhaps a quiet drive into the country would give him time to put things in order in his overfilled brain. The Poltergeist's request to find his granddaughter was one thing, an ordinary case of a missing person, they all knew how to deal with that, but the fact that the missing person had been reported by a notorious escaped convict to a kidnapped Chief Inspector of the Police Judiciaire, fairly well known himself in police circles he had to admit, changed everything. Strictly speaking, his contact with the Poltergeist should be reported to the big boys in Paris who had mounted the search all over France, but he would be worse than useless to them. He could imagine the scene: Pel seated in one of their plush leather chairs, they were bound to have plush leather chairs in Paris, his feet barely touching the floor, the ashtray just out of reach, so that every time he leant forward with his cigarette, and he would have to because they would also have thick carpet on the floors in Paris, he would be in fear of falling off the chair and flat on his face at their well-polished feet. They would question him. 'Where did you go in the car, what did you see?' And he would be obliged to reply, 'I don't know, I had a black hood over my head.' 'And the plane, didn't you hear radio instructions to the pilot?' 'I don't know. They'd put the headphones of a Walkman on my ears. All I could hear was Mahler.'

He would be to them worse than the most infuriating wet witness. But try as he might there was nothing to remember except the darkness, then finally the quiet, polite man who greeted him, shaking his hand and introducing himself simply as Jean Blanc, alias the Poltergeist. He was still dark-haired in spite of his sixty-five years, and had plenty of it. Pel passed a hand over his own sparsely thatched head and felt cheated. He was younger than his host too, he thought bitterly. He'd been a slight man, neatly but leanly built and no taller than Pel himself, which was something, although his handshake had been powerful and firm. His face was lined, as would be expected in a man of his age, but the lines were not cruel ones, they seemed more to accentuate his ready smile and the bright eyes that shone like two polished black beads. In fact he looked more like an amiable postman than a killer criminal. He'd been extremely polite and considerate of Pel's situation too, providing him with a warm and comfortable bedroom, a bathroom to himself, even a spare thousand cigarettes, the right brand too. And when his stay was longer than expected – Pel had needed a lot of convincing to take on the job of finding his granddaughter, trying to find out more about the man and his plans, but he'd cheerfully seen through that too and had told him nothing – he had suggested a phone call to his wife to put her mind at rest. Where Pel was the permanent pessimist, the Poltergeist struck him as being an optimist. Where Pel frowned and looked as if he were about to murder someone, the Poltergeist smiled and offered him another drink. Pel had to admit, and he scowled heavily at the thought of it, that unfortunately he'd almost liked the man. How in hell's name could he tell the whizz kids of Special Branch in Paris that?

Debray interrupted his train of thought.

47

'Yes,' Pel snapped, noticing a new boy hiding behind the computer maniac.

'I've been playing with my programs again,' Debray informed him happily. 'Pujol asked me for a listing of all light aircraft clubs in the area, right up to the Paris outskirts. We started to make contact with them and on the seventh call found your plane.'

Pel had removed his glasses and was reaching for the blue packet sitting with the throwaway lighter. At last he would know where he'd been.

'Unfortunately,' Debray continued, while Pujol retreated even further behind him and Pel slumped back in his chair, a Gauloise smouldering gently between his lips, 'the plane won't talk, and the pilot was paid 20,000 francs to turn his back on someone borrowing his wings. He was phoned, the cash was delivered by unknown messenger and he spent the weekend at his sister's in the Auvergne. His plane was returned intact but the tanks were empty and no entry had been made in the log-book. No one saw the plane leave or come back – it's a tiny club and most of the time unmanned. He has since been sacked from the club – they consider his actions to be irresponsible.'

'And I consider them to be infuriating!'

Another cigarette did little to calm his nerves. Pel decided a gentle trip into the country to refile the facts in his mind was the best idea he'd had that morning.

He lifted the internal telephone and buzzed the Sergeants' Room. 'The one with the least to do is to order a car and report to my office five minutes ago.' That'll get them going, he thought, as he reached for his pencils, notepads and a spare dozen packets of Gauloises, just in case.

Darcy surprised him by putting his head round the door.

'You should be busier than I am,' Pel snorted.

'I am, but I wanted to introduce you to the man with the least to do.' Darcy smiled. Pel could tell from the smile something not very nice was coming. 'He's Lage's replacement.'

Darcy swung open the door and led the way for the man with least to do.

It was a giant.

Well over six foot tall, and shoulders to go with it. And he was too good-looking for Pel's comfort. And he was immaculately dressed. He made Pel feel like the man who'd come to mend the lavatory.

And he was an Arab.

Pel looked the new man over, all two metres of him.

First he looked him over with his spectacles still perched on the top of his head. Then he allowed them to snap back on to the bridge of his nose and he looked the man over through the lenses with his head tilted back, giving the impression that he was in fact looking down at him. He noticed Darcy smiling to himself. He also noticed the new man didn't flinch once.

'Name?' Pel snapped.

'Kader Camel, sir, Camel will do, sir.'

'Christian name?'

'Cherif, sir.'

'Sheriff!'

'Yes, sir.'

'Holy Mother of God, don't tell me, you ride a horse and wear a ten gallon hat?'

'I know how to ride, but have never been called upon while on duty, and I have never, and don't intend ever, to wear a ten gallon hat, sir.'

'Well, that's something, I suppose.' Pel sighed. 'With a name like Sheriff you're going to get a lot of teasing in the police force, not to mention in the streets.'

'I'm used to it, sir. The name Camel doesn't help either, sir. There are plenty of hump jokes, but I'm used to that too. It's my father's name and I'm proud of it.'

'Mm, quite.' Pel stirred the air with a stray pencil. 'Nationality?' He knew the answer to that one, only French citizens were allowed into the Police Judiciaire, but he was just checking.

The man looked Pel straight in the eye. "French, sir. As French as you or Monsieur Darcy.'

Pel sniffed. 'You may be as French as Darcy,' he said, 'but I doubt very much that you're as French as I am.' He allowed this piece of information to sink in before going on. 'And what makes you so French?'

'My father was one of the *Harkis*. He fought for and with the French in Algeria. In recognition of his bravery they awarded

49

him a number of medals, the Légion d'Honneur included. In recognition of his loyalty they gave him his passage to France and the right to live in peace here. I was born in France, in Burgundy, I was educated at a French school, a Burgundian school, and I am now a member of the French police force, the Burgundian police force.'

Pel had the idea Darcy had briefed the man. He knew Pel thought anyone born outside Burgundy was a foreigner.

'And I suppose you were top of the class at the Ecole de Police?' he asked sarcastically. But the reply was absolutely serious.

'With a name like Camel, I had to be.'

'And I suppose you're going to be invaluable to my team?'

'I expect so, sir.'

'I beg your pardon,' Pel growled.

Still the man didn't turn a hair. 'Being of Arab descent', he said calmly, 'is sometimes more difficult in the police force than being a woman. I have to prove over and over again that I am as good as, if not better than, everyone else. You won't be disappointed, sir.'

'I certainly hope not,' Pel snorted. 'Now go and get the car and wait for me in front. And by the way,' he added, looking down at the papers on his desk, 'welcome to the team.'

'I'm very proud to be here, sir.' He turned and left, closing the door quietly behind him.

'You were a bit hard, Patron,' Darcy grinned.

'If he can stand the interview, he'll cope with the job. Police work can be far more bloody-minded than I can.'

'Yes, but the two together can be hell. We have to be strong men to cope with you both,' Darcy said, 'but he looks a bit more positive than the two wets Pujol and Rigal – one hardly notices that they're there.'

'They're just crafty, that way they keep out of trouble and avoid extra duties,' Pel replied. 'Make a note to give them a few. And by the way,' he added, 'when I get back, I want you to interrogate me again.'

'With pleasure, Patron. May I bring the knuckle-dusters this time?'

* * *

50

Pel was pleased with Cherif's driving, not that he would have dreamt of saying so. He hadn't asked for directions to Clavell, he'd simply started the engine and smoothly but gently accelerated away. The only little niggle had been when Cherif asked him to put on his safety belt. Pel hated them. They were compulsory, and had been for some time, but he still hated them; they made him feel like a trussed-up chicken ready for the chop, and he avoided wearing them whenever he could. However, as it was the first time he'd been driven by his new lightly coloured colleague, he capitulated and attached himself; perhaps he would need it. He found his driving as confident and smooth as the man himself and although Pel tried hard to dislike him intensely he found himself relaxing and allowing his mind to turn over the problems he faced.

Apart from finding out where the famous Poltergeist was hiding and returning him to Fresnes prison to finish his thirteen-year prison sentence, they were looking for his grand-daughter, of whom they knew very little apart from her academic history. They were going to have to do a lot of research to find out what she'd been up to in her spare time while the Poltergeist had been locked away for the last two years. And secondly there had been rumours about her keeping bad company. That didn't surprise Pel in the least. The research, however, he was going to have to leave to his men. Once he had the information, he could start studying it and making some guess as to where they should look next, because it was very probably going to be guesswork – that and a hell of a lot of foot-slogging, repetitious question-asking, and mostly negative results. What a pleasure police work was. Sometimes he wondered why he did it. There was only one possible answer to that: he was good at it. It was the only thing he was good at. Although, he realised, he was still married, after all these years, and to an attractive and successful woman – he wasn't quite sure how or why but his home life seemed to be a success too. Quite extraordinary, he wouldn't have married him even if he'd been paid. Marriage, he felt, had mellowed him, from intolerable all of the time, to intolerable only part of the time. Marriage, he decided, was good for a man. Nosjean was married now, de

51

Troq' looked like getting close with his titled secretary in the Palais de Justice, but Darcy still seemed a long way off, which was curious as he'd always been the one with dozens to choose from, a new woman every week, no problems in finding them or bedding them. He'd been the envy of the entire Hôtel de Police, because the girls were always beautiful. His current girlfriend was beautiful, Kate, but she was miles away down in the Tarn, for God's sake. That was no way to carry on a romance. Darcy had had to fight hard for Kate's attentions too, she hadn't just fallen into his arms like the rest of them. It was quite obvious that Darcy had got it bad, but had Kate? They only saw each other once a month or so, and apparently it didn't worry Kate in the least; perhaps she didn't know Darcy's reputation, perhaps she didn't care. Pel was feeling fatherly – after all, it was Darcy who had helped him change the wealthy widow, Madame Faivre-Peret, into Madame Pel. Perhaps he should have a word with Kate and push things along a bit; he'd like to return the favour, and she was the daughter of a friend of his. However, knowing him, he'd make a mess of it. Perhaps he'd let his wife do the talking.

Another decision made, he turned his mind back to police work. The other big problem they had at the moment was the robberies. There had been five of them over the last twenty-four months and they didn't look like stopping. They were always from the very rich, not just the rich, but the very rich, the ones who had so much money it made most people ill to think about it, but the robberies didn't seem to have been committed by someone who wanted to get back at the over-rich. They'd been chosen, he believed, because they had something distinctly worth stealing. Each time the robber, or robbers, had taken very few items, but always the most valuable. Collectors' pieces, the sort prospective buyers would pay over the odds just to own even if they couldn't exhibit them. A small sketch of Degas' *Danseuse*, two stamps, both worth a fortune, a first edition of Molière, three antique guns, and finally a priceless collection of diamond rings. Something else occurred to Pel: everything stolen had been small, small enough to fit into a coat pocket, apart from the rifle and that wasn't huge or heavy.

Descriptions of the stolen articles had already been sent out nationwide after each robbery but they could go out again all on one list accompanied by drawings or photographs where possible to jog memories. He doubted very much they would turn up because by now they'd be locked away out of sight in someone's private collection, but that was no excuse to do nothing – the police had to be seen to be doing their best even when they knew it was useless. He made a note to give the order on his return and realised his writing was far clearer than usual considering he was in a moving car. The car had stopped moving. He looked up.

'The house, sir,' Cherif said, 'is just across the square, when you're ready.'

Pel snapped his notebook closed and opened the car door to be nearly annihilated by a small boy on a pair of roller skates. He shied away like a startled foal. Fortunately Cherif was pretending not to have noticed Pel's leap to safety, but was casually walking away from the car towards the complainant's house. Pel gathered his embarrassment and his raincoat together, thanking God that it had momentarily stopped raining, although the black sky promised more of the same.

The house belonging to the cat-woman was a small, tidy, modern villa, set on the edge of an old crumbling hamlet.

The complainant, Madame Lucien, Marie-Antoinette, was large, in fact enormous, as imposing as the Pompidou Centre, but untidy and absolutely hideous. Pel considered her size and her name: apparently another parent had made a prize cock-up of choosing its offspring's label. Marie-Antoinette was not a name for a craggy mountain. She stood back from the open front door to let them in. The three of them squeezed into the narrow hall and came to a halt. She blocked the way completely but was trying to reach past them to close the door. It was an impossible scramble until Cherif obliged and she finally turned and shuffled her worn-out plimsolls towards the sitting-room, her massive hips brushing the walls on both sides of the corridor as she walked. It was a good thing people weren't equipped with wing mirrors, Pel thought; she'd have stuck fast. Fortunately the sitting-room was the largest room in the house and at last they had space to manoeuvre. Pel signalled

Cherif to carry on while he stood back to study in fascination the ten tons in front of him.

If she'd fallen over, he was sure she'd be permanently stranded on the floor, paddling like a beached whale and unable to right herself. Even her fingers, he noticed, bulged like overstuffed sausages. The poor woman moved with difficulty, swaying from side to side to enable her legs to travel forwards, while her arms stuck out diagonally from her shoulders because the circumference of her body prevented them from hanging straight down. Her head was not much better; it was covered with dyed black hair, the sort of blue-black that can only come out of a bottle, and unfortunately it had come out of the bottle a long time ago because the confused irregular parting in the middle of her head was almost white. Her top front teeth were missing. Holy Mother of God, Pel thought, what a sight; she was worse than he was first thing in the morning, and he was enough to give himself nightmares. But, he told himself severely, she was a member of the public, who had made a complaint, and was due the same courtesy and attention as a beauty queen with a complaint even though it was about something as potty as poisoning pussy cats!

Cherif, he had to admit, was doing well. Trying to keep the woman's mind from side-tracking into what she fed the local cats and moaning about not feeling very well herself was not easy, but he spoke firmly, quietly and always politely, ignoring most of what she said, noting anything relevant, and interrupting her gently when she started quoting cat-food prices. Finally, he closed the notebook and turned to his boss. 'Have you any questions to add, Chief Inspector Pel?'

'Yes, just one. Have you seen anyone at the big house, the *maison de maître*, on the other side of the square?' Pel wanted to know if Vlaxi was back in town.

'Only the nasty gardener who tried to kill my Minou. It was the day after he came to work that little Minette died in my arms. She was sick all over me, poor dear.' Her eyes were moist, remembering the tragedy. 'I laid her to rest in the garden,' she went on fighting back the tears, 'under the apple tree. You can see the little cross from the window. Poor little pussy cat . . .'

Cherif extended his courteous hand to bring the interview to a close. 'Thank you, madame, for telling us all about it. We'll see ourselves out.'

They made their escape into a downpour.

Sheltering in the car while the rain hammered on the tin roof like a set of drums in full swing, they looked at one another. Pel couldn't resist a crooked smile.

'Loony,' he said.

'Completely,' Cherif replied, returning the smile. 'Would you like to take a wrong turn and end up round the back of Vlaxi's old house, sir?'

7

As there was little to see but neat gardens and locked doors *chez* Vlaxi, Pel was happily back behind his own desk doing his impression of a damp garden bonfire and billowing smoke in all directions before his men were filtering through the door of the Hôtel de Police. First through the door of his office was de Troq'.

'Here's a copy of the fax I propose sending all over France about the robberies. I thought it would be a good idea to make a complete list of what has been stolen and may turn up in private collections, market stalls, antique and second-hand shops. Pujol's just finished it. I've checked it through, nothing's been left out.' Pel was grumpily scratching out an item on one of his lists. 'Plus,' de Troq' added, 'a copy of the fax to be sent to all Hôtels de Police informing them to check all holiday homes, in an effort to find the Poltergeist's hideout. We've omitted the coastal towns,' he pointed out. 'Darcy said you didn't hear any seagulls!'

'Good.' Pel nodded and reached for a cigarette, silently pleased by the efficiency of his department. 'And all the other reports about our missing granddaughter, fingerprints at the scene of the robberies, comparisons of technique and so on?'

'They'll be coming through shortly. Everyone's taking out their frustrations on the typewriters, even the new guy, Cherif.'

'What's he got to report, for God's sake?'

'An interview, it seems,' Nosjean replied, 'plus a number of phone calls he made to the inhabitants of Clavell.'

'About sabotaged cats?' Pel was amazed at the Arab's fastidiousness. 'Poisoning pussies, terrorising our feline friends, surely he's not going to make me read a report on that?'

'No, more about the comings and goings of Clavell. Unfortunately, he, like the rest of us, doesn't seem to be coming up with much. It's a pretty quiet place with nothing out of the ordinary bar the fishman who comes on Fridays and bread van that arrives twice a week and whose driver is apparently having a passionate love affair with a woman half-way down the hill.'

Depressing news, but to be expected. Pel removed his spectacles and looked at the young aristocratic de Troq': he never seemed to grow any older. 'And how is your passionate love affair with your titled young lady at the Palais de Justice, *mon brave*?'

It was unlike Pel to be personal but de Troq' showed no surprise; it was unlike him to show emotion at all. 'Progressing well, thank you. Both our families seem satisfied with one another.'

That appeared to be the end of that conversation so Pel tried another. 'And Nosjean,' he asked, 'how's he coping with married life?'

'Very well, I believe, although he tells me his wife is anxious to start a family. He says he hasn't finished getting used to being married yet so the idea of being a father frightens him to death.' His face broke into a smile. Nosjean, who barely looked old enough to be a policeman let alone a father, had amused the Sergeants' Room for days with his anxieties. It was old news; if it hadn't been, de Troq' wouldn't have said a word.

'Women,' Pel said knowingly, in fact knowing very little, the success of his marriage being entirely due to the patience and intelligence of his wife. 'It's better to let them have what they want – within reason, of course. And talking of passionate love affairs, tell me, in confidence of course, how's it going between Darcy and Kate?'

De Troq' knew what Pel was up to: he wanted a quick

rundown on the state of the affairs of his senior officers. A policeman with personal problems was a distracted policeman and no good to the likes of Pel. De Troq' thought carefully before replying. 'She's the only one of Darcy's women that he doesn't talk about, so I suspect it may be serious.'

'They don't see each other very often, do they?'

'No, they live too far apart.'

'When they do, does he seem better for it when he gets back?'

'Yes. But,' he added, 'Darcy always seems better for it.' Before he slipped out through the door Pel could have sworn de Troq' grinned at him.

Cherif was the next to appear. Pel removed his spectacles and reached for his cigarettes, passing a hand wearily through his thinning hair and finding even less there than he'd hoped. He sat back and waited; new boys were tiresome, particularly keen ones. Through the cloud of blue smoke he had to admit the bloke was impressive, the sort of bloke one would feel safe walking through a riot with.

'Yes?' he said, blowing smoke in his direction and trying to look harassed.

'My report on our visit to Clavell,' the good-looking Arab replied, placing several papers on the corner of Pel's desk. 'Not important, except that the gardener employed at the Vlaxi house is an old boy from the next village and has three cats of his own. He swears he didn't put down poison for even the mice. He's paid by banker's order to keep the place looking tidy. He met the owner a long time ago, he says, and hasn't seen him since, but as long as he keeps getting paid, he'll keep on doing the work. Shall I keep digging too?'

'When you're not needed for something more important.' Pel had to admit Cherif showed initiative and he hadn't wasted words on a self-complimentary speech. Pel had been at the interview with the fat cat-woman – Cherif wasn't to know he hadn't been listening. It would all be in his report anyway; he'd simply told him the one thing he had marked down for Cherif to check. Pel looked down at his lists and crossed off another item, 'Vlaxi's gardener'.

'Tell me,' he went on, trying out a smile and managing

to look worse than ever, 'how do you feel after your first full day?'

'Looking forward to tomorrow, sir.'

Keen. Pel didn't suppose that would last past the first crisis with leave weekends and private life in general cancelled.

'And I suppose they're looking after you in the Sergeants' Room?'

'Yes, sir.'

'And Misset?'

'No more annoying than a fly in winter, sir.'

'Carry on.'

'Sir.'

There was a smile lurking in Pel's expression: he checked it quickly and replaced it with a more comfortable frown. Cherif had started well but he was a bit heavy-handed on the sirs. It made him feel like an elderly general. Respect was all very well, but there were limits – he'd have to have a word with Darcy and get him to calm their coloured colleague down. And what the hell did he mean about Misset? No more annoying than a fly in winter?

The men were in, the reports were in, most of the inhabitants of the Hôtel de Police were on their way home leaving a skeleton staff on duty. And Pel. After the reports had been finished he had to read them. He stared at a page of bad typing that Bardolle had struggled over. It amazed everyone that he had managed it at all with his prize fighter fists, but at least when he was in front of the antique typewriter, thrown out of the typing pool a hundred years ago, his tongue sticking between his teeth and a heavy frown clouding his cheerful country face, there was no danger of being blasted from the room by his booming voice.

Darcy pushed his head round the door to wish him a good evening before he left. While there was plenty of work, for the moment there was no panic on so Pel's men made the most of it to leave only a few hours late.

Pel looked up briefly and grimaced. As Darcy's head was disappearing again he was called back.

'What do you do with flies in winter?' Pel asked.
'Squash them!'

As he turned the millionth page that evening, it occurred to him that reading reports was one small bit of police work that he could do at home, in the comfort of his own sitting-room with his own wife while she listened to classical music. Although he was not a fan he had grown accustomed to Mozart, Delius, Bach and the rest of the bunch, even finding them quite soothing after the noise of human chaos all day at work. Madame, being an intelligent woman, had long given up trying to convince her husband of the merits of opera and chose instead the more peaceful movements for the evenings when he was there.

She did so this evening, and while Madame Routy crashed the crockery into the dishwasher in the kitchen, and Pel settled himself into his comfortable armchair, Madame Pel placed the Brandenburg concertos on to her newly acquired compact disc player. Pel had been flabbergasted by the cost of her new musical set-up, but as she had gently pointed out, she could afford it. Her hairdressing salon, Nanette's, the most expensive in the city, was doing as well as ever, and so were the two high-class boutiques she'd opened in case her customers from Nanette's had any money left after paying for their hair. Apparently they had.

The crashing from the kitchen had ceased, Madame Routy had retired to her own quarters, Bach was gently smoothing the wrinkles in Pel's brow, his wife was sitting reading in the other armchair, and he had a glass of finest Scotch whisky in his hand. Pel looked round the attractive sitting-room of his home and found it hard to believe; if anyone could see him they'd think he was a very successful man. How had it happened? He hadn't done it, he was sure – it had to be his wife. Until he'd married her his housekeeper had terrorised him, his clothes looked as if they belonged to a tramp and his house looked like a heap of bricks and shutters and doors dumped in an abandoned field. This was quite a change, he thought. He felt contentment; it was an unusual feeling for Pel. Then the file slipped from his knees and scattered dozens of papers like confetti all over the carpet. Happiness didn't last long in Pel's life.

As it was Sunday the following day, Pel allowed himself the luxury of an extra thirty seconds in bed until guilt overcame him at the thought of all those criminals already hard at work, and he crowbarred himself from the covers and staggered to the bathroom. A pale, unshaven face, topped with pale, thinning hair that stood on end, looked back at him from the mirror. Good grief, thank God I haven't got my glasses on, he thought. If I could see myself properly I'd be terrified.

Pink and polished from the shower, Pel installed himself opposite his wife at the dining-room table for breakfast to find her in conversation with their housekeeper.

'But, Madame Routy, how do you know he's such a terrible man?'

'Seen it in the papers, haven't I? Drugs, guns, murder, slave trade, he's done the lot,' she retorted.

'About whom are we speaking?' Pel inquired in his best employer's voice.

'I don't know about you,' came back the employee's chiselled reply, 'but we were talking about the Poltergeist.' Pel felt momentarily crushed.

'There was a reconstruction of his escape from prison on the television last night,' his wife explained.

'They did it in a helicopter,' the housekeeper interrupted. 'It's always by helicopter, isn't it? Vaujour in 1986, piloted by his wife, Nadine; in '87 it was Philippe Truc de Roche from Nice; '81, I think I'm correct in saying, there were two, Daniel Beaumont and Gerard Dupré; and another three in 1992, you must remember that one. All by helicopter.'

Pel raised his eyebrows at his well-informed housekeeper. He had long suspected her of being an undercover criminal herself; now he was convinced.

'When are they going to cover the exercise areas with anti-helicopter grilles?' she demanded.

'When they can afford it,' Pel replied: as with so many things, it was all a question of money.

'Not soon enough, that's my opinion.'

'Madame Routy feels very strongly,' Pel's wife intervened,

hoping to avoid full-scale war between her housekeeper and her husband, 'that the Poltergeist's been at large long enough and if he's not caught in the immediate future he'll be up to his old tricks again.'

'A massacre, that's what it'll be,' Madame Routy said, warming to the subject. 'A veritable blood bath.'

'I doubt it very much,' Pel said. 'The Poltergeist was very select with his crimes – they were carefully planned, and he left the least possible amount of mess after him – and I'd like to point out that he was never convicted of murder. However, I would be interested to hear about the reconstruction, if you have time,' he added, 'after fetching the coffee.'

As Madame Routy worked up to full revs about prisons, prisoners and most other subjects vaguely connected with the escape, Pel and his wife silently worked their way through their breakfast of coffee and croissants. Pel gave the impression of not listening to a word, studying his coffee throughout the speech; Madame, however, looked up from time to time and nodded at their housekeeper.

'And after all that,' she was saying, 'they went on to report on the disappearance of the old rogue's granddaughter, Laura. Of all the nerve, as if you poor souls at police headquarters haven't got enough to do, and now you've got to look for a criminal's lost family. It wouldn't surprise me if she was the one who organised his escape and they've buggered off together.'

'Madame Routy!'

'Excuse me, madame. I think I'd better tidy up the kitchen before I go to my sister's for Sunday lunch.'

Pel was smothering laughter behind a soggy croissant.

Darcy soon put a stop to Pel's mirth when he rang shortly afterwards.

'Seen the Sunday papers, Patron?'

'Haven't had a chance yet. What's in them?'

'A very handsome picture of you, and of course Sarrazin's scoop story.'

Pel picked up the Sunday papers. Naturally the leading story was a political crisis. Pel sniffed; he thought little of politicians and even less of their prima donna behaviour over crises. The important story of the day, that of a Chief Inspector's temporary disappearance, was slotted in with the dwindling reports on the whereabouts of the Poltergeist. Alongside was a less than becoming picture of Pel.

'I look more like a villain than the Poltergeist,' he commented to his wife as they read through the story.

The headline Sarrazin had chosen was inevitably sensational: POLICE CHIEF KIDNAPPED. POLTERGEIST PLAYS HIS PART.

'Well, there's the first bit of ad-libbing,' Pel said. 'But the rest looks all right.'

'Chief Inspector Evariste Clovis Désiré Pel . . .' Pel sighed. Sarrazin had certainly done his research, damn him. Was it a joke, or plain viciousness that had made him print all his Christian names? He wasn't sure whether it had been a joke or plain viciousness when his parents had chosen them. They'd always been an embarrassment to him, but unfortunately there was no way of getting rid of them. He continued to read. '. . . was kidnapped from in front of his own Hôtel de Police between 6 p.m. and midnight on 15th April. He was hooded and first taken by car, then plane, then car again to an isolated cottage. No one knows where. It was only when he was inside behind locked shutters that the hood was removed; the identity of his kidnappers, however, has not been revealed to me, if indeed the police know themselves, and although I was called personally to the Hôtel de Police to see the officers in charge of the case they were unable to give me any clues. The purpose of this little adventure was to brief the Chief Inspector about the missing granddaughter of the famous escaped Poltergeist. Although her disappearance has already been reported by her maid some weeks ago, it was felt that not enough progress had been made and a well-known detective like Monsieur Pel should be enlisted. Perhaps they didn't realise at the local gendarmerie, where her maid went to report her absence, who Mademoiselle Laura Lebon was? Chief Inspector Pel, who has earned himself the reputation of a policeman who always gets his man, told me the Poltergeist is, according to his information, willing to give himself up when his granddaughter is safely returned home.

'Do we or the police believe him? Has his granddaughter been abducted or has she run away, sick of her criminal heritage and the hold her grandfather has over her? Now that he's free again, does she no longer feel safe? Does she know something she shouldn't? Is this why she must be found? In any event, as I was told yesterday by Chief Inspector Pel himself, Laura Lebon is officially a missing person; she is a French citizen, and is entitled to protection (from her grandfather or her enemies), and it is therefore with diligence that he will undertake the finding of this girl. Unfortunately, although this request was made on behalf of the Poltergeist, he was unable to give me any information as to where the escaped criminal is hiding, but will work just as diligently in his efforts to help the Special Branch find a wanted and dangerous man.'

There followed a brief description of the granddaughter and an old school photograph her maid had given Sarrazin showing Laura aged fifteen. The girl was now twenty-one and inevitably looked nothing like the blurred photograph. It certainly looked nothing like the picture Pel had distributed to his men.

'Well, he didn't stray too much from what I dictated,' Pel commented.

'And he makes you sound like Bruce Wayne of Gotham City, a real hero,' Madame said, smiling.

'Who in God's name is he?'

Inevitably the story brought the Big Boys from Special Branch storming down from Paris and on Monday morning they were waiting in his office to question and requestion Pel on the events during his few days' absence. While he hung on to his patience, his nerves and his tongue, he tried to co-operate. They finally left, having wasted a great deal of time, but with no further information than Sarrazin had given the whole of France, and no more information than Pel had himself – except, of course, and he had no proof, that he had spent the weekend with the Poltergeist. The man he'd seen didn't look anything like the face they had on file, which was grey and drawn with pale blue eyes, nothing like the polished black beads Pel remembered.

It had been a strange experience altogether. To begin with, Pel had been infuriated anyone could be so sure of themselves as to kidnap him right outside the Hôtel de Police and spirit him away for a couple of days in the country. However, as he'd grudgingly settled in, he couldn't say it had been unpleasant. Unnerving at first but not unpleasant, although he'd told Darcy he'd suffered terribly. He remembered the first evening meal. 'I'm not guilty of drug-smuggling,' his host had said. 'I wouldn't touch the muck, I'm not an assassin. And anyway, it's too profitable simply robbing the rich.'

'A veritable little Robin Hood.' Pel couldn't resist it.

'Hardly, *mon ami*. I don't give it to the poor, I keep it for myself, thereby avoiding all possibility of joining them in the workhouse. I steal from those who can afford it, who have an excess or are well insured. Let's face it, all insurance companies are thieves – they deserve to pay up occasionally.' Pel had found his head nodding spontaneously. The man was a crook, but a hospitable and amusing one. Watching the dawn arrive just before his departure on the final morning, Pel had briefly considered admitting his host to the Bigots' Club, of which he was secretary, treasurer and honorary member. There was only one other member, his wife's Cousin Roger. Perhaps, he thought, he should boost the membership list and allow his kidnapper . . . The proposal was turned down immediately; kidnappers were not allowed in his club.

He called Darcy into the office. 'Okay, now the ponces from Paris have gone home, it's your turn. Have another go.'

'With or without the knuckle-dusters?'

'Just get on with it, and stop grinning.'

'Change places with me.'

'I beg your pardon?'

'I want you sitting this side of the desk in the small uncomfortable chair.' Darcy was enjoying himself. Pel was shocked but agreed to change places. After taking his seat, however, he announced that the hard chair was not good for his ulcer and he'd have to change back if he was going to concentrate without interruptions from the pain in his stomach. Pel had no ulcer but, like all French children, he'd learnt enough about the workings of his body at school to turn him into a hypochondriac as soon as he grasped the essentials. Pel was better at it than most.

As Pel gained his own personal chair Darcy opened fire. After squabbling for some time, Darcy trying unsuccessfully to be a bully, they accepted it was useless. Pel was still the Patron and every time Darcy became verbally violent Pel's eyebrows came down into a perfectly practised curtain of bad temper and he threatened to fire him. They were getting nowhere.

'Damn it, Darcy,' he growled, 'you're not trying.'

'You, on the other hand, are very trying. So far the only thing you've told me that I didn't know already was that you were served a very fine kir, and that your host knew the aperitif was named after our Maire of long ago who invented the damn drink.'

'You didn't know that?' Pel exclaimed. 'How dare you work for me in the city of Dijon and not know that? You're fired!'

'Of course I knew where kir comes from,' Darcy said patiently, 'but you hadn't mentioned the fact that you'd been drinking it with the Poltergeist the last time I questioned you. And, Patron,' he added, 'firing me isn't going to get you anywhere closer to remembering something useful.'

'Neither is blathering on about noises and smells or food and drink – which reminds me, I'm thirsty.' He looked briefly at his watch. 'I've had enough, and I'm hungry. Let's go for a beer and a rubber pâté sandwich across the road. You never know, it might be edible today.'

Since the introduction of the law prohibiting smoking in public places, Pel had been perturbed that it might prohibit him from the pleasures of the Bar Transvaal. However, as the bar was situated across the street from the Hôtel de Police, the owner realised immediately he'd go bankrupt if he tried to stop his clients, mostly harassed policemen, smoking on the premises. Although the law was the law, he'd found a nice way round it.

Stuck neatly to the door was the information that the Smokers' Room was inside, while the terrace, a larger area, was strictly No Smoking. As it was still chucking it down, the rain ran in rivers off the sagging awning to splash on to the tops of the terrace tables; there were no non-smokers out there. Pel smiled to himself and fought his way through the fog inside to the bar.

Chewing his way through half a crisp fresh baguette filled with pâté which in his opinion tasted like canned cat-food, Pel watched the immaculate Darcy drink.

'By the way,' he said, 'that makes me think of the coloured gentleman who has just joined our team.'

Darcy looked blankly over his glass of beer.

'The Arab.'

'Hardly coloured, Patron, just lightly tanned.'

'Whatever, tell him he can consider the cat case his own. I can't think he'll make a mess of it even though he's a novice – there isn't much to make a mess of for the moment. In fact, he did quite well the other morning. And while you're at it, tell him to call Vlaxi's number from time to time. A gardener is being paid to tend his lovely lawns so he may be preparing a comeback.'

'He may also be preparing for the place to be sold,' suggested Darcy.

'Possibly, but a phone call or two doesn't cost much time or money, and there's no one spare to sit and watch, especially as it may only be innocent couples looking at a house for sale. Get him to find out if the house has been registered with any estate agents, or the local Notaire. We may just get a lead on where he or his band of undesirables are operating from now.'

'I think you'll find he's already started,' Darcy replied, attacking a microwaved hamburger that he'd just been served. Pel watched while he removed the cellophane wrapping and took a bite.

'How can you eat that muck?'

'The same way I eat anything,' Darcy replied pleasantly. 'With my teeth. You ought to try one sometime – a floppy hamburger gives your gums a rest from being lacerated by our delicious crusty bread.' Darcy chewed briefly and swallowed, followed it by a mouthful of beer and asked Pel how he'd got on with Cherif when they'd gone out together.

'Not bad, for an Arab,' Pel replied grudgingly. 'How's he going down in the Sergeants' Room?'

66

'Misset did his best and asked our Monsieur Camel if he would prefer one hump or two in his coffee, but Cherif shut him up pretty smartly with a remark that showed Misset to be the fool we all know he is.'

'Oh.' Pel looked at Darcy, who was contentedly chewing again. Misset was a clot and needed forever putting in his place. He was pleased Cherif had started so promptly. 'What was the remark?'

'That one learnt at Maternelle the difference between a camel and a dromedary and that having acquired this knowledge it was surely not necessary to ask if a Camel had one hump or two. He suggested that perhaps Misset should return to playschool for a refresher course!'

'Good God! Poor old Misset!' But Pel smiled inwardly, at the same time trying desperately to recall how many humps a camel had.

'He slunk back to his desk while Cherif helped himself to two lumps of sugar.'

Two, of course, Pel thought. He was delighted to have remembered, his education had been complete after all.

The lunch hour was over: it had lasted a bare twenty minutes. A message came by phone that Darcy was needed back at the office and he quickly swallowed what remained of his beer. As he turned to leave, Pel informed him that he was going to see his wife at Nanette's hair salon to try the range of perfumed oils she sold to her wealthy customers. 'I'm determined to identify what I smelt at the Poltergeist's house. You think it's important, and I think you may after all be right. And talking about wives,' he added, 'when are you going to get yourself one?'

8

Pel pulled the collar of his mackintosh up round his ears. He would have liked to pull it up over his balding head, but that was for kids. He shrugged to himself; what remained of his hair was going to get rearranged, and he would end up looking about as well groomed as a road sweeper on a blustery day. Staring out at the new day early on Tuesday morning, he realised the *météo* hadn't made a mistake. They'd said more rain, and more rain was precisely what they were getting. It was a record according to the specialists, but then it always was, Pel thought sourly. Even so, the non-stop downpours were becoming rather tedious. Pel didn't like rain; it made him soggy round the collar. He didn't like high winds; they boxed his ears like an angry uncle. He didn't like hot sunshine either; it made him perspire far too freely, and his feet felt like they were standing in bowls of soup. In fact, Pel summed himself up, he didn't like weather. And there was an awful lot of it about at the moment. As he stood by the front door contemplating the few metres between him and his car, Yves Pasquier, his next-door neighbour, was preparing to dash for the school bus.

'Want to borrow my snorkle, Chief Inspector?' he shouted cheerfully.

It was then that Pel realised the boy was hidden behind a large pair of goggles. He waved to his young friend. 'Thank you, I'll manage,' he replied, 'but I'd get a pair of windscreen wipers fitted to those things if I were you.'

As he entered the city limits he noticed the locals fighting their way to work, heads bent against the wind, pushing straining umbrellas in front of them in an effort to find some protection. Everyone was scowling. There was no one on the street corners or outside the cafés passing the time of day; they were all concentrating on not being drowned.

However, Darcy found Pel sitting looking smug when he arrived in his office.

'Well, it's not the weather,' he said, 'so what's cheered you up, Patron?'

'I know what the smell was! My wife is a perfume fiend and having tried all the exotic oils at the salon, which were no good at all, she finally handed me an uninteresting bottle of coloured water they use for the occasional gentleman client. That was it. Lavender water.'

'Lavender, that means Provence. It's well known for its production of lavender. It's a bit early in the season but the morning sun on the damp countryside would have made the smell stronger, enough for even you to notice.'

They'd finally narrowed it down to the upper part of the Gard, Bouche du Rhône, Var and the Vaucluse departments. It was something. A phone call to Avignon was made in the hope of enlisting their help in scouring the countryside for the hideout where Pel had been held. But help was not forthcoming.

The weather was even worse in the south of France, and Darcy went back to report to Pel looking grim.

'What's up, *mon brave*? Has the Eiffel Tower been washed away in the storms?'

'No, Patron, but virtually a whole village has.'

'Inform me.'

'It doesn't really concern us,' Darcy explained, 'but the local police won't have time to check on the holiday homes in the area for a few days. The Vaucluse has been declared a disaster area. The sheer quantity of water pouring into the valleys from the surrounding hillsides simply caved in the river banks, washing away houses, new and old alike. The water level continued to rise, flooding fields and streets. A whole caravan site was swept away, with the residents inside. A very weary chap from Avignon police telephoned to apologise for their temporary inability to help us with our search. He said they'd been working with insufficiently equipped firemen and non-existent emergency services since before five this morning. No one expected it to happen in Provence. They've got seven dead and so far twenty-nine missing.'

What a wonderfully depressing way to start the day, Pel thought. Thank God he lived in Burgundy. He looked out through the window darkened by rain; it was still hammering down relentlessly. It was enough to make a man worry rats.

After the usual morning meeting, the day settled down to be dull and grey, orchestrated by the constant roar of the skies depositing gallons of water on anyone silly enough to step outside. Fortunately for Pel's men, most of their footwork had been completed and questions could now be put by phone. Their files on the Poltergeist's granddaughter and the recent robberies were filling up nicely. Members of the public wandered in to make complaints or a nuisance of themselves but the detectives did their jobs quietly and without agitation, glad to be inside for once. They were all aware that it was usually on a day like today that all hell broke loose and everyone turned out into the streets to swim their way from door to door. Pel's team were keeping quiet and dry, hoping no one would notice.

It didn't last long.

As darkness crept over Burgundy, early because of the black canopy overhead, extraordinary though it was, fire was reported. The *pompiers'* fire engines wailed out of the city. Everyone held their breath and stopped putting on their coats: it was well after six and the moment they'd looked forward to all day, time to go home. At first they thought it had been a pile-up on one of the main roads out of town – the conditions were terrible and the visibility awful – but news came through eventually that it was only a barn blaze at a local farm. A sigh of relief was heard from the Sergeants' Room; something as simple as that wasn't going to concern them and drag them out into the awful weather. There was far too much of it about that evening and no one wanted to partake of it.

Little did they know it was going to be the key in a murder case.

When Pel heard the following morning where the fire had been, he had the distinct feeling that life had it in for him. 'Clavell again!' he exclaimed. 'Tell me more.'

'Not much to tell, sir,' Cherif replied. 'The straw went up and put the livestock in danger. It could have been spontaneous combustion or an accident with a cigarette end, we don't know yet. The locals rallied round and organised the evacuation of the animals to a nearby field; the fire brigade did the rest. The farmer was insured, any damage is covered. Foul play is not suspected.'

One person however was not of that opinion.

During the afternoon Cherif knocked at Pel's door and asked for advice.

'It's the cat-woman, sir,' he explained. 'She says that while

70

the whole village was watching or helping with the farm fire, she was watching something else entirely.'

'Someone strangling Minette or Minou, or whatever her silly cats are called?' Pel suggested venomously.

'She says it was something we would like to know about.'

'The woman's potty,' Pel said decisively.

'I quite agree, but should I follow it up? Cécile says I should.'

Pel ripped his spectacles from his forehead, nearly setting fire to himself as he caught the end of his Gauloise on his ear and sent a shower of sparks on to his shirt front. 'And what the hell would she know?' he demanded as he swept away the cinders.

'She's completing her thesis on criminology and has some very interesting opinions,' Cherif explained apologetically. 'She suggests I should follow it up on the off-chance the cat-woman did actually see something of interest to us.'

Pel, of course, agreed, but he wasn't going to admit it.

'There's no time today,' he said. 'Pick me up on your way out of the city tomorrow morning. We'll see the woman then.'

'What time, sir?'

'Seven sharp,' Pel said, thinking he'd got his own back by making Cherif get up early. It hadn't yet occurred to him that in order to be ready he too would be doing the same.

As they arrived in Clavell it was obvious things were not as they'd expected. Even though it was drizzling copiously a small crowd of housewives had gathered in the square and were looking towards the cat-woman's house. Outside was parked a smart new Opel Vectra – belonging to her husband, Pel presumed. It was parked neatly in the short drive leading to the front door. Behind this was a mud-splattered four-wheel-drive vehicle sporting more aerials than seemed good for it. A car radio could be heard crackling faintly as they got out and approached the house. Pel noticed the red serpent and sword sticker on the front windscreen. 'Doctor,' he said, pushing past a group of whispering women towards the open front door.

The mountain of flesh lay sprawled at the bottom of a

71

highly polished wooden staircase, hideously twisted under a torn cotton nightdress. The doctor was kneeling beside the cat-woman; a stethoscope connected them.

'I'm sorry,' he said. 'There's nothing I can do. She's dead.'

A man with a worried frown, sitting at the table, gasped and buried his head in his hands to weep. A woman standing beside him covered her mouth to stifle an exclamation. Another woman turned to go, but between her and the door was Pel.

'Close the front door,' he said to Cherif. 'No one's to leave.'

'Who the hell are you?' The doctor was standing now, looking directly at the two policemen.

Pel explained, allowing the gathering the benefit of his identity card with its red, white and blue stripe.

'Sorry,' the doctor said, extending his hand for an introduction. 'I'm Dr Boudet. I thought you were just a couple more sightseers. I had to fight my way through the crowd when I arrived.'

'I understand,' Pel replied. 'How did she die?'

'Fell down the stairs, I should think,' Boudet replied. 'You were damn quick to get here, although I don't think you're needed. She must have slipped or tripped at the top – an accident.'

Pel wasn't so sure and he told Cherif to radio for a team of experts from the city, together with an ambulance for the body, while he watched the doctor continue his work. Pel had told him that he would request an autopsy, at which Boudet had raised an eyebrow but said nothing, preferring to tend to the shocked members of the household. The weeping man at the table was shaking now, repeating to himself, 'I didn't mean it,' while the woman beside him was trying to console him, although openly crying herself. They both received a couple of capsules to calm their nerves and were helped over to an uncomfortable-looking leather sofa.

'Husband, Monsieur André Lucien, and cleaning lady,' the doctor informed Pel, 'both in a state of shock. They found the body when they came in together this morning.'

It was Pel's turn to raise an eyebrow.

'It's a strange household,' Boudet explained. 'Nothing's quite what it seems. If you think she was pushed, and personally

I don't, I wish you luck with the untangling of this family's problems. I've known them eight years and am only beginning to understand.'

Cherif briefly questioned the other people in the room and took all their names and addresses before allowing them to leave. No one had seen anything; they'd all arrived after the doctor's car had skidded to a stop in the square and he'd been seen running into the house. Sightseers.

Before leaving, Boudet quietly asked permission to be present at the autopsy. 'She's a special case,' he said. 'It'll be fascinating to see what makes up the tonnage.'

While they waited for the experts Pel spoke to the bereaved couple on the sofa. The husband, in spite of being in a highly emotional state, was surprisingly coherent. He was a good-looking man with black hair, greying at the temples, straight teeth and pale brown eyes. He was neatly dressed in modern clothes, not at all what Pel would have expected as husband of the fat woman who could only have been described as a mass of human debris, even when she was alive.

'I didn't mean it,' he said again.

Pel waited to hear the rest.

'Last night, I was so sick of her complaining and whingeing – she never stopped,' he sobbed. 'I told Arlette I wished she was dead.'

'Arlette?'

The cleaning woman clasping his hand replied, 'C'est moi.'

Pel looked her. She was slightly older than the husband, with a careworn face as if she'd always worked hard to earn a living, but she wasn't bad-looking; on the other hand she wasn't particularly good-looking. She had large blue eyes and a lot of leg, he noticed; apart from that the only remarkable thing about her was her hair. It was dyed blonde and was so tightly frizzed it looked as if it had been fried in oil.

'Dédé often comes round to my place to talk,' she went on.

'Dédé?'

'André,' she explained, looking at the man weeping beside her. 'He needs someone to listen to him. His wife only ever complained and she had everything. Look at this house, it was

73

for her, the furniture and fittings, all for her, everything Dédé did was for her.'

'And last night?'

'She'd been worse than usual,' Dédé said softly, 'saying I didn't want to take her to see her mother any more. *Mais merde!*' he exclaimed suddenly, looking at Pel for sympathy. 'She's been dead eight years.'

'Obsessed with the cemetery, she was,' Arlette explained. 'Always putting flowers on some relation's grave. If only she'd paid a bit more attention to those living, specially in her own home. Her son can't stand her and Dédé had had as much as he could take.'

'Your son, monsieur, where is he?'

'I don't know. I think he's away on a business trip – you'll have to ask his wife.'

While Pel explained to Prélat from Fingerprints, who had just arrived, Arlette took her fried hair into the kitchen to make a soothing camomile tisane for anyone in need.

'Look at the wooden stairs,' Pel said. 'They're so highly polished they're almost like a mirror – see if you can get some footprints off them. The housework can't have been done yet this morning, so you might be lucky. Also the banisters, the windows upstairs – well, you know the ticket. My man Cherif will follow you up to look for anything else.'

'Sheriff?'

'He's my sergeant,' Pel said and left Prélat to work it out.

The death, a possible manslaughter or murder, had to be reported to the Juge d'Instruction. Pel was delighted to find it was young Judge Casteou who came to Clavell briefly to see the body before it was removed, something she was obliged to do. She'd arrived, looked, made a few notes, nodded at Pel who was busy with the bereaved husband and left. She'd once told Pel that the etiquette of her profession demanded that the Judges d'Instruction confine themselves to their chambers; it was up to the police to be out and about, until she was expected to appear as an expert, among experts, hemmed in by formalities. Translated, it meant she didn't interfere. Not only was she efficient, she was also pretty, which was a vast improvement on her alternative, a pompous plump man. When Pel arrived in her office later that morning her sunny smile made up for the soaking he'd taken running from the car. Without wasting time they discussed the case, agreed an autopsy was called for and signed the relevant papers. Pel left, feeling it was a pleasure doing business. Until he stepped in a puddle and had to suffer a soggy sock all the way back to his office.

The autopsy was carried out early that afternoon and when the results came through Pel wasn't surprised to find it was Boudet, the dead woman's family practitioner, who brought them. Following him into the office, however, was Cham, police surgeon and assistant to Minet, head of the Pathology Department.

'We can't give you a murder, I'm afraid,' Boudet said, 'but we can give you a wonderful cocktail of food and drugs.' Behind his small spectacles, he was a big man, built like a rugger forward, and looked as if he enjoyed his job, particularly the moments that made most people clutch at their throats and gasp for water.

'Inform me.'

'She fell down the stairs late last night and finally died in the early hours of this morning. Most of that time would have been spent in a state of semi-consciousness or completely out.'

'Can't you be more precise? The corpse was barely cold.'

'Indeed. Normally food plus time elapsed after its consumption equated to state of digestion of the deceased gives us the time of death,' Boudet explained while Pel's eyes began to glaze over: equations of that sort were not his problem, it was the answer he wanted. 'If not,' Boudet continued, 'there's always the state of the brain tissue. Well, there are other bits and bobs but that's about it, really. In her case, though, the food factor could be considered debatable because she never stopped eating, and the brain tissue was not all it might have been thanks to years of misuse of medication.'

'Get to the point, man.'

'Give us a chance, Pel, you'll see the relevance of all this in a minute. There were no wounds other than those sustained

75

by falling down the stairs. No stabbing, no shooting, no strangulation,' Cham explained. 'However, the contents of the dead woman's stomach make interesting reading. Fifteen croissants, seven *chocolatines*, half a kilo of uncooked meat, raw potatoes, various salads, tomato, lettuce, carrot, tinned artichoke hearts, dried cat-food, almost a kilo of dissolved sugar, a litre of vanilla ice-cream, what we believe to be a tube of toothpaste, and so it goes on.'

'Good God!' Pel looked at the long list. 'She had all that for supper?'

'No, she ate it during the evening and night, it was mostly undigested. She was', Boudet explained, 'a compulsive eater. I'd been trying to treat her for it for over five years, but because of her mental state – she was a depressive and therefore not entirely balanced – I was unable to give her the normal medication to help her lose weight. She was crafty too. It was only last week that we discovered that she'd been consuming vast quantities of Valium, a drug I had prescribed in small doses, ten milligram capsules, to help her sleep. My secretary discovered it when entering the Medical Centre's monthly prescriptions on the computer. This woman was dissatisfied when I refused to increase the dosage and had gone in turn to my partners, there are three of them, asking them to prescribe something to help her insomnia. Knowing a bit about her case, two of the three immediately prescribed Valium, surprised I hadn't already, which is what she told them, and the third finally prescribed it after two more consultations. Each one of them was called to her house independently, so no one knew what was going on until it all appeared on the computer. She must have had enough Valium to send an army to sleep. Increasing the dose gradually, she could have been taking up to fifty milligrams in one go.'

Pel studied the doctor. He was young like Cham, but where Cham was built like a string bean Boudet was more like a prize marrow. 'How many had she swallowed last night?' he asked.

'Enough to put the ordinary person to sleep permanently, but in her case, as she was more than a little overweight, I would say enough to make her very drowsy.'

76

Cham nodded his agreement. 'Certainly sleepy enough to fall headlong down the stairs,' he added.

'And she took these pills as she felt she needed them?'

'Her husband, André, tried hiding them, as he did with most of the edibles in the house, but as we've seen by the contents of her stomach she was cunning enough to find sufficient food to have been feasting most of the night.'

'Her husband said', Pel told them, 'that last night he had wished her dead. As their family doctor, do you think . . .?'

'No,' Boudet replied immediately. 'Strange though it may seem, he still loved her. She's undergone a complete metamorphosis, you know – eight years ago she was a bombshell, blonde and slim with just the right amount of curves and angles. He longed for the day she'd be back to normal. He's paid a fortune in wonder drugs, cures, clinics and health farms.'

'Could he afford it? He told me he was an engineer for the EDF. The electricity board doesn't pay that handsomely.'

'If he couldn't, his son coughed up. He's doing well now and, like his father, couldn't bear the sight of his deformed mother. André refused to admit she was beyond repair. I'm sure he wouldn't have deliberately engineered her death.'

'And the cleaner, Arlette?'

'I doubt it.'

'And the son, wherever he is?'

The doctor shook his head and placed the report on the desk. Pel took a quick look at the list of goodies found in the woman's stomach.

'Cat-food? Toothpaste?' he asked.

'She'd eat anything,' explained the doctor and Pel wondered if she'd have eaten the carbonised casseroles his housekeeper cooked for him before she'd been tamed by his wife. 'You have to understand,' Boudet explained, 'eating for her was an illness. Her husband tried to hide anything and everything. Sometimes he refused to do the shopping for days so there was nothing left in the house but she'd always find a way, shouting to the *boulanger* to deliver a dozen croissants, raiding the freezer to crunch her way through boxes of frozen food, and apparently now it's cat-food and toothpaste. Frankly, I'm not surprised.'

Pel, however, made a note to question everyone again,

together with the villagers, in an attempt to find out what she had seen, if she'd seen anything, that was so extraordinary she'd called the police.

9

As his men filed out of the room after the morning meeting, Pel was summoned to the Chief's office. He'd been occupied for nearly an hour on the phone and wanted to hear of the progress they were making. In fact what he heard was of the progress they were not making. The Chief was not pleased.

'I'll sum up what you've just told me, shall I?' he said between clenched teeth. 'The antique robberies, nothing; the Poltergeist's hideout, nothing; the Poltergeist's whereabouts, nothing; the Poltergeist's granddaughter, nothing; a suspected murder in a small hamlet called Clavell, nothing. We have a sheriff in the Police Judiciaire de la République Française and a young, disruptive, though attractive, you assure me, criminologist lodging in the Sergeants' Room. At least Misset is happy. Pel,' he sighed, closing the files on his desk and arranging them into a pile, 'it doesn't sound too good, does it?'

Pel lit a cigarette and inhaled so deeply that the Chief was tempted to look and see if the smoke was seeping out from the bottoms of his trousers.

'I've had Monsieur le Procureur on to me this morning,' he said instead. 'As our boss, so to speak, he's wanting to know what we're doing to stem the robberies. Last night there was another one.' Pel raised an eyebrow and exhaled nonchalantly. 'His own home.' He paused while Pel recovered from a coughing fit that succeeded in turning his face purple. 'They came back from dinner in the city and found they were missing a priceless sixteenth-century gold chalice recovered after the Germans made a dash for it at the end of the war, scattering contraband along the edge of their route. The Procureur's father used it as a shaving mug for months until he finally got home and his mother cleaned and polished the thing. He told me in voluble terms that not only does it represent freedom to his family, it's worth a bloody fortune.'

'Was it insured?'

'Of course it was!' The Chief was hanging on to his temper by the skin of his teeth. He'd hoped to impress Pel with his story, but apparently he'd had very little effect at all.

'So at least he won't be out of pocket?'

'Pel!'

'The Procureur', Pel continued in his best pompous voice, 'is entitled to the same treatment as any other French citizen. Just because he has your personal telephone number does not entitle him to preferential treatment.' He gasped at the end of his cigarette. 'How did the buggers get in this time?'

'Down the chimney.' The Chief was beginning to feel exhausted. He looked up at the clock on the wall: it wasn't yet nine. 'It's one of those big country chimneys which opens out into a fireplace the size of my sitting-room,' he went on hurriedly before Pel could interupt. 'They slid the flat hat off the top of the aperture, left it on the roof, and came down like Father Christmas, bringing with them a great deal of soot. The Procureur's wife is in a state of collapse.'

'They should have it swept more often,' Pel interjected. 'Once a year, and a certificate to prove it – if not, they'll be prosecuted in the event of a chimney fire.'

'Well, now it has been swept,' the Chief snapped back, 'well and truly, by the burglars, and I'm the one getting it in the neck. So stop being a pompous ass and do something about it!'

Pel rose to leave the room. The Chief wasn't going to let him get away that easily. 'And don't send de Troq',' he said. 'The Procureur will not be impressed by titles like other idiots. He wants a real-life Chief Inspector, that's to say you!'

As he closed the door behind him, Pel wondered sarcastically what 'Chief Inspector' was if it wasn't a title.

Never one to underplay a situation, Pel recruited Darcy, Nosjean and de Troq', together with a couple of juniors, Annie Saxe included in case Madame le Procureur still needed catching as she collapsed in a swoon, and of course Prélat and his team from Fingerprints, to go and investigate the robbery of the golden goblet.

79

As they left, Pel asked Annie how their little criminologist was coping with the members of his team, Misset in particular.

'She threatened to break his nose for him yesterday.' Annie smiled. She remembered almost doing the same thing shortly after her arrival. 'So I think she'll be able to look after herself.'

'What's she writing up today then, the hazards of working with lecherous policemen?'

'I haven't a clue. She left during the afternoon yesterday for a number of important tutorials. She'll be back shortly.'

'So what's Misset doing in her absence?'

'Bothering the girls in the typing pool.'

The Procureur was on his high horse, as was his wife. Fortunately for the police he had had the sense to stop her and their *femme de ménage* clearing up the mess. Pel and his men stared at the soot-covered room; not only was it covered in a fine layer of black dust, it also smelt abominable as only old damp fireplaces can. While the men from Fingerprints got to work in the chaos, Pel, accompanied by most of his team, attempted to question the Procureur and his wife.

It wasn't going too well. He was incensed that anyone should have the nerve to steal from the Chief Prosecutor's house. While Annie tried hopelessly to soothe the nerves of his wife and their daily help, Pel tried just as hopelessly to soothe the nerves of the house owner.

'It's a violation of privacy!' he was shrieking. 'How dare they come in here and help themselves to our belongings! Just wait till you catch the devils – I'll have a few things to say to them and to the judge when it comes to trial. You won't be seeing these chaps for a damn long time.'

Pel sighed. He understood the feeling – it was the same as anyone who had been robbed and faced the aftermath. 'We're doing our best,' he said limply.

'Your best is not good enough!'

'Perhaps we should tackle these robberies from a different angle. The robbers are not, as far as we can tell, known to us. We've had all the known thieves in for questioning but, although we discovered a number of small misdemeanours in passing, they all have alibis. Perhaps,' he suggested, 'it is someone you know, monsieur?'

'A friend of mine? Are you suggesting that my friends are a band of robbers?'

'No, monsieur. But I'm sure your friends are very well placed in society and have housekeepers, gardeners and so on. It only takes one of them with a big mouth in a bar or a little too much to drink one evening and a whole crowd of unknowns are graced with the information that you had in your possession a very valuable gold goblet.'

The Procureur visibly calmed down. 'Ah, I see what you're driving at. Then you'd better get on and question all the employees in the homes of my friends.'

What fun, Pel thought to himself – along with all the domestics of all the other robbed house owners, not to mention their friends' domestics too. It was going to be a long day. In fact it was going to be a long week, if not a very long year.

There was one bit of good news when Pel arrived back: they were getting closer to finding the hideout. Rigal had been left to man the phones with a large map of the south of France and instructions to study it for mountains that would cause an air pocket noticeable enough to put Pel's heart in his mouth in a light aircraft. Having spent most of his life at Brest in Brittany, as far away from Provence as geographically possible for a Frenchman to live, Rigal knew very little about it. However, not daring to complain, he sat down and studied the map until the phone on his desk interrupted his calculations. It was the answer to his prayers. Avignon, in spite of their floods and disaster, believed they had unearthed the house for which they were searching, a small dwelling sitting in the middle of vineyards and lavender fields. Asked what the local police should do, Rigal had a brainwave and told them to seal the place off until further instructions were given. Cheerfully he took himself along to Pel's office to find he had just returned from his outing to see the Procureur.

'Not a million miles from the Gorges de Verdon,' Rigal finished his announcement proudly. 'It was probably the canyon that caused the aircraft you were in to hiccup.'

81

Pel scowled through his smokescreen. 'It did more than hic-cup, I can tell you,' he said. 'So what are they doing about it?'

'I told them to seal it off and await your instructions.'

'Good. Give me the telephone number and name of the officer in charge.'

Rigal's initial joy evaporated. He looked at his feet, pushed them gently around on the floor and wondered how the hell he was going to tell his bad-tempered boss he'd forgotten to ask. Pel guessed.

'Get out!'

Rigal fled for the door, grateful he'd got away with his life.

After ten minutes and a lot of apologising on the phone, he reappeared with the information. Silently he placed it on the desk in front of Pel.

'Congratulations,' Pel said without looking up. 'Now go back to sucking your thumb in the Sergeants' Room.'

As Commissaire Clouet at Avignon pointed out gloomily, there were an enormous number of *résidences secondaires* in Provence, half of which belonged to English, Dutch, German and various other nationalities, who opened them up for the summer, but left them to rot for most of the rest of the year, and with the weather being what it had been, even the French owners hadn't been to their houses much. It was, he informed Pel, still raining. It was in Burgundy, too. Pel stared out at the sheet of grey persistently falling from the sky. They were nearly at the end of April and they'd barely seen the sun – what was happening to his beautiful Burgundy? Soon they'd all have lawns like the English and would be drinking afternoon tea. Horror of horrors!

Commissaire Clouet's mournful voice broke into Pel's thoughts. 'We've recovered most of our missing persons. One of the dead was found nine kilometres away, in the branches of a tree.'

Sympathetic though he would have liked to have been, Pel had his own problems. 'You told one of my men you've found the house we're looking for.'

'To be honest, we didn't find it – we haven't done anything but help mop up the catastrophic floods for days now – but when I arrived this morning I opened my post as I do every morning. My secretary opens everything official but I always have a certain amount of personal stuff and prefer to handle it myself.' Pel was gritting his teeth but waiting patiently. 'One of the envelopes contained the following address: Lamotte, Bonnieux, 84. It was delivered by hand, we believe last night, although it had a stamp on it crossed with the word Dijon – that's what made me think it concerned you rather than us. I hope I'm not wasting your time.'

'So do I. What else do you know?'

Clouet continued. 'I sent a couple of chaps out there immediately and they've just got back to say the place is empty but there are signs of a struggle: a bashed-in door, overturned chairs, that sort of thing. I've sealed off the property and now await your instructions. What exactly are you looking for?'

'A man.'

'The house was empty, no man.'

'I'll send someone down – in fact . . .' He paused briefly to allow himself to catch up with his brain which was doing double time. '. . . I'll come myself. I'll be with you this afternoon.'

It had occurred to Pel that he was the only one who would be able to recognise the interior of the house, and although the Procureur and the Chief would complain that he wasn't handling the robbery of the golden goblet personally twenty-four hours a day, if he was quick he could make his escape without them noticing. With him he took Cherif, partly because he was one of the few left in the building – everyone else was out questioning domestics and their families – and partly because his driving didn't frighten the living daylights out of him. But mainly because he didn't have the stomach for a whole day with Misset, the only other option.

They made good time down the motorway, arriving on the outskirts of Avignon just after midday, ravenous and with a raging thirst. Choosing to continue to the Hôtel de Police, they were disappointed to find that Commissaire Clouet had already left for lunch and was not expected back until two. Pel was furious and sat chain-smoking in his office with a scowl on his face black enough to frighten away the bravest inspector. Shortly, however, on the instructions of Cherif, a tray of food arrived and, having consumed an omelette laced with locally pressed olive oil, a crisp green salad and a lump of fresh bread plus most of a carafe of rośe wine from a neighbouring farm, Pel allowed his scowl to become a mere frown. It wasn't Burgundy by any means but it wasn't as bad as he'd expected.

Clouet, when he arrived, was a melancholy man, almost as tall as Cherif but a great deal thinner. He had an adam's apple that bobbed up and down when he spoke and an out-of-date droopy moustache that curled down round the corners of his mouth on to his chin, giving him the final touch of looking as if he was mourning his mother. However, he wasted no time in showing Pel the letter he had received.

'I presume you've had it over to your Forensic Department?' Pel asked.

'First thing I did,' Clouet replied. He was if nothing else efficient. 'The paper is mass produced and can be bought in any of our thousands of supermarkets; it's in fact a medium quality typing paper, very common. The lettering comes from a jet-spray computer printer, sounds extraordinary, but that's how it's done nowadays. I ordered a search for such a machine and found four in this very building. There are another seven at the *préfecture*, a dozen in the council offices – they're virtually standard issue. I've compared copies from nearly a hundred machines around the city and it is impossible to tell the difference. Our man from Forensics told me it wasn't worth trying to trace the printer. The letters are no longer tapped out and therefore become distorted or bent through long use – they are sprayed on to the paper. He explained it in very technical terms which were a little beyond me – computers are not my subject – but what it boiled down to was that the printer was not traceable from this letter. The envelope is the same as the paper, mass produced and bought almost anywhere in the country. There were no fingerprints, no smudges, no perfume, no mud splashes. I'm sorry,' he said, looking sadly at Pel, 'but the letter is only the transport of a message, it has told us no more than the address.'

Before the man burst into tears Pel thought it would be wise to beat a retreat from his office and visit the address.

They found it well hidden, three kilometres off a tiny country road that wound through vineyards and olive groves. The house itself was built in local pale stone and was long and low, hiding in a shallow valley of lavender with more vines clinging to the gentle slopes of shale and gravel. Although it was no longer raining as they got out of the car, the ground was still moist and in the diluted sun that filtered through the scudding clouds Pel again smelt the perfume of lavender. Round the house a barrier in red and white plastic tape had been placed, guarded by two severe-looking police officers. They demanded identity cards just to prove they were taking their job seriously, but Clouet shrugged them off and ducked under the tape.

It was the hideout to which Pel had been brought all right – he recognised its interior immediately, even to the large earthenware casserole still sitting on the stove. A couple of chairs had been upturned, the table pushed to one side and two empty bottles of Nuits-Saint-Georges lay broken on the floor.

'We've been over the place for footprints, fingerprints, the odd hair that may have fallen or a bit of fluff or cotton from a piece of clothing. They were very careful. We have one or two bits and pieces, carefully under lock and key – they'll serve, we hope, in proving a specific person's presence here but are worse than useless in helping us identify them. There were, correct me if I'm wrong, a number of men present, three perhaps, and sorting out which hair or minuscule piece of fluff belongs to who is impossible until we have them in front of us.'

Clouet was thorough. Pel nodded at what he'd been told. He wandered into the bedroom where he'd slept. The bed was stripped and the vase which had contained fresh tulips now only held the wilting remains. When he'd been there it had been a cheerful clean little room, now it looked sordid and neglected.

The other rooms were the same. The long country table was now dusty and covered with damp leaves blown in through the splintered door; the six heavy chairs, one of which had its back broken, lay haphazardly across the room among the debris of broken plates and glasses. Pel stared at the fireplace:

where there had been a crackling log fire, now there were only cold cinders. In the soot on the brick back to the chimney was scratched a word – or at least a few letters. It was high up and almost out of sight but it was definitely there.

Clouet joined him in staring at the letters: >1A+/. Both men had taken out their notebooks and were copying what they saw. It meant nothing to either of them. 'I'll get a bloke from Photography over,' Clouet said. 'I'll also be asking why it wasn't spotted before.'

Pel's mind was racing, however. 'Have any of the locals reported anything suspicious?' he asked.

'Not a thing. My men questioned the owners of the house at the beginning of the drive. They're a middle-aged couple who work in town, with two children normally at school, and Grandmère. She's always in the house, she can't drive and spends her days looking after the vegetable garden, doing the darning and preparing the evening meal. If anyone had gone to the house she would have seen them. She told us about a large black car that arrived two days ago and left again almost immediately but since then no one's been past.'

'I don't suppose she got the number of the car?' Pel asked idly.

'No, she only just managed to notice it had four wheels.' Apparently witnesses were no better down south. 'But she is an old woman whose eyesight is failing; I suppose one must make allowances.' Pel didn't feel like making allowances for anyone.

'Can this house be seen from there?'

'No, it's hidden completely by the slight slope in the ground. It's invisible from all sides, until you're a matter of a few hundred metres away.'

With a frown on his sad face, Clouet looked at Pel, wondering where his train of thought was heading. Having heard of his reputation, however, he had more sense than to interrupt or bother him with his own questions. Chief Inspector Pel would let him know in good time if he felt like it. He followed him outside. Pel was lighting a cigarette and looking out at the horizon which was not far due to the undulation creating the valley.

'Any other way of getting here?' he asked, suddenly turning and facing Clouet.

'Only through the vineyards or lavender fields, there's no other track.'

'Even for the tractors that come to spray the vines?'

'Yes, naturally. There are farm tracks that arrive from all directions, but none that cross the boundary of this small property. I've had the map out and looked up the Cadastre reference for ownership all around. I've also questioned the local farmer on the other side of the hill. He and his son don't come across this land, even when there's no one here; in any event since the pruning finished in early March they haven't been near the place.'

'So to get here, without passing the house at the end of the drive, one would have to tramp on foot through a couple of kilometres of rough and very muddy agricultural land?'

'Unless one came by motor bike.'

'It wouldn't get through the mud.'

'A *trail* bike might.'

When they were back in Clouet's cheerful grey office, looking out at the newly established cheerful grey clouds that were chucking it down directly outside, Pel explained to Clouet's cheerful grey face.

'You've been pretty thorough,' he said, trying to cheer up the site of a major depression, 'but I'm surprised no one noticed the letters scraped in the soot. Perhaps they were put there after your men first visited it and before they sealed it off. If indeed they are relevant, which they might not be.'

Miserable though he looked, Clouet was intelligent and honest. 'I think it's far more likely that my chaps simply didn't notice it – after all, they weren't sure what they were looking for, still aren't, really.'

'Someone sent you the address of the house I've been looking for for over a week. Why? A well-wisher wanting to help us with our inquiries? Our interest in this house is only known to the members of the Hôtels de Police. It hasn't been reported in the newspapers or on television, and if a member of the police force knew about it he would have come forward in person with the information expecting at least a metaphorical pat on the back.'

'A member of the gang, then,' Clouet suggested, 'who's got cold feet about how the affair is going?'

'It could be,' Pel agreed. 'Get your men from Fingerprints to go over the house a second time and fax me a photo of the back of the fireplace as soon as you have it. In fact it'll probably arrive in my office before I do.'

10

The Chief was sitting and listening with interest as Pel's men made their reports. He'd promised the Procureur and his wife some action, if not satisfaction, and he knew very well that he'd be answering questions himself today, so he was there to get the answers from Pel's team well in advance. Out of recognition that the Chief was present, Pel started with the robberies. He had in front of him the paperwork his men had prepared the previous day while he'd been in Provence and the pile was an impressive one. He'd glanced briefly through it on his arrival at the Hôtel de Police and discovered that in the space of twenty-four hours the servants, domestics, gardeners, casual handymen, even visiting labourers of the Procureur and his friends had been questioned. A number of interesting names had popped up, for instance Pierre la Poche, a well-known pickpocket, who was working as second gardener at an impressive *maison de maître* belonging to a local business man. The man had always been a show-off, in Pel's opinion, so perhaps he deserved to have a pickpocket on his staff. Or perhaps Pierre la Poche was going straight? Perhaps crime was going out of fashion? Perhaps he'd fly to the moon for his holidays?

'So what have we got?' Pel asked de Troq', who immediately stood up, notes at the ready. 'As briefly as possible, if you don't mind. There's a lot to get through.'

'We collected the names and addresses of the Procureur's and his friends' domestics. The reports of the interviews carried out yesterday were completed late last night. There are fifty-seven reports for fifty-seven interviews for twenty households. No one worked for more than one household, either in the Procureur's circle of friends or the other robberies.'

'How many suspects?' the Chief inquired.

'None.' The Chief's face fell. 'After a lot of hassling and a few embarrassing questions about who wasn't necessarily in bed with his own wife, we finally managed to establish alibis for all fifty-seven.'

'The Procureur will be delighted,' the Chief sighed.

'However, Debray fed all the information we have on the robberies themselves into his computer to see what it could make of them.'

'With the exception of the diamond robbery,' Debray explained, 'it became very clear that there are common denominators. Each case deals with collectors' pieces, the most valuable in a collection. In the diamond case it was the whole collection but that is still, as with the others, small enough to fit easily into a coat pocket. In every case, including the diamond robbery, the point of entry and exit is a small aperture and often high up.'

'Like a chimney,' the Chief commented.

'Exactly, which leads us to believe that it is one small agile man who knows what he's looking for and probably even has a buyer ready . . .'

'Why a man?' A female voice was heard from the back of the room. Everyone turned, realising it wasn't Annie. It was Cécile Ortille, their criminology student. 'I can see that Napoleon's pig-headed soldier's philosophy is still alive and well in this Hôtel de Police.'

'I beg your pardon?'

'Chauvin,' she replied, 'he was the one that started chauvinism. Although, to be fair, he wasn't against women, he was against anyone and anything that wasn't French.'

'Quite right too,' Pel muttered. 'May I ask,' he said, through still clenched teeth, 'what this valuable piece of useless information has to do with our inquiries?'

'Certainly. Why do you think it's got to be a man? A woman would be very capable of doing it.'

'Or woman,' Debray corrected himself. 'Although, we presumed a man because burglars usually are.'

'Marguerite Marty wasn't, neither was Marie Davaillaud.'

'They were the exceptions and they weren't robbers, they were murderesses. Marie Davaillaud poisoned eleven people.'

'They were acquitted too.'

'Shall we leave the feminist arguments until later?' Pel growled, trying to intimidate the student with one of his best scowls. 'Who the hell let her in?' he said to Darcy in a whisper loud enough to wake the dead.

'So we're talking about collectors' items?' The Chief gathered the meeting back together again.

'We'll do the rounds today,' de Troq' said. 'I don't think there's much point in trying the antique shops but we'll cover them anyway. I'm hoping, with a little help from the computers in the insurance agencies' head offices in Paris plus Debray translating for us, that we may be able to build up a list of collectors nationwide. It'll be a lengthy job but worth it, I think. Personally I believe these pieces would not have been sold in this area, they're too distinctive and therefore easy to trace. Unfortunately, once sold they could disappear for ever, as often happens with stolen paintings: the buyer contents himself with ownership and resists the urge to display.'

'What we need, then,' the Chief summed up, 'is to find just one of the stolen items to give us a lead as to where to look.'

'It would be very helpful,' de Troq' agreed. 'Unfortunately, single items like these are too easy to hide, either on a person, in a parcel or in a suitcase. They could be in America, Australia or Timbuktu by now.'

'Thank you, de Troq'.' The Chief sighed wearily. 'I shall enjoy saying that to the Procureur.'

Brochard had spent the previous day dragging Bardolle and his foghorn voice round the diamond dealers of Paris. While Bardolle's hefty country figure received a number of sideways looks, Brochard, always appearing so young and innocent as if he'd recently climbed off his mother's knee, got most people talking. It was assumed that Brochard was a young spoilt rich boy and Bardolle his bodyguard and in the end they'd quite enjoyed themselves. Unfortunately, however, as they had to tell Pel, no collection of diamonds had come on to the market, complete or recut.

'A number of dealers mentioned an Arab sheik, however,' Brochard pointed out. 'Apparently he was in Paris to celebrate his third marriage and was looking for a unique collection of jewellery to offer as a wedding present to his new young bride. The word is he found what he was looking for from a private seller and has since left the country.'

'Possibly our diamond robbery?'

'Could be. Unfortunately, the sheik's name was a very complicated one, and as no one we spoke to actually did business with him, it remains a mystery. We spent most of yesterday evening, after dealing closed, going through the newspapers hoping to find a brief report on his visit, but we found nothing.'

'Sarrazin?' Pel suggested, knowing the freelance journalist always knew more than was good for him.

'Even Sarrazin, when we tracked him down, couldn't come up with an answer. There are so many rich oil sheiks now throwing their money about in Europe that they pass unnoticed. The limousines are a dozen deep outside the most expensive shops in Paris, London and Rome, all for the blooming Arabs.'

Cherif, sitting quietly to one side of the room, looked up briefly and caught the eye of Brochard, who blushed and smiled apologetically. 'No offence meant,' he said.

'None taken, I'm French.'

'But we can assume', Pel concluded, 'that the diamond robbery was also done with a specific buyer in mind – supply and demand, like the others.'

'That's the only connection we came up with,' de Troq' agreed. 'That and the fact that the burglar got through a tiny window. Male or female,' he added, bowing his head towards Cécile.

'Keep trying to find the sheik who bought the diamonds. The embassy may help you . . .'

'They refused,' Brochard told them.

'Perhaps I could help,' suggested Cherif. 'Speak to them in their own tongue. I could be looking for a long-lost uncle, brother of my dying father.'

Pel agreed it was worth a try, then the meeting moved on to the death under suspicious circumstances at Clavell. Darcy was in charge while Cherif was doing the leg work, the paperwork and being general dogsbody, so that Pel could give his attention to more pressing matters like disappearing escaped prisoners and dissatisfied robbed prosecutors.

The investigation of the dead woman at Clavell was, however, turning out to be a tricky one. Instead of having the satisfaction of uncovering one suspect, or at the most two, Darcy and Cherif had in fact found eleven people, all with a reason for getting rid of the fat woman.

'It's a complicated family,' Darcy explained. 'The dead woman had been suffering from depression and obsession with her health; she called the long-suffering doctors out every day, Sundays included. This has been going on for at least five years. The husband is sick and tired of the situation and in fact is having a long-standing affair with the woman who comes to do the housework. She is also sick of the situation and longs to set up home with him but he's unable to abandon his responsibilities. So there are two suspects. The son is twenty-seven and a business man in the city who hardly ever goes home to see his parents, apparently because he was badgered non-stop when he was there, badgered non-stop to get married as soon as he left home and finally was badgered non-stop to give up going away on business trips and supply his mother with a grandchild. He, I'm told, blames his mother for his wife's inability to conceive plus his father's misery which weighs heavily on his shoulders. We've checked and he's away visiting suppliers at the moment; we're going to have to wait until he gets back to speak to him. However, in the mean time we've asked around the village and, according to the neighbours, whenever he came home he did nothing but shout at his mother. His wife hates her and refuses to speak to her or about her, which gives us suspects three and four. Beyond that there are the husband's parents who loathe the situation and blame the dead woman for all the unhappiness in their son's family. The husband also has two brothers who are delighted the situation has come to an end and finally there are two men and a woman in the same village who could be counted as suspects because the dead woman spied on them and threatened to denounce them to their respective spouses and families. All three are being unfaithful. I've discounted the doctors who were pestered by her because that's their job and it was getting ridiculous, but given the time we'll obviously be questioning them again.'

'*Génial*,' Pel sighed. 'Usually we have to search for months to find just one suspect and here we have a dozen or so to choose from. Keep at it.' He was looking as fed up as the Chief, but then Pel always looked fed up.

As the chairs scraped on the floor and the men rose to leave, Cécile's voice was heard again loud and clear from the back of the room.

'What about the Poltergeist?'

Pel looked quickly at Misset, who was in the room. He wasn't supposed to know anything about their personal search for the escaped prisoner and his granddaughter; he was still photocopying all the articles he could find in the newspapers on the man. He had a bright idea to stop him asking questions.

'Misset is doing his best,' he replied.

'Misset!' Cécile cried. 'However do you expect to find the Poltergeist with him in charge? The man hasn't got a fucking brain in his head.'

The whole room had fallen silent waiting either for Cécile to be expelled permanently from the Hôtel de Police or for Pel to explode on the spot. Neither happened.

'You are wrong, my dear,' Pel replied silkily, 'it's just that he doesn't use it very often.' As he rose to leave he told Darcy to get rid of the girl, and fast.

Although he could see she was becoming a nuisance, Darcy however simply told her to become invisible.

'But it's ridiculous,' she complained. 'Misset can't handle something as important as that alone. Anyway, I thought Chief Inspector Pel went to Avignon yesterday – didn't he find anything at the house?'

Darcy studied the girl. 'You', he said slowly, 'have been listening at too many keyholes. That is not why you are here. Softly, softly, Cécile, or you might find yourself out on your ear with nowhere else to go for your crime and punishment research.'

'Are you threatening me?' she retorted, her beautiful green eyes flashing wildly.

'No, just warning you.'

Nosjean was sitting worrying about the possibility of becoming a father. He wasn't too keen on the idea and he was sporting a deep Pel-style frown when Annie Saxe arrived to grab him by the arm, oblivious of his problems, and whisk him off to Paris. She'd managed to track down the lawyer who was handling the Poltergeist's appeal and was determined to speak to him.

When they arrived he carefully and politely explained that he wasn't at liberty to discuss the case, nor who was paying his bills, although he did admit that he was preparing a case for the Appeal Court on behalf of the Poltergeist, which was likely to bring to light evidence against at least one known scoundrel still uncaught. Furthermore, he suggested the Poltergeist had been framed, very cleverly, and this had led to his condemnation to a long prison sentence two years ago. The man was professional, slick and, beyond whetting their appetites, silent. However, as Nosjean pointed out, someone had to be paying him and had been paying him for over eighteen months. He had insisted it was not the Poltergeist. He had seen him briefly at Fresnes prison, that was all, well after the payments had started.

'So the question is,' Nosjean said, 'who the hell is supplying the money to continue researching his defence? This chap's services don't come free.'

'I can't imagine it's his old company of bandits he left behind,' Pel admitted. 'Usually when the boss is safely behind bars there's someone very ready and willing to take over, even to the extent of keeping him behind bars. I only saw three men with him, the driver, the man behind the gun and the heavy on the door, just hired help.'

'But family loyalty?' Annie asked.

'Explain.'

'His granddaughter,' she said. 'Could she be paying the bills?'

'She's a law student.'

'And disappeared. The rumour was that she was keeping bad company – isn't that why the Poltergeist released himself from prison? Because he was worried about her. Has she taken up his old habits or his old gang, or both?'

'I doubt the boys he had working for him would accept a woman for a boss, even in this day and age of feminism. I doubt too that at her age, twenty-one, she would be capable of it. However,' Pel puffed pensively on his millionth Gauloise of the day, 'if the second-in-command was her boyfriend, and that sort of thing isn't unknown, it's always possible. You'd better find her.'

'We're looking,' Nosjean said. 'Annie spent her first day in the law school yesterday. She's registered herself as a student and spoken to her professors, her friends, male and female, even the girls that serve in the canteen.'

'She just disappeared in a puff of smoke.'

'Like her grandfather.'

Pel was puzzling with the letters he'd noticed scraped in the soot on the back of the chimney at the Poltergeist's hideout.

'What do you make of it, Darcy?' he said, turning the paper round so the letters were now upside down. They made no more sense than they had before so he put them back the way they had been originally.

'>1A+/. Do you think it's a chemical formula?' Darcy suggested. 'Or a code for a safe deposit number?'

'Or the name of his girlfriend in Russian,' Pel added. 'We're getting nowhere and we're wasting our time. Give the thing to Debray and let him play with it on his computers. You know what his brain's like when it's linked into his IBM, maybe he'll come up with something.'

Didier Darras burst into the room, causing Pel to raise an eyebrow and light another cigarette.

'Patron,' he gasped, 'I think we've got something. The old boy whose château was robbed, he's in with de Troq", someone offered him his stolen gun at a bumped-up price.'

* * *

'It's preposterous,' Pel heard as he approached de Troq's desk with Darras. 'Absolutely bloody preposterous, d'you hear?'

De Troq' was entirely in agreement but in his smooth educated way was gradually calming the Baron de Charnet down, although, Pel noticed, he was doing it from the other side of the room.

'If the pistol can be positively identified as your stolen property, you will naturally have it returned to you, after any proceedings, without parting with a centime.'

'Knew you'd understand, that's why I came t'see you.' De Charnet was already looking more cheerful when he noticed Pel hovering behind him. 'What the dickens are you doing there, young man?'

Pel reeled as the Baron's halitosis hit him. He took a large step to the left to avoid a repeat performance.

'Can't stand having someone lookin' over my shoulder,' de Charnet said, apparently oblivious of the effect he was having. 'Comes from my Resistance days, I s'pose.'

De Troq' was wincing, Darras was trying hard not to snigger, while Pel surprisingly was allowing the corners of his mouth to suggest a smile and inclining his head slightly to suggest a bow. The Baron had called him 'young man'. However, studying the old boy, he realised the Baron was virtually prehistoric, in comparison with which Pel was a mere boy.

De Troq' made the presentations, managing to make his boss sound extremely important. The Baron looked him up and down, rose, offered a limp handshake and refolded his long limbs back into his chair. Pel perched like a small balding parrot on the edge of the desk: a small balding parrot determined on catching lung cancer. He was smoking wildly as usual, puffing out great clouds of blue smoke that hung like an umbrella of pollution over the industrial zone.

'There's a magazine,' the Baron was explaining for Pel's benefit, 'silly affair, very exclusive, supposed to keep us titled chaps in contact, can't stand the thing myself, neither can any of the old-school types, but there are a few young upstarts who like to keep it going. It was one of these chaps, Vicomte Rouvier, wears suede shoes and a lot of jewellery, very suspicious sort.' Pel looked down at his own suede shoes. 'He got in touch with me,' de Charnet continued, 'rang me up on the telephone, said he'd seen my little ad in the magazine – thought it was worth a try, never know what you might turn up, and I wasn't wrong, was I? He said he had just what I was looking for and would a little semi-automatic Gaulois interest me? Well, of course I said it would. He brought it to the house this morning. Wanted cash for it. After beating him down a bit, asking a ridiculous price, greedy young tike, I agreed and said I'd have the money for him tomorrow. Thought you'd like to be there when he turns up.' The ancient face of the Baron looked around him as if inviting applause.

'An excellent idea, sir. We'll be hiding in the bushes.' De Charnet's wonderful schoolboy enthusiasm was catching, even Pel was at it. He coughed, inhaled deeply at the end of his cigarette and pulled himself together. 'Are you sure it was your pistol?'

'Absolutely. This gun wasn't mass produced like nowadays, you know. And it has little marks on it from use in the war. Definitely my gun, no doubt about it.'

11

Much to everyone's surprise, not least that of the baffled *météo* men, who had predicted rain, rain and more rain, the following morning brought a sudden drop in temperature. A gale during the night had swept the sky clear and left no cover; without the thick cloud Burgundians woke shivering as if they'd lost their bedclothes. Grumbling, they staggered to open the shutters to be greeted by clear blue skies and sun bright enough to dazzle them. By eight o'clock the saturated countryside was steaming gently. Even Pel didn't fail to notice the cacophony of birdsong.

As he stepped outside, he looked across to the next-door house. He was feeling cheerful enough to have a short conversation with Yves but there was no sign of his young neighbour, not even the wagging end of his mophead dog. He caught sight of his mother, however, at the kitchen window; she was a pretty young woman, and an agreeable replacement for the fourteen-year-old boy. They'd been fortunate with their neighbours – they could have been landed with a family with four teenage boys all revving up their *mobilettes*. Not that he'd notice, he thought; he was hardly ever at home, what with pressure of work, unsolved robberies, fat women falling downstairs and breaking their silly necks, escaped prisoners, disappearing granddaughters. He sighed: it was never-ending. Pel's habitual gloom had returned; he felt better and allowed himself to light his first cigarette there standing on his doorstep. Having realised what he'd done it was then necessary to bolt for his car and accelerate hard down the road to make a quick getaway in case his wife happened to be watching him, or of course the housekeeper – he was sure she was a self-appointed spy.

Pel's driving had never been much better than that of an eighteen-year-old who had just failed his test, and he managed to leave half the rubber from his tyres on the road outside his house. During the course of his approach to the Hôtel de Police, he startled a dozen dogs out for a springtime frolic, terrified three innocent office workers who were late for work, and scared the living daylights out of a commercial traveller, who had to stop for a brandy to calm his nerves.

However, Pel arrived safe and sound unaware of the havoc he'd caused on his way. The duty sergeant on the front desk, as usual, wished le Patron a good morning. Pel, as usual, didn't notice and continued up the stairs to his office without even a nod of the head. It was all absolutely normal.

Having sifted rapidly through the papers on his desk, Pel did his morning exercises, blinking rapidly for a couple of seconds just to let his brain know he was watching if it was thinking of slacking, filled his pockets with spare packets of Gauloises and prepared to leave with de Troq' for de Charnet's château where they hoped to leap out of a suitable bush and arrest a young count who was selling stolen property, de Charnet's stolen property to be precise.

'Odd that,' he said as de Troq' came through the door, car keys in his hand.

'Yes, sir.' De Troq' hadn't a clue what Pel was talking about, but knew him well enough to wait until it was explained.

'Trying to sell de Charnet his own pistol.'

Cécile, their student, slid quietly through the door holding what she hoped was a placating cup of coffee for the boss.

'Coincidence?' de Troq' suggested idly.

Pel patted his stuffed pockets, reconsidered, withdrew a half-empty packet and allowed himself just one more before leaving. Through the first thick clouds of smoke he noticed Cécile hovering by his desk.

'What do you want?' he growled. 'No such thing as coincidence in our line of work,' he retorted to de Troq'. 'There's a bit of luck, lots of hard work and far too many forms to fill in.'

Cécile was trying not to cough and failing.

'Put it down, girl,' Pel said, 'there, here, anywhere. In fact take it away, I'm going out. I haven't got time to sit sipping coffee all day, I've got work to do.'

Half an hour later he regretted having sent her away. He was still in his office, de Troq' was still standing by the door, but he'd put the car keys in his pocket. They weren't going anywhere. Between them sat an extremely happy Baron de Charnet with what looked like a small canon across his knees, and beside him a young man with beautifully waved hair, perfectly manicured fingernails, an impeccably cut suit, but brown suede shoes. Together with a gold watch, a heavy gold bracelet and a number of sparkling rings, he was wearing a pair of very old handcuffs.

'The bounder turned up early,' de Charnet announced, 'but I was ready for him. Thought the old Mousqueton Rival wouldn't work. Every single one of my guns is in perfect working order,' he said proudly, 'as he found out when he tried to make a run for it. Didn't fire at him, of course, might have damaged something vital. It's killed a few tigers in its time.' He hooted with laughter, filling the small office with the foul smell of stale garlic. Pel took most of the blast, being directly in front of him. He nearly passed out. Instead he lit another cigarette: perhaps the strong French tobacco would diffuse the Baron's breath.

'Told him we were on to him and the police wanted a word,' the Baron continued. 'Told him he'd made a mistake coming to me with the pistol, I knew exactly where it came from. Frightfully cross he was when he heard it'd been stolen from me. Don't think he knew till then. Went all red in the face and started swearing. "Bugger me," he said, "I'll kill the bastard." So what do you make of all that?'

Pel could stand it no longer. De Troq', who was standing behind the cabaret, was smiling at the old boy's story and Pel's discomfort at having to smell it. It was time he suffered the same fate.

'You've done extremely well,' he said, standing up and opening a window. The morning was still fresh but freezing was better than the smell of rotting rubbish dumps. 'A bit of quick thinking and you've saved the police a lot of leg work.' Pel had been looking forward to his trip into the countryside to partake of a bit of nature. Yesterday he'd been dreading it, but yesterday it'd been pouring with rain. However, it was time to get down to business, preferably without having to send for the gas masks. 'De Troq', I'd like you to take the Baron across the road while I talk to this young man. Offer him a brandy, I think he deserves it.'

That wiped the smile off de Troq's face but he did as he was told. On his way out the Baron gave his final instructions. 'Be mighty grateful if you can get this thing cleared up pretty quick. The end of term's coming up soon.' Everyone in the room wondered what the hell he was blathering on about. 'Got a number of school parties coming to visit the relics at the château, *voyages scolaires* and all that. Some of them are awfully young, no more than babes, little chaps from the Maternelles, so I don't want a bunch of cops and robbers charging about the place. Oh, and when you want to remove the *menottes*, here's the key. Thought I'd mention it – those handcuffs are antiques, can't have you cutting through them to get the chappie out. You'd be cutting up police history.' With a parting gale of stale breath that nearly flattened Pel against the wall he left with de Troq' following at a polite distance.

'Excuse me.' A voice was heard from behind the antique handcuffs. 'I don't usually smoke Gauloises but do you think I could have one? Two of us smoking might deaden the stink more quickly.'

Pel first unlocked the handcuffs and the man rubbed his wrists. 'Those things hurt. I'm sure he put them on too tight deliberately. It's a good thing the police have changed to plastic now.'

'The police have changed to plastic straps,' Pel pointed out, 'not because they are more comfortable but because they are less dangerous. There were worries about Aids contamination in the unlikely event of the metal ones nicking a tiny fold of skin.' The prisoner stared momentarily at his informant then rapidly searched for wounds. Satisfied there were none, he fell like a drowning man on the packet of Gauloises Pel pushed towards him.

'He drove me here in his ancient Peugeot Darl Mat. Beautiful old bus, only one I've ever seen, but Christ, it's slow and every time he spoke to me, which was often, you've heard how he goes on, he turned to face me. Imagine three-quarters of an hour cooped up in a confined space with that. He wouldn't let me open the windows either. God, I was nearly sick.'

Although it didn't show on his face, Pel couldn't help smiling to himself. Perhaps he'd found the police a secret weapon. Lock the Baron into a small cell with a captured villain and you'd have a confession in no time. On reflection, he decided, that was cheating; the accused wouldn't stand a chance, he'd confess even if he wasn't guilty.

The count was still feeling ill and on Pel's instructions coffee and croissants were sent for. Pel was in need almost as much as the pale young man opposite him who hadn't eaten since lunchtime the previous day. The Bad Breath Baron on an empty stomach was enough for even Pel to take pity on him. Cécile arrived looking smug, clutching a tray from the bar across the road, but on seeing the handcuffs sitting on the desk, her face fell. Having glanced at the man slumped in the chair just behind her, she rapidly put their breakfast down and scuttled from the room.

Watching him tackle his breakfast Pel realised that he was probably no more than twenty years old. His chin, what there was of it, still looked incredibly smooth; he couldn't have been shaving long. While he had all the appearance of an aristocrat there was something missing. Not that Pel knew that much about titled people. He'd always wanted to be one, but – he glanced down at his suede shoes – he'd never be able to afford to replace all his footwear, and if he did, he'd never have the time to polish leather. God knows where de Troq' found the time, his shoes always shone like brass. He just had to accept it, he wasn't born to be a baron.

He startled himself as well as the young count by his next question.

'Why do you wear suede shoes?'

The young count nearly choked on his croissant but after a quick swallow of black coffee he recovered enough to answer.

'Why not? They're easier to keep clean.'

Without the ancient handcuffs, the man looked more at ease. It was now only the bracelets and watch that jingled gently against the desk top.

'Why do you wear so much jewellery?'

'It impresses the girls,' he replied, deftly catching crumbs.

That was it! Pel knew now what was missing. Arrogance. De Troq' didn't need to wear any ironmongery round his wrists to impress the girls. They were impressed at five hundred metres by his shining arrogance, if not his shining shoes. De Troq', like de Charnet, like any other real aristocrat, knew he was better than the crowd; he didn't have to prove it by dressing up like a Christmas tree.

He sat down, stubbing out his cigarette and reaching for another in the same movement.

'Name, address and occupation,' he said, 'and don't give me the rubbish about being a count, I want your real name, address and occupation.'

The man opened his mouth, thought better of what he was going to say and closed it. He started again.

'How did you know?'

'You noticed the detective standing behind you, by the door? Slight chap, neat haircut, highly polished shoes.'

He nodded.

'That was Detective Inspector the Baron Charles Victor de Troquereau de Turenne.' Pel after many years and much practice had said it all without a single mistake. 'We know a thing or two about barons and counts at this Hôtel de Police. Titles don't impress us, it's the men who wear them that should make an impression. And you don't. To me you look very ordinary, like the rest of us poor mortals who have only Monsieur to prefix our names.'

'It fools quite a few people quite a lot of the time.'

'So tell me all about yourself. So far you'll be booked for handling stolen goods – let's hope it doesn't get worse. In fact, if you didn't know they were stolen it could get better.'

Was this an offer of a deal? He didn't know Pel and thought it might be.

'Jean-Paul Pradier, 6 rue de la Gare, Avignon. Painter and decorator by profession.'

'Avignon, go on, you're beginning to sound interesting.'

'My dad was a painter and decorator too. I joined the firm when I was sixteen, school didn't interest me, I wanted to earn money. Dad has a good reputation and decorates for all the best families. I've been in some pretty monied places with him.' As he spoke, all pretences at being posh were slipping away, leaving an ordinary young man with dreams beyond his station. 'I've been in châteaux and film stars' houses – not just in the servants' quarters either, I've been in the sitting-rooms and bedrooms, advised the owners themselves on what colour to paint them, well, my dad did. I found with the wink of an eye and a nicely turned phrase, copied from the toffs, I could work my way into a few of the daughters' beds. Mothers too when I got braver. Unfortunately my dad found out and gave me the sack. So I took off and made a new start as the Count Jean-Paul Rouvier. Got myself invited to the right parties then into the right beds, and little presents and hand-outs started coming my way. Worked well for a while. Then for some reason they stopped playing the game.'

Pel realised sadly that that was exactly what it had been for the rich women: a game. Pradier had merely been a toy, a temporary amusement to display at parties.

'So when this advert turned up with the gun, I jumped at the opportunity.'

'I think, *mon brave*, you jumped in the wrong direction.'

'I was set up.'

'You were still handling stolen goods.'

103

'I didn't know that.'

'Didn't you?'

Pradier was photographed and put behind bars until they decided what to charge him with. It was obvious to Pel he wasn't the brains behind the robberies, in fact he doubted whether he had many brains at all. He'd get on well with Misset.

Just in case, however, his identification sheet was faxed to Montpellier; if he had a record, they'd find it there in their vast files and fax it back. It was also faxed to Clouet in Avignon. There was always the possibility that while he might not have a record he might have a reputation and Clouet or one of his men would be able to enlighten him if he'd been bending the law or stepping on any toes.

While Pradier was sulking in the cage, along with a drunk and disorderly and a voluptuous woman of over fifty arrested for soliciting business in the bars along the canal at nine thirty in the morning, Pel sulked in his office.

Two weeks ago life had been nice and peaceful. Thanks to the torrential rain they'd suffered crime had been slack; no one liked robbing, raping or ransacking with an umbrella in his hand. There'd been just a couple of million cases to solve. Policemen had gently cantered all over Burgundy in an effort to solve old cases: it'd given them a breathing space and the chance to make the crime statistics look more healthy. At least nobody'd been complaining. Now the Procureur was pestering the Chief, who was pestering Pel, who was inevitably pestering everyone else at the Hôtel de Police.

The series of robberies dated back over a period of eighteen months; each one was daring, precise and scrupulously clean. They'd taken one piece, chosen from many valuables, and gone. Gone in a puff of smoke. Even now with their first mistake, Pradier trying to sell back to the original owner, it seemed like a dead end. He'd received the advert and the gun by post, no idea where it had been posted but thought it might be Avignon. The advert cut from the magazine had been stuck to the outside of a small cardboard box which contained the tiny gun. The cutting described the gun briefly and gave a phone number, adding finally that cash would be paid. He hadn't found it at all odd, he'd said, to receive the gun; he simply thought it was a little present from a secret admirer.

All that apart, there was still the Poltergeist on the loose, apparently kidnapped, which bothered Pel. He'd made a promise to find his granddaughter and that wasn't showing much sign of progress either. And of course the dead woman at Clavell, did she fall or was she pushed? It was quite obvious from the medical reports that she was drugged to the eyeballs, but by her own hand and not in an attempt at suicide, by simple stupidity. There was no evidence of violence, just that she'd fallen down the stairs and broken her neck, dislocated her shoulder, crushed two ribs under her immense weight and bruised her huge body from top to toe, not that she was in any state to care any more. It was always possible that it wasn't an accident, although he was beginning to think that that was after all the most likely answer. A dozen people had motives for wanting the fat woman out of the way but none of them felt like the murdering kind. He'd have to have another go at them, and the son, when he got back from his business trip – they still hadn't managed to contact him.

'Patron, look at this!' Misset was standing framed in the door of Pel's office, red in the face and obviously out of breath. He'd sprinted up three flights of stairs from the files in the basement and was suffering.

'One knocks normally,' Pel said coolly, watching the perspiration break out all over Misset's forehead.

'But this is important!' Misset bleated.

'For the love of God, close the door. It's making a draught and I've got a cold coming on.'

Misset did as he was told and with a flourish presented Pel with a photograph he'd been clutching tightly in his fist.

'Very interesting,' Pel agreed as he saw the Poltergeist sitting under a parasol enjoying a cocktail with none other than their favourite local gangster, Carmen Vlaxi. Both of them were a great deal younger but there was no mistaking their identity. 'So where's the journalistic bit of information that goes with it telling us who took the picture and describing the happy couple and what they're supposed to be up to?'

105

'There wasn't any,' Misset said, frowning. 'Odd, isn't it? There was just the photo – no inscription, no date.'

'You mean, this isn't a news cutting?'

'No, it's just an old photo I found half-way down the file I'm working through, and, Patron, doesn't Vlaxi own a house in the same village as the recent suspected murder?'

Pel looked over his glasses at the detective who normally kept his brain ticking over in neutral. 'He does indeed,' he said. 'What made you notice that?'

Misset was looking pleased with himself. 'I overheard a conversation in the Sergeants' Room.'

He'd been eavesdropping again. Pel pushed his spectacles up on to his forehead and reached for the smouldering Gauloise sitting on the edge of an overflowing ashtray. Suspicions and ideas were whizzing silently about inside his head, causing a deep frown to implant itself on his face, which made him look more bad-tempered than ever. Misset prepared to bolt for the door; he knew Pel only too well and was quite ready to make himself scarce. For the moment, however, he held his breath. Pel was thinking and mustn't be interrupted.

At last he snapped his glasses back into position, looked sharply at Misset and stubbed out his cigarette with precision.

'Get the photograph over to the experts. First Fingerprints, then let the Forensic Lab have a go at it. I'd like to know where it came from and how it got there.'

Misset breathed a sigh of relief.

'By the way,' Pel added, 'you were quite right to come and show me.'

Misset smiled at the first compliment he'd received from Pel for years. He opened his mouth to speak.

'Don't spoil it by trying to talk to me,' Pel snapped. 'Get on with it!'

His frown deepened: Vlaxi and the fat woman, both in the same village. Could there be a connection? Highly unlikely, he decided – in fact, impossible. Just a coincidence. But he didn't believe in coincidences in crime.

* * *

As Pel was preparing to leave for lunch his phone rang. It was Clouet in Avignon.

Pel stared at the phone as if it would bite him. Clouet's shrill voice was streaming out in high excitement.

'Pradier's a local boy, bit of a playboy, likes to hang around the night-clubs and spends all summer on the beaches on the Mediterranean getting the all-over perfect tan. In the winter he's taken to going to the posh ski stations in the Alps and lounging about in the lap of some rich old dear who is willing to pay to have a youngster on her arm. He's never been booked for anything, he's relatively new at the game and is easily scared. He's been hauled in a couple of times when a husband has complained about him hanging round his wife, and has backed off immediately. He wants money and the good things in life, not trouble. His ambition is to marry a rich wife who will keep him in the manner to which he is trying to become accustomed.'

'Not a hardened criminal,' Pel summed up.

'No, a rascal.'

Pel allowed Clouet to collect his thoughts; there was obviously more to come, or he wouldn't have phoned. A simple fax would have been enough to cover the information he'd just given him.

'We've been having a competition here,' he suddenly announced. 'I set the members of my team a puzzle for their spare time,' he laughed at his own joke, 'as if they had any. Remember the letters we found scratched in the soot on the back of the chimney at the hideout of your missing man?'

Pel had found them but he let it pass. He nodded, felt foolish realising Clouet couldn't see him and finally grunted his acknowledgement into the mouthpiece.

'I had my computer chaps have a go at it, as I suspect you did. But they came up with absolutely zero. It baffled me so I took a copy home one night and my teenage children agreed that it looked like one of those problems you find in those silly puzzle magazines. It gave me an idea. I had dozens of copies made and distributed them among my men, offering a free meal at the new McDonald's here for the first to crack the puzzle.'

Pel lit a fresh cigarette with impatience. He hoped the end of the story was worth waiting for. He wasn't disappointed.

'The letters were very probably scratched rapidly and therefore badly but if you turn the arrow head round you have a V, the number one could be an L, then A, the plus sign could be an X on its side, and finally I. Put that lot together and . . .'

Pel had been scribbling idly on a notepad. Suddenly he sat up.

'*Vlaxi!*'

'Exactly,' Clouet agreed triumphantly. 'We've done a check and he moved into your area not long ago, a matter of a couple of years. Know him, do you?'

'Know him? Yes, we do, very well. Thank you, Clouet, tell your chap I'll go halves and he can take his whole family to McDonald's.'

'Thank you, my son'll be delighted.'

'Bright boy,' Pel announced and slammed down the phone.

'Darcy,' Pel shrieked down the corridor. Things seemed to be moving at last. The break they'd been waiting for had turned up. Vlaxi the old rogue was up to his old tricks again. He must be back in the area. And the woman at Clavell who'd died. She'd said she'd seen something that would interest the police, that was the day before she fell down the stairs. She could see the back of Vlaxi's house and garden from the upstairs window of her house. And the photo Misset had just shown him. This was it.

Unfortunately it wasn't.

'Darcy's gone to Clavell with Cherif,' Annie told him.

'What the hell for?'

'A body has been found in a swimming pool there.'

12

Dead bodies are never attractive, but drowned bodies, particularly when they have been immersed for any length of time, are particularly ugly. This body was bloated and looking nasty. The face was so puffed up its features were barely visible. Darcy and Cherif watched as a rubber-suited Forensic man gently floated their floater to the edge of the swimming pool. The owner of the pool, Monsieur Ferrier, was standing with his arm round the shoulder of his wife, who was clutching a handkerchief to her mouth; their three children, aged eight, ten and twelve, stood beside them fascinated by the appearance of a corpse in their own back garden.

'Take him out very carefully on the plastic sheeting.' Dr Cham from the Pathology Lab stood by the pool giving instructions. 'We don't want him falling to pieces in the water.'

Madame Ferrier gasped; the children jostled for position to get a better view in case their corpse did decide to disintegrate before their very eyes.

When the excitement had calmed down, the body gone with Cham to be examined and the few dozen neighbours sent home to gossip amongst themselves, Darcy and Cherif accompanied the Ferrier family into their modern and spotless kitchen.

'What'll they do with him?' The eight-year-old gazed at Darcy hoping for a gruesome reply.

'Cut him open and see what's inside, silly,' the twelve-year-old replied with superiority.

'Will they really?'

'That's about right,' Darcy agreed.

'They'll examine what's in his stomach to see what he had eaten, they'll take out his blood and test it to see if he was drunk, they'll cut up his liver and kidneys to see if he was healthy . . .' The twelve-year-old was thoroughly enjoying himself: he obviously watched too many American films on television.

'I'm going to be sick,' the ten-year-old said, turning a deeper shade of green, and promptly threw up all over her brother's shoes.

'That'll learn you to be rude,' the eight-year-old chirruped.

'That's enough!' Madame Ferrier's patience snapped. She turned to her husband, 'Why don't you take these gentlemen through to the *salon*, dear,' she said. 'I'll tie and gag the kids in here.'

Darcy couldn't help smiling: the scene reminded him of his

beautiful Kate and her raucous boys. He longed to see her, in fact he longed to see them, even though they had the ability to interrupt almost every time he got Kate in a passionate clinch. He'd just witnessed a classic moment from family life in the Ferriers' kitchen, an older child taunting a younger child until finally someone had deposited their breakfast on the floor, but for all that he found children amused him. Darcy decided he might, only might, quite like being a father. *Mon Dieu!* What was he thinking of? He wasn't even married yet. But if he married Kate, he'd be marrying the two boys too, a ready-made family. What a thought! It was time to change the subject but he surprised himself by looking forward to thinking about it later in the day.

Ferrier was pouring out small glasses of Armagnac for them. 'I don't know about you, but I could do with a quick one. I expect my wife's got the *eau-de-vie* open in the kitchen. What a bloody start to the day.'

He downed his drink in one and helped himself to another before settling into a hard leather chair. 'The kids'd been pestering me to take the winter cover off the pool the moment the sun came out. Spring's a bit late arriving this year so they were getting frantic. This morning I finally agreed. We've got a day off today for the Maire's birthday or something,' he explained. 'I'm a teacher – not at their school, thank God – so we thought if this weather was going to last we might just brave the icy water in the wet suits we have for sailing on the lakes.

'I started unclipping the heavy duty rubber bands at one end and we were carefully folding back the cover when my daughter started having hysterics. To be honest, at first I ignored her. Sandwiched as she is in age between the two boys she has a tough time and can be known to use her femininity rather than her intelligence to get what she wants. That's to say she screams until we let her have her own way. There'd been an argument about who was going to be first in the pool and . . . anyway, I ignored her. It was only when we got more than half the cover off that I saw why she was screaming. There he was, lying motionless on the bottom of the pool. Ugly bugger, wasn't he?' He swallowed the second glass of Armagnac and took a third. 'I think I'd better go and see how my wife is coping,' he said suddenly and left the room. Both Darcy and Cherif had noticed his face was the same shade of green as his daughter's.

'Dr Cham's working on the body now. He may be able to tell us something by this evening,' Darcy told Pel on his return to the office. 'I've checked Missing Persons and no one from the village or surrounding countryside has been reported as missing – but that means nothing, of course, he could be from anywhere, especially if he was murdered and put there deliberately.'

'You noticed other wounds to suggest murder?' Pel asked, resigned to yet another problem on the case book.

'No, but as Ferrier explained, the winter cover is held down tightly with metal clips and heavy duty rubber bands – alone, you wouldn't be able to get under the cover without detaching the clips or the bands, and having done so you'd certainly not be able to reattach them from inside the pool, so at least we know it isn't suicide.'

'Or accident, it seems.'

'Cham'll tell us how he died. In the mean time, while we were at Clavell, Cherif wanted to take a look at the barn that went up in flames. He's a fastidious man, isn't he? I nearly refused, I had a bit of thinking to do, but decided in the end it wouldn't do any harm.'

'And?'

'And I nearly got my leg bitten off by a savage alsatian dog and my head bitten off by the farmer. He's a very unpleasant peasant, told me to mind my own business, they were well insured, thank you very much. He's convinced it was spontaneous combustion, happens sometimes, he said and slammed the door in my face. But we've been doing some checking: spontaneous combustion occurs between eight and eighty days after the hay's been cut. His hay was cut last July, nine months ago. Also with spontaneous combustion it ignites internally where the heat builds up and burns outwards. The firemen who attended the fire said the blaze was at one side burning towards the middle. Their opinion was a carelessly dropped cigarette or match.'

111

'What do you think?' Pel asked, hoping it was precisely that but knowing that if Darcy was bothering to tell him all this it was because he suspected foul play. Darcy was a good cop and Pel always listened to him even when he didn't want to hear what he was saying.

'I don't think it was an accident. Particularly now that Cherif tells me it was the night of the fire the dead woman at Clavell claims to have seen something that would interest the police. She said something about everyone watching the fire at the farm. Everyone except her. I'm wondering if it was set alight to draw attention away from another event in the village, one that wasn't supposed to be noticed.'

'I don't suppose it was our long-lost friends the Poltergeist and Vlaxi holding hands in the twilight, was it?' Pel told Darcy about Misset's discovery.

'Good grief, I didn't realise those two knew each other.'

'Neither did I. But apparently they do or did – and well enough to enjoy what looks like a bit of spare time together. Quite matey they look, don't you think?'

'Where was it taken? Vlaxi's house at Clavell?'

'Hardly, there are palm trees in the background. I've got the experts working on it now. They may come up with nothing – it's what I'm expecting, it's too long a shot – but you never know, this may be my lucky day.'

Pel was getting the feeling that Clavell was a quiet den of iniquity; he mentally added barn fire and body to his list of starring attractions. The little hamlet appeared to have more than its fair share of skeletons in cupboards. And there was still the elusive son of the fat woman to find. Was he innocently on a business trip or was there something more? Pel wasn't satisfied with the business trip theory, not now. Acting on a hunch he reached for the telephone and dialled the office number of one of his wife's cousins who was conveniently an accountant in the city and often agreed to pass on snippets of interesting information.

Pel was quite surprised to hear the delight in Cousin Roger's voice; he accepted that they got on well but he often wondered how anyone could like a cantankerous detective as much as Roger seemed to. After the initial niceties and the inevitable

112

invitation to share a riotous Sunday with Roger's wife, four children, uncountable dogs and cats, not to mention the unfortunate alcoholic goldfish who always got what was left in the glasses after lunch poured into their tank, they became more serious.

'What are you after this time then, Pel? You're always after something when you ring me up.'

He hadn't realised he'd been so transparent but Roger seemed happy enough, so he decided to carry on.

'Do you know a type by the name of Lucien, Christophe Lucien? He's a local business man. I'm told he sells farm produce to supermarkets.'

'I don't know him personally,' Cousin Roger replied, 'but I do act for a couple of his clients, a producer of *fois gras* and another of wine. We also have the accounts of a number of supermarkets in the area who handle his Produits Paysans. The whole thing started very quietly a long time ago, five years perhaps; he set up a stall in the supermarket at Talant to see what happened. He manned it himself and after three or four weeks found he was running out of things to sell so he installed a pretty girl behind his counter and went off to find more farmers to supply him. Now the thing runs itself, the stalls are self-service and the pretty girl is his secretary. In the last eighteen months he's changed his car, updated all the supermarket stalls, moved house and established himself in smart new offices. He seems to be riding high, or so they say.'

'Suspicious?'

'You've only got to look at the accounts of his farmers and his supermarkets to see that it's legitimate. Everyone involved is happy.'

'So he's a real success story?'

'It looks that way, and I must say it's a pleasure to come across one from time to time – there've been a hell of a lot of people going under with the recession.'

So that was that: his hunch had been wrong. Pel replaced the receiver, deciding patience was a virtue that he would have to cultivate. It appeared that Lucien was in fact on an innocent business trip, nothing more, and that they would simply have to wait for him to come home to them.

Darcy dropped into the offices of the Juges d'Instruction to request a search warrant for Vlaxi's house in Clavell and as expected, because there was no real reason for such a search, it was refused. As Judge Casteou apologetically pointed out, there was no evidence that anything strange was going on there, no evidence that anyone was or had been in residence for a long time – in fact the place had been locked and shuttered for well over a year, as Darcy knew only too well.

'But a gardener's been pottering about. It has been suggested that he's been poisoning the local feline fraternity causing much agitation to one very large lady, who incidentally is now dead, possibly murdered.' Darcy half-heartedly tried to persuade the pleasant judge to sign the warrant. But she smiled back at him shaking her attractive head.

'If I remember correctly, the gardener has been questioned and it looks highly unlikely that it was him trying to kill the cats. I'm sorry, but I can't agree to you busting into an apparently abandoned house: you have no real reason to.'

Darcy was obliged to agree it had been more nosiness than evidence that had made him ask. On his way back to his office his thoughts strayed to Kate. He had an ache developing, worse than a toothache – if he didn't see her he'd go mad. What if she didn't want to see him? What the hell was he thinking of? But for the first time in his life, after dozens of beautiful girls being madly in love with him, Darcy was praying that Kate really was in love with him. How could he be sure? Life would be unbearable without her; there'd be nothing to go on for, no future, no reason. Darcy stopped dead in his tracks. He must be in love. Good God, Darcy was in love. It had finally happened. After all the other girls he'd had and tossed aside, he'd finally met the one who'd turned his insides liquid and had him biting his fingernails down to the quick worrying in case some other bloke was chatting her up. He'd always had more than one girlfriend at a time, bed-hopping was his hobby, but the thought of Kate in the arms of another man . . .

'Kate! Will you marry me?'

'Yes! Who is this?'

'What do you mean, who is this?'

Kate dissolved into rich velvety laughter. 'Daniel, darling, just for a moment I wondered if it was really you.'

Darcy burst into Pel's office; he had to tell someone. But when he saw Pel's gloomy face he decided he'd save the news until later.

'It's Vlaxi,' Pel announced dully.

Cham was sitting opposite Pel. Both of them were puffing professionally on their cigarettes.

'Tell Darcy what you told me.'

'I've taken the fingerprints from our dead body in the swimming pool at Clavell. Although you didn't recognise him because he was too bloated by the water for even his own mother to recognise him, the prints don't change. They were badly wrinkled when we got him out but after we'd dried his hands carefully and let the skin rest for a couple of hours the prints reappeared. It's Vlaxi.'

'*Merde!*' Darcy drew up another chair and sat down. 'That means that our lead of Vlaxi in the photograph with our missing celebrity is in fact a dead end after all.'

'I'm afraid so,' Pel agreed, 'particularly as Vlaxi's been dead for six months or so.'

'Since the end of September, beginning of October, I estimate,' Cham confirmed, his adam's apple bobbing up and down energetically. 'As you can appreciate, after a certain length of time it's difficult to be more specific, but the swimming pool was closed up at the end of September and to be in the state he was in he would need to have been immersed for more than four months.'

'By the way,' Pel interrupted, 'don't owners of swimming pools have to treat the water in the winter with chlorine or something? Didn't Ferrier notice anything then?'

'He poured it into the inspection hatch which is sunk into the paving stones surrounding the pool. A quick blast with the filtration unit and the chlorine was stirred nicely in.'

'Ah, just wondered,' Pel said. 'Carry on, Cham.'

'However,' Cham said, 'I've examined the body and done the initial autopsy. He was indeed drowned.'

Pel and Darcy looked at each other. It wasn't what they'd expected. They'd expected a shooting, stabbing, drugs overdose, at least a simple poisoning.

'But not in the swimming pool,' Cham concluded.

Darcy decided it was time for a cigarette.

'His lungs were ballooned and filled with water, as was his stomach. But not with chlorinated water from a swimming pool – with ordinary tap water, hot tap water. We found traces of *calcaire* and rust from the inside of an old *chauffe-eau*. We also found traces of soap, which suggests very strongly that he drowned in his bath. Another fact that confirms this is that I'm convinced he was dressed after he died. His clothes were put on him by someone else. They didn't bother with underclothes or socks and shoes but they did button him into a shirt and trousers and jacket, all fairly easy to put on.'

'Drowned in his bath – not exactly the spectacular exit I would have expected from a villain like Vlaxi,' Pel said. 'Is it easy to drown in the bath?'

'Extremely,' Cham said, 'as was proved in the Brides in the Bath case in Great Britain. They discovered in the end that if you lift and gently pull the legs of your victim, his head slides under the water. The water rushing up the victim's nostrils shock him into unconsciousness and the rest is easy.'

'So he was murdered?'

'It looks likely,' the pathologist agreed. 'Drowning yourself is pretty near impossible unless you tie yourself to a lump of concrete, and drowning by accident in the bath is rare unless you're either very young, very old, or very ill. He was none of these.'

'*Parfait*, another murder.'

13

Nosjean and Annie Saxe had been working together on the Poltergeist's granddaughter's disappearance and were slowly but surely making progress. It was, as it often was, two steps forward and one step back, an exhausting and frustrating process, but overall they were crawling forward with their investigation.

After Annie had spent days sitting, sometimes snoring, her way through boring lectures at the University in an attempt to ingratiate herself with Laura's friends, then hanging about until the early hours in student cafés listening to excited conversations about how the students were going to change the world and wondering if there had ever existed a student who hadn't been through the same farce, she realised that thanks to four years' police work, particularly the last eighteen months with Pel's team, she felt middle-aged. She was small and neat with a thatch of wild red hair and green eyes that shone like newly cut emeralds. She looked about eighteen and she'd been perfect as a plant at the law school, apart from the odd yawn that was noticed, and all students yawned from time to time. Her comrades had accepted her story of late arrival due to her parents moving house, a reasonably common occurrence at French universities as most students live not far from home, and she settled down to study law, precisely as Laura must have done. The lecturers paid her no particular attention but she did stick to the back of the lecture hall and deliberately missed the tutorials. She'd enjoyed herself and learnt a bit too. Law, she decided, was, apart from being so long-winded and filled with words she didn't understand, an interesting subject, and her fellow students, although they never seemed to sleep, which found her dropping off at any given moment, were a delightful bunch of normal, high-spirited and well-balanced young people – apart from their politics, of course. However, she remembered her severe father calming her mother when she'd found a membership card to the Communist Party in one of her older brothers' pockets: 'Not to be a Communist before you're thirty is to have no heart,' he'd told her, 'but to be a Communist over forty is to have no head. He'll grow out of it,' with which he left the table and went off to watch the local rugby match, leaving a suitably stunned and silenced wife. She'd learnt a lot from her father; most of it was the shut up and listen philosophy, but it had served her well and in doing just that she'd been able to build up a pretty good picture of Laura Lebon. Finally enrolling in the gymnastics club, just as Laura had done, and surpassing herself thanks to the hard rugby training her five brothers had given her when she was little, she'd seen a picture of the missing girl pinned to the wall of the changing room, taken just before she'd disappeared. It looked nothing like the two others they had at the police station. The girl had chameleon qualities. Her hair had changed completely; where it had been bubbly light brown curls, it was now short blonde and spiky. The glasses she'd worn had gone, to reveal large blue eyes, and her mouth, once a nondescript pair of lips, with a bit of help from her make-up bag was full and wide. Looking at the picture, Annie felt that she almost knew the girl and that under different circumstances they'd have got along like a house on fire.

Nosjean had been to Switzerland and back in an attempt to discover something from her old finishing school, where she'd never finished, and came back disappointed and tired. The inhabitants had been polished, snobby, and loose. He'd been propositioned by three girls and one teacher. After he had turned them all down – naturally, he was a married man now – they were thoroughly foul to him. He came away feeling scruffy, common and extremely old-fashioned but at least able to face himself and, of course, Mijo, his wife. He had, however, discovered very little, except that Laura had not been liked. The Principale of the establishment had told him quite plainly that she was a headstrong girl, discontented to learn etiquette and cookery. 'She won't spend the rest of her life planning dinner parties and ticking off nanny,' she'd said curtly. 'More likely end up running the Revolution', she'd added under her breath.

'Which one?'

'Any revolution. Do you know, she temporarily turned fifteen of my girls into women's liberationists! It was dreadful, simply dreadful. It took us weeks to get them back to normal.'

Although he was disheartened, Nosjean too was beginning to like Laura: she was obviously bright and stood up for herself. No one was going to push her around. But she was the Poltergeist's granddaughter – it was to be expected.

On his return, Nosjean departed for Paris to see once again the lawyer working on the Poltergeist's appeal. The famous lawyer hadn't been available, having flown to New York to answer questions on a television programme about the difference between justice in Europe and America – he was, Nosjean was told by his efficient secretary, bilingual of course. Therefore, Nosjean had to content himself with the secretary, who was only too willing to sit and chat all afternoon. A question of when the cat's away, Nosjean thought to himself. She was a great deal more forthcoming than the lawyer and gave him the details he asked for, including the dates on which the payments for preparing the appeal had been received.

When Nosjean got back to the Hôtel de Police he called Annie over to help him collate all their information. He also enlisted de Troq' and Didier Darras, who were still puzzling over the robberies of the rich and famous. When Pel put a furious face round the door of the Sergeants' Room the four of them were so engrossed they didn't look up. Pel was furious because he'd wanted to spend a happy day hassling the inhabitants of Clavell, on three counts. The first, the floater that had turned out to be Vlaxi taking a prolonged and definitive dip in his neighbour's pool; the second, the large lady who had seen something she wasn't supposed to and then fell or was pushed to her death at the bottom of the stairs; and finally the fire at the farm which now looked very much like arson. It was all happening at Clavell and he'd been looking forward to finding out exactly why. Unfortunately the Chief had called him to a meeting with the Procureur, the Juge d'Instruction, the local MP, the Préfet, the head of the gendarmerie, the Maire and various other local dignitaries, all of whom wanted to know what the hell the police were up to and when they would be making an arrest so that they and their friends would be able to sleep in peace.

So he hadn't been to Clavell after all; Darcy had gone instead. It wasn't fair, he sighed, especially on such a beautiful day, when the sun was shining, the birds were singing and all was right with the world – well, almost. Walking towards the Chief's office, Pel had worked himself into an ecstatic state of bad humour, perfect for answering all the silly questions he was inevitably asked.

However, standing in the Sergeants' Room, his hands on his hips, scowling over his glasses and through the smoke coming in a rush from his nostrils, he looked like a local friendly dragon, and when Nosjean finally noticed him he couldn't help smiling. He knew his boss well and was happy to be able to cheer him up slightly – he hoped; one was never quite sure with Pel.

'I think we've got a connection, Patron.'

'I wish I'd got a connection to a desert island where politicians and self-opinionated civil servants were shot on sight,' Pel growled.

'You'd be bored, sir,' Annie grinned.

'Nonsense, I'd be a crack shot in a matter of days.' The corners of his mouth lifted and hesitated. For Pel it passed as a smile. 'So what's the connection?'

'We've been checking dates with de Troq' and Didier's robberies,' Nosjean explained. 'They coincide. The robbery takes place about a week to ten days before the Poltergeist's defence lawyer receives a payment. Without exception. There's more than enough stashed away now to cover the appeal.'

'When did they start?'

'Shortly after our phantom friend was convicted.'

'So now you suspect there'll be no more robberies?'

'If what we've been thinking is correct, then no, there's no need. Unless of course our robber has got a taste for it.'

'And what we're thinking is that our robber is employed by the Poltergeist?'

'It looks likely.'

'Pradier?'

'No. If he'd stolen the gun in the first place he surely wouldn't have been dim enough to try and sell it back to the owner shortly afterwards. So we don't think it's Pradier; he was only supplied with the gun and de Charnet's phone number.'

'A deliberate move to bring our attention to Pradier?'

'But why?'

'Now that's what we've got to find out, *mes braves*,' Pel said. 'It would be very helpful to ask the Poltergeist but as he's still missing we're just going to have to do it the hard way.' He picked up Laura Lebon's photograph from the desk. 'Who's this?'

'The Poltergeist's granddaughter,' Annie told him.

'She's changed.'

'A bit of make-up here and there can do a lot for a girl. It's a vast improvement, *n'est ce pas?*' Annie was saying, 'What do you think, Patron?' but Pel was already on his way out of the room.

'I wouldn't 'ave fed 'er to me dogs,' the gnarled old peasant said, his red face crinkling into a broad smile. The soggy yellow cigarette stub stuck to his lower lip seemed in danger of falling into his wine but miraculously didn't move. Darcy decided it'd been stuck with Superglue. The grimy stubs of his teeth sat crookedly in his mouth like abandoned gravestones, but his small dark eyes glittered with alertness.

'Don't miss nothing in this place,' he said proudly. 'F'r instance, a lorry arrived a couple of weeks ago, driver said it was calves from the co-operative for the farm here. Well, that's normal enough to be sure, but the driver didn't look right, too flippin' clean.' He took an energetic gulp at his wine before tearing off a lump of pale brown bread. He chewed on it with difficulty; it looked as tough as old leather and far less appetising. 'And another thing, them calves didn't moo.' He went on laboriously chewing, the cigarette stub still hanging from his lip. 'Born here, I was, in the next-door barn. I know all the comings and goings of this place and that fat old *poule* was a bad'n, no one'll miss 'er now she's gone.'

Hector Jean-Michel Rataboule, Clavell's oldest inhabitant – he looked it, and, when the wind was in the wrong direction, he smelt it – was polishing off the rest of the bottle of sharp red wine together with the mouldy-looking end of a dried peppery sausage with his bread. It was nine thirty in the morning and, having been out in the fields since dawn, he was having his breakfast.

'Got a few acres here that I inherited from my Papa, grow enough vegetables to sell at market, got my poultry for meat and a couple of cows for milk. Branching out this year – I've installed six sheep down by the river. I'm going to make some money with the lambs. It was while I was down there, tending the lambs, I saw something bloody queer the other day. I was sat by the weeping willow, in the shade – the sun was bleedin' 'ot yesterday, got me all of a lather – I was sat there taking in the scenery with me dogs all panting and puffing, when what should I see but that big shiny red car of 'is pull into the farmyard. He'd come along the bottom of the valley, 'ardly anyone uses that road now, 'cept us farmers for our animals, those with cars comes in from the top off the main road, but there 'e was creeping along, scared silly the 'oles might damage 'is beautiful red car. Then blow me down, 'e turned into the farmyard and came down the side and round the back out of sight. Except to me, of course – 'e was straight in front of me sittin' in the branches of the willow. Well, 'e 'ates old Gastou the farmer, always 'as done, but there they was as chummy as you like, 'ad 'is arm round 'is shoulder even, chatting away like brothers.'

'What sort of car?'

'Red.'

'Do you know the make?'

'No, I don't, but it's like them cars you see on the telly.'

'I don't suppose you heard what they were talking about?' Darcy suggested.

'The burned lucerne,' the peasant replied casually, his mouth full again. 'I couldn't rightly 'ear but I could see clearly. They was looking at the *cadavre* of the barn and gesticulating – 'e was trying to calm old Gastou down. Then it 'appened,' he added dramatically.

'What?' Darcy and Cherif were on the edges of their chairs.

''E gave Gastou the money. Looked like a lot to me. Just couldn't figure that one. It was only cattle fodder that went up in flames, the animals next door were safely got down to my field when it happened, did it myself, everyone else was in a blind panic. First I got a right ticking off for interfering, then he came along with a bottle to apologise and says it's because 'e doesn't like strangers in his barns. Me a stranger! I've been here longer than 'e has. Next thing I know, 'e and the city bloke, and there's not a lot stranger than that sort, are all matey, exchanging smiles and money. Not that they knows I know. Gastou thinks 'e's a snob – well, 'e is, don't talk to any of the village people, and 'e's ticked us all off for making the roads dirty with our tractors, them that's got them, in winter with all the mud. Messes up 'is shiny polished mudguards. What the 'ell does 'e expect us to do, pick the buggers up and tiptoe past 'is bleeding front door? Or perhaps get down on our 'ands and knees and scrub the road clean? Interfering townie.'

'Who's e?'

'Young Lucien, of course,' the old man replied, astonished they hadn't realised in the first place. 'The fat woman's son.'

So he was back. His business trip was over, but although they'd left messages at both his home and his office he hadn't come in to see the police as requested. Which meant they'd have to go out to him.

Darcy and Cherif arrived on his immaculate doorstep that evening. His house was at the end of a cul-de-sac behind white-painted gates. It was modern and grand, with white pillars on the front verandah and a pair of lions sitting on the gate posts. Larger than its neighbours, the house was in the middle of a small development of two- and three-bedroomed bungalows; *chez* Lucien looked as if it was showing off. Everything about it was polished and expensive although, Darcy noticed, it was

123

in bad taste. The garden was well stocked with exotic trees and shrubs, and displaying their bodies quite unashamedly were half a dozen startling white marble statues of busty nymphs. Eventually the front door was opened by a small round woman brandishing a large feather duster and a broad naïve smile. She had a cobweb caught in her hair. She could have been pretty but looked as if she didn't bother or simply didn't care. Not at all what they'd expected of the wife of a business executive with a flashy red car. Perhaps she was the cleaner.

Having inspected their credentials she invited them in and asked them to sit in the spotless but dark sitting-room. It smelt of furniture polish and newly washed floors. The two policemen tiptoed in and perched themselves on the edge of a hard leather couch. All the shutters had been pulled half closed at the windows so very little light came into the room. Through the shadows, however, Darcy noticed more expensive junk scattered round the fireplace, most of it nude ladies and posters of film stars.

She'd noticed he'd noticed. 'My husband loves the *beaux-arts*,' she announced proudly. 'He spends quite a lot of time and money on sculptures and paintings.' She flicked an electric switch and for a moment both policemen blinked into the spotlights. Once their eyes adjusted they were able to gaze at the dozen or so pictures hanging round the room. They were all large, all famous – Renoir, Gauguin, Rubens were the three Darcy recognised immediately – and all of women in a state of undress. They happily shared the walls with the handsome faces of James Dean, Marlon Brando, Alain Delon, Jean Gabin and so on, but in spite of Madame's pride, they were no more than posters in elaborate frames.

'Aren't they wonderful!' she exclaimed, clutching her feather duster to her ample bosom. 'He travels a lot, you see, so he has the opportunity of meeting people and sometimes to make art discoveries.'

That sort of art discovery, Darcy thought, could be done at the local Euromarché, the hypermarket on the edge of town. They had a poster counter crammed full of art from Hard Rock

124

to Van Gogh, and portraits ranging from the voluptuous Bardot as a young starlet to a chimpanzee sitting on the lavatory, but he wasn't about to disillusion the poor woman. He'd seen enough of her art collection, however, and decided it was time to get down to business.

'But he's not home yet,' she replied to his question.

'May we wait?'

'You'll have to wait a long time,' she said. 'He won't be back until next Tuesday.'

'But . . .' Cherif had opened his mouth for the first time and was about to make a mistake. Fortunately he noticed the meaningful look on Darcy's face and shut up. Instead he opened his notebook and scribbled hastily.

'Do you know where he is?'

'Oh no, he travels around an awful lot, hardly ever at home. Export, you see,' she said proudly.

'What does he export?'

'All sorts of things, but mostly food. Pâté, *fois gras*, good wines, *confit de canard*. Luxury foods, you know.'

'Does he work in this area much?'

'He works in all areas, taking orders from the shops and giving orders to the peasants. That's who he deals with, you see. He buys from them, it's all genuine farm produce and made by hand. It must be marvellous for the poor peasants who have no contact with the outside world, beyond, of course, the local market, to think that my husband is sending their pâté, or whatever it is, all over France.'

'I thought you said he was in exports?'

'Yes, he is. He exports all over France. There isn't a department he doesn't export to.'

Cherif crossed out 'export' in his notebook and replaced it with 'national distribution'.

'What car does he drive?'

She squealed. Darcy could hardly believe it, she actually squealed like a fourteen-year-old at the turn of the century.

'She's red,' she said, her eyes rolling in ecstasy. 'She's red and shiny. Oh, she's beautiful, with air-conditioning, stereo, electric windows . . .'

'The make, do you know the make?'

'An Opel Calibra.' Darcy had been expecting a Ferrari or at least a Porsche.

When she came through the door she made quite an impression on the assembled policemen. They stopped what they were doing and strained their necks to take a better look. She was beautiful, dressed in a classic navy blue suit that showed enough leg and gentle curves of her body to make quite a few mouths hang open. She was tall and slender and when she took her sunglasses off she had large dark brown eyes. She smiled and walked towards the desk. Seven policemen fell in love at first sight.

De Troq' and Darras came through the door behind her, arguing pleasantly, before turning off to go up to the Sergeants' Room. Both men took a long look at the lady. Darras was smitten. De Troq' approached the desk cautiously.

'Kate?'

The lady turned and accelerated her smile towards de Troq'.

'Charles, how lovely to see you again.' The listening policemen found her voice as dark and smooth as the thick hair that tumbled on to her shoulders.

De Troq' took the lady's hand and kissed it, clicking his aristocratic heels at the same time.

'I thought I recognised you,' he said, 'but I wasn't sure. You look different.'

'Not dressed in dungarees and clogs. I decided I'd better make an effort if I was coming all this way to see Darcy.'

In between swooning and staring, the Hôtel de Police was slowly losing interest. This lady belonged to someone. First they thought it was the Baron de Troq', that was understandable, she had his class, but now it turned out she was Darcy's. That was understandable too, she had his looks.

As Darcy was still out de Troq' took Kate up the stairs and along the corridor to tap lightly at his boss's door. Having just returned from an afternoon in hell with the local law-makers, in Pel's opinion, a bunch of over-stuffed, self-important pains in the backside, he was not in a good mood. He'd just decided to smoke himself into an early grave, at least it might save him from murdering one of the local dignitaries, when he heard the knock on his door. For the love of God, he thought, what now?

But it wasn't what he'd expected. Kate stepped through the door and brought a ray of sunshine into Pel's office. Immediately he leapt up, fussed about opening windows – he could hardly see her through the fog – dusted her chair with his handkerchief, thank God he'd taken a clean one that morning, and generally behaved like a mother hen, much to the amusement of de Troq'. Pel knew Kate's father well, Pel's wife liked Kate's mother, which helped enormously, and not long ago the police had had occasion to chase one of their dishonest residents down to the Tarn and use Kate's huge old house as their headquarters. That was how Darcy and de Troq' had met her, and after a brief tussle Darcy had won.

Before they left that evening, Darcy handed his files over to Cherif.

'You may be new to the job, but you're bright – do something with those, will you? And by the way, don't call me tonight, not even if they drop the bomb.'

Cherif grinned over the files. 'She's a very fine lady, Darcy. Have a good evening.'

Darcy slapped him on the shoulder in happy high spirits. The cases weren't coming together at all but his life seemed to be. He took Kate's hand and made his exit proudly, recognising the looks of lust and longing that followed them.

Pel's wife was pleasantly surprised when her husband returned that evening. He was carrying a bunch of hideous gladioli but he'd bought them himself and she was very flattered. Then he'd announced that they would be eating out: this he saved to say in front of Madame Routy, simply to have the pleasure of watching her face fall. He hoped she'd spent all afternoon in the kitchen slaving over a hot stove. It was more likely that she'd spent the afternoon in front of their television in one of the comfortable armchairs with the sound turned up from

127

unbearable to unbelievable, but by the look on her face, he had the idea he might just have won a small victory.

'So, tell me, Pel,' his wife asked when they'd finished their meal and were enjoying their coffee and cognac, 'what's all this in aid of?'

'The meal we missed when I was carted off unexpectedly. I owed you one.'

'Oh.'

Pel realised he'd said the wrong thing.

'And', he added hastily, 'Kate's come up to see Darcy and he's over the moon, behaving like a young stallion again. It's infectious, made me think of when I was courting you, my dear.' He hoped he hadn't overdone it.

She smiled back at him. 'How romantic of you.' She took his hand. He hadn't overdone it after all. 'How is Kate?'

'Different,' Pel replied. 'She looked sophisticated and polished, put the fear of God into me when she first walked in. Not the way I remember her at all.'

'She'll have changed her clothes and put some make-up on to come to the city, I suspect. You'd be surprised how a woman can change her appearance with a dab of lipstick and swapping her jeans for a pretty dress.'

Pel stared at his wife. Annie had said almost the same thing, but she'd been talking about Laura Lebon. He was just starting a silent argument with himself about coincidence when his wife interrupted with a piece of surprising news.

'I'm so pleased for Darcy,' she was saying. 'Kate'll make him a wonderful wife.'

'Wife!'

'Yes, her mother telephoned me this morning. Kate's looking for a house in Burgundy and wondered if I could advise her as to the areas likely to appeal – you know, where there are good schools for her boys. She's planning to move as soon as Darcy's set a date for the wedding.'

'Good God! Darcy's finally getting married!' For a moment Pel looked shocked, then he swallowed the last of his brandy. 'It's about bloody time.'

* * *

128

Pel being Pel, even when he was out with his ever-patient wife, was still a policeman and on their way home from the restaurant he couldn't resist the temptation of popping into the Hôtel de Police just to make sure it was still in one piece. Although it wasn't late the main entrance hall was quiet and they made their way arm in arm up the stairs towards the detectives' offices. De Troq' was just coming out of the Sergeants' Room and he clicked his heels and took Madame's offered hand, bowing his head in true old-fashioned style. Pel thought briefly that he might cultivate the same movements but rapidly decided that while it was charming on de Troq' it would be ridiculous for him to attempt it, almost as laughable as a duck doing ballet lessons.

'Madame, what a pleasure to see you. Would you permit me to borrow your husband for a matter of seconds on police business?' De Troq' was at his best.

He always amused Pel's wife. 'I've never come between Pel and the police, Charles, so of course you can borrow him, particularly if it's only for a matter of seconds.'

'It's Clouet,' de Troq' said, once Madame had been left comfortably seated in Pel's office. 'He rang not long ago. He was furious.'

Pel's eyebrows shot up. Clouet was a melancholy man not given to tempers, even mild ones, so he was surprised to be informed that he was furious.

'Apparently he has just found out', de Troq' went on, 'that the Drugs Squad working that section of the south coast have had an eye on Pradier for quite some time.' Pel understood all; there was nothing worse than having some special squad investigating in your area and behaving like prima donnas towards the local police. 'He is believed to be a delivery boy for an organisation distributing drugs nationwide. Unfortunately they only have their suspicions and can prove nothing. They've done a lot of digging and asked exhaustive questions. Pradier appears to be clean, however . . .'

'However, there's no smoke without fire,' Pel said.

Before Pel had managed to close his office door for the first time the following morning it started opening again. Cherif ducked his head and entered. Pel sighed: why had he stopped growing so soon? He would have loved to have been two metres tall. Why should Arabs have all the luck?

'I saw the Arab sheik who bought our stolen diamonds. His description of what he bought corresponds with our description of what was stolen. I went to the Louis XV yesterday evening.'

Only the best, Pel noticed; it was the most expensive hotel in Paris and he doubted that personally he could afford a beer in its bar, let alone a room for the night.

'I was received with great courtesy into his suite of rooms and was told that the diamonds he had bought, with cash incidentally, had already left the country with his new wife on a private plane. He'd had to stay behind to complete a business transaction. He was profusely apologetic and insisted he had no idea they were stolen. He promised they would be returned immediately and asked for an assurance that his money would be reimbursed.'

Pel sniffed. 'Is that all?'

'No, sir. He had contacted a number of dealers with a view to buying a collection but the diamonds he bought were presented to him by a young woman with long blonde hair and beautiful blue eyes. He presumed she represented one of the original firms. She was extremely pretty and very shapely. She spoke with a very well-educated voice.'

'I suppose your Arab sheik would recognise one?' Pel asked sarcastically.

'He would, sir. He was at Cambridge in England and l'ENA, the most élite school in France.'

As Cherif left, Pel idly shuffled files round on his desk before setting off slowly for the Chief's office. The description the sheik had given them didn't fit anyone. Laura Lebon in the most recent picture of her was blonde and blue-eyed, but she'd had short hair which stood on end making her look as if she'd caught her finger in an electric plug. Although striking she was not classically pretty and certainly not shapely – in fact, in the photo Annie had taken from the gym she looked distinctly flat-chested – but she was well educated, extremely well educated. It seemed only sheiks and criminals could afford the best nowadays.

Pel puffed aggressively on a cigarette while Darcy sat in the other chair looking relaxed, confident and full of the joys of spring. Perhaps Kate had something to do with it. He'd always looked like the hero out of a Disney cartoon but today his teeth were sparkling more brightly, his shirt collar was whiter than white and he gave the unbelievable impression of having slept well and being ready to attack the day ahead. Pel never gave that impression.

On the other side of the desk their ex-champion boxer Chief was pretending to interest himself in a telephone conversation with a big-wig from the city who was apparently boring the Chief to tears.

Once a month he called Pel into his office to see how things were going so he could make his monthly unofficial report to the Maire, the politicians, the bore on the other end of the telephone and any other very important person who decided to take an interest and pull rank to stick their nose in and find out what was happening at the Hôtel de Police. Unfortunately, because of the nature of the recent robberies, robberies of wealthy and therefore apparently influential people, not to mention the Procureur himself, there were far too many very important people sticking their noses into police affairs. The Chief sighed; he longed for a quiet month with just the usual million muggings, bombings, break-ins and banditism.

Pel had just come from his own morning meeting where as usual he'd listened to his men's comments and given his instructions for the day. This helped him to feel organised and momentarily under control. Unfortunately the day invariably organised itself and took off at high speed leaving most of Pel's team, particularly Pel himself, gasping for breath and trying to catch up with it.

The pencil the Chief had been chewing finally gave up and disintegrated into a pile of damp splinters. He replaced the receiver and began spitting out the remains.

'Sometimes I wish murder was legal,' he said.

'Who'd run the country?'

The Chief stared at Pel. 'What do you mean?'

'If murder was legal, within five minutes there'd be no politicians, no councillors, no tax men and naturally no footballers.'

'What have footballers got to do with it?'

'Too much,' Pel growled and stubbed out his cigarette viciously.

Pel's brain and his way of using it were beyond the Chief, particularly first thing in the morning when he started complaining about footballers. As far as he knew, they didn't have a single robbery, knifing, or even a slight grievous bodily harm connected with a footballer. He changed the subject.

'Let's have it,' he said. 'The case load and what's happening.'

'What's not happening.'

'Whichever way you prefer to put it.' The Chief sighed: this morning was going to be a long and difficult one, and Pel was not helping.

'The Poltergeist', Pel started, 'has been positively identified all over the country, seen by everyone from a baby in its pram in Paris, to an old dear of ninety-three staggering out to feed the poultry in the back yard. She claims he was hiding in the barn. Plus, naturally, all the usual nutcases – one saw him up a tree, another claimed he telephoned to find out if it was raining in Perpignan. However, on the positive side, Avignon have confirmed that it was indeed him at the house where I was taken and that I wasn't in fact dreaming. They've matched his fingerprints from prison records with the dabs they found all over the cottage. They also found my fingerprints, another confirmation that I wasn't making it all up, plus a number of others, unfortunately unidentified, one set of which appears to belong to a young female, which surprised us all – there was certainly no woman there when I was staying and they've found no further evidence of her existence. The things in the bathroom were masculine along with what few clothes were left in the cupboard. She's not on record, so either she's not a criminal or she's simply never been caught, which doesn't help. Clouet's inquiries, covering a substantial area of the south of France, going into three departments, have however brought us nothing. In my opinion, and from what I told you of my visit, all the food, wine and other necessaries were bought in small quantities, in several supermarkets, possibly all over the place. We've tried asking questions at the obvious places on the route between Fresnes and the hideout but unfortunately the hundreds of cashiers involved just don't remember. As they pointed out, they each deal with thousands of customers a day and most of the time they're not looking at the purchaser but at the purchased, trying to find, as one girl succinctly put it, the bloody code bar, which gives the price to her computer cash register. One other little thing Clouet has told us is that the Drugs Squad are keeping watch on Pradier, the young fool who tried to sell de Charnet his own gun, and while I was considering the fact that they can pin nothing on him Darcy came in to tell me about the peasant Rataboule in Clavell – he needs complete renovation, filthy old boy apparently, but his brain is still in good working order. Now he –'

'Pel!' the Chief interrupted. The peasant might have a brain in good working order but it was nothing compared with the way Pel's could leap about. He was finding it impossible to follow the train of thought. What the hell had a peasant's brain got to do with the disappearance of the Poltergeist? 'Could I have the abridged version this morning? We've all got a hell of a day ahead of us, so let's keep it short, shall we?'

'Certainly,' Pel said. 'Poltergeist, no news. His granddaughter, no news. Robberies, no news. Death at Clavell, no news. Vlaxi drowning, no news – '

'Pel!'

'Sir?'

133

As Pel and Darcy left his office, the Chief pulled out his handkerchief and mopped his fevered brow. If murder was legal, he thought, Pel would be his first victim. If only he wasn't such a good policeman. He had to admit that. He was good for the police and good for the city. He was no good for the Chief that morning; thank God it was over for another month. Perhaps by next month things would have calmed down and Pel would have solved all their problems. But even if he had, the Chief sighed, there'd be a whole new set of problems. Roll on retirement.

What Pel had said was sadly true. They had conscientiously followed up all the leads they had; thousands of kilometres had been covered by foot and by car in an effort to take their investigations one step further. Days had been spent in that pursuit but the trails had gone cold and they were no further forward. Pel sighed and stared at Darcy as if it were his fault. Darcy didn't flinch; he was immune to Pel.

'We're going to have to use the press,' Pel said.

'Sarrazin'll be delighted. Which story are we going to give him?'

Pel looked down at his list of cases. The Poltergeist's escape was top of the page but the national dailies already had the story – since the first moment the Poltergeist had been missed at Fresnes, in fact – and while the appearance of various different photographs on various front pages had brought the usual overwhelming crowd of nutters claiming to be responsible for his escape, his kidnap, even his capture and his death, the Special Police from Paris were apparently as stuck as Pel and his team were.

'The granddaughter,' he decided, 'Laura Lebon. We've got a recent photo of her, the one Annie pinched from the gymnasium. Have it blown up and if necessary the girl's face touched up discreetly. Blow-ups tend to go fuzzy and people don't look at them properly. I want her on the front page, but at the bottom – don't tell Sarrazin who she is, just give him the photo. And while you're about it,' he added, 'get the photo in shop windows and at supermarket check-outs. She was last seen at the law school so cover a radius of say ten kilometres with the photo.'

'Who'll take the calls of identification? There'll be millions, even if the girl was only passing through heavily disguised as a Martian.'

'Rigal,' Pel suggested, 'and why not ask our criminology student to man, or should I say woman, seeing she's a feminist, the second phone. It might keep them both out of our hair for a day or two. They're about as useless as each other.' Pel had nothing against women, nothing at all, he loved his wife dearly, and Annie Saxe was growing on him daily, but they should, like the men around him, have their uses. Pel didn't believe a woman should be just a pretty face; she had to have a brain, and use it. He would have been staggered to find he was not far off being a feminist himself. However, so far Rigal had done very little except whimper and retreat to his corner, like a puppy to its basket, and Cécile had damn well interfered in police work which didn't concern her and which had, in Pel's opinion, little to do with the criminology thesis she was supposed to be putting together. In fact, after the first couple of times he'd seen her, he'd failed to notice her work files anywhere although he had tripped over her crash helmet regularly and had almost charged her with the possession of an offensive weapon when she'd sped past him that morning extremely noisily into the courtyard at the back of the Hôtel de Police. However, it was pointed out that a Kawasaki 249cc motor bike was not considered in law to be an offensive weapon, particularly as no injury was caused, to which Pel had bellowed that his nerves were in an advanced state of collapse thanks to her Nagasaki 999. Coming back from Darcy's office he was thinking about it and had succeeded in working himself into what looked like explosion point. Men leapt through doorways and flattened themselves against the walls as Pel in profound scowl stamped past. As he passed the door of the Sergeants' Room he shouted for Annie Saxe and as she cantered along at his heels he told her to get Cécile's fingerprints on file fast. 'We'll need them one day,' he said to the protesting policewoman. 'You'll see, there are criminal qualities in that girl, totally lacking in responsibility to her elders.'

'But what reason shall I give, Patron?'

'Anything you like. Tell her I like being bloody-minded, tell her it's standard practice for anyone working with the police, tell her I'm sending her to the moon and her dabs must be sent in advance, but most particularly tell her that if she doesn't watch out I'll personally order her wretched bike to be taken to the breaker's yard.'

Pel felt better after his short outburst and settled down to listen again to Darcy, who'd appeared clutching a staggeringly thick pile of newly typed reports. 'We've done all we can so far about the robberies,' Darcy pointed out. 'Lists of stolen goods, together with photos or drawings, have been faxed all over the country, the scenes of the crimes have been gone over with a fine-tooth comb and dusted for fingerprints, footprints, faceprints and any other sort of print you can think of. The victims, their staff, friends, families, associates, dustmen and so on have been interviewed. I'm afraid we'll have to force ourselves to be patient. One of the stolen items should turn up eventually and until it does we've come to a very dead end. Apart from the bogus count from Avignon, of course, Jean-Paul Pradier, although so far he's told us nothing. He seems to be as confused as we are. Let's face it, it was a pretty lousy trick to bait him with the pistol and send him straight back to where it had been originally stolen. He'll have to be released or charged today.'

'Unless he was deliberately sent back to tell us something,' Pel suggested.

'It's always possible, but so far he's told us nothing.'

'So far,' Pel repeated, 'but if I had more men at my disposal I'd have the silly little devil followed.'

'They'd probably follow him to the first bar where he'd get drunk at the expense of some unsuspecting woman and end up sleeping it off in her bed.'

'Release him and tell Misset to tail him.'

'You're not serious?'

'I damn well am,' Pel growled. 'Tell Misset to tail him. For forty-eight hours, to see where he goes. If there's nothing interesting he can come home after that. Pradier is our only lead that's still vaguely tepid, so let him lead us.'

136

Darcy made a note and turned his attention to the case of the accidental death of the fat woman at Clavell.

'An accident after all,' he said. 'From the doctor's report, the autopsy report, her medical history, family history and the fact that our experts found nothing to suggest foul play, we're going to have to accept a verdict of accidental death.'

'There's something else,' Pel said stubbornly. 'She saw something she shouldn't have.'

'Perhaps that's got nothing to do with it, perhaps she made it all up to attract attention to herself, and anyway, now that the inquest is over, permission has been given to bury the body. They've already started digging for tomorrow's funeral.'

'Eh?' Pel's brain was on the same road as Darcy's but in a completely different carriageway.

'She was a very large lady,' Darcy explained.

'That's the understatement of the year.' Pel thoughtfully dragged at the end of his cigarette as if drawing inspiration from its tobacco. 'Let's have one last bash at it. I'm not a hundred per cent satisfied with the autopsy report.'

Darcy resisted a sigh. The inquest had been satisfied but Pel had something on his mind, something that was leading them all over the place, poking about in all the dirty little corners, first the Pradier tail, now the Clavell investigation. However, he knew his boss too well to suggest it was all a waste of time. Pel's mind was notorious; there was method in its madness, though for the moment Darcy couldn't see it.

'I could send Cherif back to check the statements,' he suggested finally. 'See if we can jog a few memories.'

'Alone?'

'No, Angelface is back from his holidays, I thought he could go along as chaperone, make sure Mr Super-Arab doesn't step out of line.'

'Aimedieu, he's quiet and careful – yes, that's fine. Tell him to get a sample of the cat-food the woman dished up, if it's still around. On second thoughts, it'll probably have been thrown away, tell him instead to dig up one of the dead cats.'

Darcy looked momentarily startled.

'Yes,' Pel agreed, 'I know it's a strange request but I've got stranger. He's to take the cat's corpse to the lab and ask Cham to do an autopsy on the thing.'

Darcy made his notes, wondering to himself what Cham's reaction was going to be to such a request. 'Is that all?'

Before he could reply there was a knock at the door and de Troq' appeared.

'Yes?' Pel snapped.

'Monsieur Rataboule, farmer at Clavell, to see Darcy, Patron.'

'Wheel him in.'

They smelt him before they saw him. De Troq', however, guided him respectfully to a seat as if he were a guest of honour.

'Been having a poke about,' the peasant said, nervously rolling his grubby beret into a ball. Here in the city he was like a fish out of water and smelt as if he'd been that way for a number of weeks. 'I don't want no trouble but I got to thinking about those calves that didn't moo . . .'

Pel looked questioningly at Darcy but he was concentrating on Rataboule. 'Tell me about the driver of the lorry,' he said.

'The driver? What d' you want to know about him for? He didn't say nothing but good morning and jangle his bracelet at me. I'm telling you, I don't think them calves was calves at all. Slipped into the barn last night, didn't I, after lights out. There had been calves there – well, I knew that, it was me what got them out when the hay store went up – but the far end's been roughly partitioned off, didn't notice when I went in for the calves that night in the dark, and there it was different.'

'What was different, monsieur?' Darcy asked patiently.

'There was still straw on the floor, there was buckets scattered around, and a dripping tap and so on, but it smelt different.'

Both Pel and Darcy were amazed he could smell anything beyond his own stagnant scent. 'It didn't smell of cattle,' he said.

'What did it smell of?'

'Humans.'

Pel sighed. 'How do you know, monsieur?'

'Humans eat meat, cattle don't. Cow shit and human shit ain't the same.'

15

After Rataboule had been delicately thanked and shown out, the windows thrown open and a few dozen cigarettes smoked to smother the lingering smell, Pel reached for the phone. Darcy listened as he spoke to young Judge Casteou, requesting a search warrant for the farm and outbuildings plus sniffer dogs. Being Pel he got what he wanted shortly after silkily inviting Judge Casteou to lunch.

Replacing the phone, he looked up at Darcy as if surprised that he was still there. 'What about you?' he asked.

'I'm seeing the husband and the cleaning lady, surprising them at their places of work, see if they've set up home together yet – plus I'll try and collar the elusive son. His wife's expecting him home today.'

'That leaves Vlaxi's drowned and bloated corpse to deal with.'

'I've got Debray to contact Interpol and he's collating any information that turns up about Vlaxi's movements, together with everything we have so far, which is quite a bit, as to his known associates, business deals, so on and so forth. I'd still like a look into his house but that would be asking too much of Judge Casteou, specially as she's just agreed to the search warrant for the farm.'

'Vlaxi's house'll keep. When we can come up with a good reason for Vlaxi being murdered then we'll have our search warrant.

Darcy looked up and grinned at his boss. 'A good reason for killing Vlaxi?' he said. 'There are dozens.'

'I agree, but we need something that would pass muster with the judge, not simply the statement, he was a nasty little devil.' Pel reached for his packet of cigarettes, drew one out, horrified himself by finding there was already one in his mouth, alight and smouldering, and pushed the packet aggressively towards Darcy as if it was all his fault. 'What I want to know,' he said suddenly, 'is where that photograph of Vlaxi and the Poltergeist came from and what for the love of God it has got to do with us.'

As Darcy was preparing to leave, another of Pel's ideas emerged from beneath his frown. 'Have you noticed how, every time we seem to be stuck, we keep getting little titbits of information? Just enough to set us off again. The address of the hideout, the word scratched in the soot of the chimney, Pradier turning up to sell de Charnet his own gun, the photograph of Vlaxi under a palm tree with the Poltergeist, even the report of our cat problem at Clavell floating on to my desk if I remember correctly. Everything seems to point to Clavell and Vlaxi.'

'But he's dead,' Darcy pointed out flatly.

Pel wasn't to be discouraged, however. 'Clavell then. Is someone feeding us information? We appear to have the perfect partner. If that's the case perhaps the best thing to do is act dim and let them get on with it. Sit back and let this partner person hand me the clues.' Pel picked up the photo of Laura Lebon. 'In the mean time,' he said, 'send Debray along. I want him to play with this on his computer. I've got an Identikit game for him.'

Darcy turned and left. Pel had never been one to sit back and let anyone hand him anything. As he strode down the corridor towards his own office Darcy thought about it; the more he thought about it, the more he was convinced that Pel had finally pickled his brain with overwork or with all the nicotine and tar he consumed in a day. It was hardly surprising. On the other hand, could he just be right? The old bugger usually was.

Sarrazin was hopping about like a poodle waiting to be let out. 'For God's sake, calm down,' Darcy said to the agitated journalist.

'Give me something, and I'll give you a surprise worth having.'

Darcy smiled to himself. His instructions were to give Sarrazin the story about the missing granddaughter, so he casually agreed and explained what they wanted. Sarrazin looked slightly deflated that it had been so easy.

'Who is this bird anyway?' he wanted to know. 'She's not a bad looker.'

'Her name's Laura Lebon.'

'So who's she, when she's at home?'

'That's just the trouble, she's not at home and hasn't been for quite some time. We need her to help us with our inquiries.'

'And for me to prove to her family that the police are doing their job. Why's she so important anyway? Missing witness? Stolen from the hands of the police or running scared from a pursuing murderer?'

'Christ, you do have a sensational way of seeing life!'

'All in a day's work, *mon brave*, all in a day's work.'

'To be honest,' Darcy explained, 'we're not sure how important she is or may be. All I can tell you is that she's missing and it's time we found her. So what have you got for us?'

'Just a moment! This isn't what I'd exactly call a scoop – tell me a bit more about her. Is she the suspected murderer of the dead woman at Clavell, the long-lost lover of Vlaxi, a female cat burglar who's causing you all the trouble with the rich and famous or simply a famous escaped criminal's runaway granddaughter?'

Darcy's eyes flicked up to look at Sarrazin's serious questioning face. 'Christ,' he said again, 'you do have an extraordinary imagination.'

Surprisingly Sarrazin pursued the subject no further and handed Darcy a photograph. He looked at it briefly and handed it back. 'Seen it,' he said.

Sarrazin's eyebrows shot up and came down immediately in a dramatic frown. 'How come?' he said. 'It was in my private dark room, negative and everything. I got this picture years ago. At the time I was at Formentor in Majorca photographing celebrities from behind a handy palm tree. It was *the* place to go. I also got Anthony Quinn, Alain Delon, Maurice Chevalier, to mention just a few, plus a dozen or so delicious little dolly birds.'

'All you'd get now is coach parties from St Etienne, Lyons and the outskirts of Paris.'

141

'In those days it was very exclusive.'

'And you thought your photo was an exclusive too?'

'I know it is. I took pictures of all sorts of people on the off-chance that they would become celebrities as well as the celebrities themselves. I heard about Vlaxi being found, know obviously, like the whole of France, that the Poltergeist has escaped, and something went click up top. I hunted out this photo for you and there they are happily sipping cocktails together.'

'So where did our copy come from?'

'Has it got anything on the back? Date, name, place, title, for instance?'

'Not a thing.'

'Then it has to be stolen.' Sarrazin looked horrified. 'Or be the copy I gave to Vlaxi or the Poltergeist. I was always very correct about that; anyone I photographed had the chance to buy. Often they told me to get lost but sometimes I was lucky and they ordered a copy. Occasionally they even bought the negative, terrified I might let it fall into the wrong hands, but how could anyone . . .'

Darcy couldn't resist grinning at the affronted news-seeker who frequently invaded the privacy of anyone he felt like for the sake of a story but who now was astonished to find it had happened to him. 'My God, I think I've been robbed,' he said unbelievingly.

After a stunned Sarrazin had left his office, Darcy went along and told Pel, who chewed the end of his pencil, grunted to let him know he'd heard and waved him away. Potty, Darcy thought, definitely going potty.

He left Pel chewing pencils and headed for Lucien's house. He'd told Pel he would follow up the death of the fat woman at Clavell and decided he'd start with the son. He took Pujol along for the ride, who proceeded to stuff every available pocket with extra notepads, cigarettes, tape measures and other paraphernalia he felt necessary to have about his person when accompanying a senior detective on an inquiry. Darcy wanted to tell the new recruit to stop fussing about details but, realising that he was only doing what he'd learnt during his training and that often it was the details that counted in a complicated investigation, he said nothing and waited patiently while Pujol filled up. Darcy expected a quick trip out to Lucien's lovely villa, a quiet word with the man about his whereabouts, a gentle cruise back to the Hôtel de Police, a peaceful afternoon pushing papers round his desk before a long evening with Kate. Unfortunately that's not the way it worked out.

Lucien was still not at home. His dim wife told them sadly that he'd not come home from his business trip but had telephoned to say he had a very important lunch appointment and would probably be back that evening. 'He's a dedicated man, you know,' she said. No more dedicated than a policeman, Darcy thought bitterly as he plodded back to the car and the realisation that this was after all going to be a long day that could possibly spoil his evening. But he had the address of Lucien's office. Maybe Lucien was spending the day with his secretary: she might be more interesting than his wife, she was supposed to be pretty at least. It was worth a try. Darcy told Pujol to get him there as fast as possible.

Pujol took him at his word and took every corner on two wheels. Darcy hung on to his seat for fear of being flung out of the door and hung on to his temper by the skin of his teeth. When the squealing of the tyres allowed him to be heard he managed to make Pujol understand that although their mission was urgent, it wasn't a question of life and death and he could release the accelerator pedal from its imprisonment beneath his over-heavy foot. They finally came to a stop in front of the block of offices where Lucien worked. The plaque on the door three floors up announced 'Produits Paysans' and the neat little secretary, all blushes and bosom, announced that Lucien was no longer in the office: he'd come in early that morning but now she wasn't expecting him back for the rest of the day.

'He might have gone to see his girlfriend, or he might have gone straight out to see the peasants,' she said, extricating a nail file from her desk drawer and gently going to work on sharpening her claws. 'It's his day for visiting the workers.'

'His words or yours?' Darcy scowled at her. Pel would have been proud of him.

'Oh, his,' she replied without looking up.

'Tell me about the girlfriend.'

'Not much to tell.'

'Try.'

'She's taller than me,' she said, 'brown hair and green eyes, quite attractive really in spite of her flat chest,' she added, looking down proudly at her own well-endowed front.

'What's her name?'

'*Chérie*.' Darcy raised his eyebrows. 'Well, that's what Monsieur Lucien calls her, "darling", either that or "*ma petite*".'

'Do you know where she lives?'

'No idea.'

Pujol was copying the interview into his notebook word for word. Having finished, he blinked three or four times and waited for further information, his pencil poised and ready to scribble.

'Okay,' Darcy sighed. 'Perhaps you would be kind enough to give me the addresses of his peasants.'

The girl looked up directly at Darcy and actually fluttered her eyelashes at him. 'If I give you that,' she said in a low voice, 'what will you give me?'

Momentarily Darcy stared back, lost for words. In the old days he would have been only too willing to give her what she quite obviously wanted, a quick trip to a secluded bar followed by a long trip round his bedroom. 'If you don't give me the list,' he said slowly, 'I might just give you a kick in the pants. So look slippy and let's see some action.'

Her eyes opened wide but she didn't move.

'Arrest her,' Darcy said, turning to Pujol, 'for obstructing a police officer in the course of . . .' Pujol was spilling pencils from every pocket. The girl however had dropped her nail file and was making a successful sprint for the filing cabinet. In thirty seconds Darcy had the list in his hands.

With Pujol driving again they set off for the first address while Darcy phoned in the vague description of Lucien's girlfriend to Pel, who acknowledged the call and made no comment. Things were obviously no better back at the office. Perhaps it was a good thing they'd be spending the day chasing about the countryside.

They went from farm to farm, producers of pâté, *fois gras, confit de canard*, honey, *boeuf bourguignon*, not to mention the thousands of different wines ranging from grotty to bloody marvellous. They started at the top of the list, which was his first appointment, and worked their way down, but each time it was the same story: Lucien had been there but he'd just left. They missed him every time. Darcy skipped a couple of names and headed for one towards the end of the list.

'Producers of excellent wine' it said on the wooden board at the gate. They were met by a bored-looking youth wearing torn jeans, long hair, a black T-shirt with a skull and crossbones on it, and an outsize ear-ring that dangled dangerously from one ear. If he turned round quickly, Darcy thought, it could blind him in both eyes. He opened the door and allowed them into the spacious farmhouse kitchen. In one corner, next to a fireplace large enough to hold a conference in, was a television set almost as large; coming from it was a terrific amount of noise. The youth threw himself back on to the sagging sofa opposite the gyrating screen. Darcy and Pujol installed themselves at the vast kitchen table.

'Do you like Twisted Sister?' the youth asked unexpectedly.

'Sorry, I've never heard of her,' Darcy replied honestly.

'It's a group,' the boy on the sofa pointed out. 'How about Slayer? Iron Maiden, Metallica, Guns 'n' Roses?'

'I think I've heard of Guns 'n' Roses.'

'That's because they've been on the Top Cinquante. It's surprising really, a lot of the rock groups of the sixties are back at the top. I was really amazed to find Dad had been a fan of Led Zeppelin.' The boy, about seventeen years old, had a bright and intelligent way of speaking although he looked terrifying, and as Darcy was running out of time to track down the elusive Lucien he decided to try a few questions on the rocker on the sofa instead of enduring the long wait for his parents.

'Do you know Monsieur Lucien?'

'That's not a hard rock group,' the boy said, grinning.

'No, it's the man who comes to see your parents about selling their wine in supermarkets all over France.'

'Oh, that creep. Yes, I've seen him, why? Has he done something wrong?'

'No, but I'd like to talk to him.'

The boy slid off the sofa and turned the television down. 'You can beat him to a pulp for all I care. When you catch him perhaps you'll let me know – I'd like to put in a couple of punches myself. He's been harassing my parents for some time now, not to mention flirting with my sister. She's only fifteen, dirty old man.'

'He's only twenty-seven or so himself,' Darcy pointed out.

'He's too old to make suggestions to my sister.'

Darcy felt ancient. 'How exactly has he been harassing your parents?'

'He wanted to borrow a barn a few weeks back, the one over the side of the hill, asked if it had running water and a lock on the door. My parents asked him what he wanted it for and he told them that was none of their business. My dad said it was, because it was his barn and he'd have to know before he could say one way or the other.'

'Is that all?'

'It doesn't sound like much, does it?' the boy admitted. 'But it was more his attitude, or the way he said it, if you know what I mean. It was after that he started making suggestions to my sister. He called her over to his big flashy red car to talk to her and to look down the front of her dress. She backed off all pink in the face and he laughed out loud and said she had a nice juicy little pair, not quite ripe but nearly ready for picking. I nearly smashed his face in there and then.'

'He was coming to see your parents today, wasn't he?'

'Yeah, but he called to say he couldn't make it.'

'I don't suppose you know where he called from?'

'His car, the rotten slob's got a phone in his car.'

'Is that all he said, that he couldn't make it?'

'Nope, he also said if two men came looking for him, policemen or otherwise, we were to say he'd just left.'

Bingo! His little secretary had told him they were after him.

'How do you know, did you take the call?'

'Yeah, I haven't seen my parents all morning, I got up a bit late. I think Dad's out on the tractor spraying the vines, and Mum's gone into town with my sister to do the shopping. Anyway, I've done as I was told, I just said it a different way, *n'est ce pas?*'

146

Unfortunately, it didn't bring them any closer to finding the elusive Monsieur Lucien.

Misset, however, had had more luck. But of course being Misset he didn't realise it.

Reluctantly, he had taken up his position behind Pradier and had tailed him around the city all morning, dragging his feet as the day became hotter and more humid. He wrenched at his tie to loosen it and mopped his fevered brow with a damp handkerchief. The temptation to give up and hide in an air-conditioned bar with a nice cool glass of beer for the rest of the day, saying to Pel later that he'd accidentally lost Pradier, was hard to resist. However, he knew his boss and his wrath, so he kept on following. Fortunately for Misset, Pradier spent most of the time wandering from bar to bar or walking aimlessly in the park until finally he slumped into a restaurant chair and seemed to be waiting for someone. Sitting at a small table with a *pastis* comfortably installed in front of him, he waved away the waiter offering a menu. He glanced at his watch then at the entrance to the restaurant. Misset watched from behind his beer at the small bar in the corner. Pradier kept looking from his watch to the entrance for half an hour or so until at last an expensively dressed young man entered, looked briefly at the congregation, spotted Pradier and seated himself opposite him. They obviously knew each other and happily sat together ordering their meal. Misset decided it was safe to leave them to it.

Just before midday, as Misset was leaving the restaurant, Cherif and Aimedieu arrived in Pel's office to report on their morning in Clavell.

'Put it on paper,' Pel said, only glancing at the two men.

'I think you'll want to hear this immediately,' Aimedieu insisted.

'I doubt it, but go on, I'm listening.'

'The dogs arrived at the same time as we did with the search warrant. They went through the outbuildings showing some

147

excitement at the far end of what we were told was the calves' barn. They followed their noses round the back of the house to the dustbins. Eventually the handlers turned up three small plastic bags. They've gone off to the lab to be analysed. We went back to the barn but there was nothing there expect a rude word scrawled on the door.'

'A rude word?' Pel looked up.

'*Rlla*, Patron,' Cherif explained. 'It's Arab for *merde*, shit. I don't think it was painted there either, it was smeared in what looked more like mud, but smelt worse. We scratched a sample off and sent it along to the lab with the plastic bags at about ten o'clock.'

Pel was at last looking interested. 'When will we have the results?'

'They said by lunchtime.'

'That's any minute now. Get the lab on the phone, Aimedieu.' He turned to Cherif. 'What else?'

'After we'd finished at the farm we went to Monsieur and Madame Lucien's house.'

'The fat woman's place?'

'Yes, sir. There was no one at home, which meant we had no trouble digging up the cat you requested. Aimedieu also had a quick look in the dustbin there. He found the remains of a bag of cat-food. Both cat and food went to the lab when we got back a few minutes ago.'

Pel had closed the file he'd been studying and was now studying Cherif. 'There's more?'

'A little. We spent the rest of the morning asking questions. One young woman finally remembered seeing a man climbing over the garden wall of Vlaxi's house and setting off at a run for the main road. She didn't think it odd at the time but decided this morning that it may be, particularly as she now thinks he wasn't wearing any shoes.'

'Did you get a description of the man?'

'Dark-haired, ordinary height, ordinary build – I'm afraid she isn't the most observant witness in the world,' Cherif apologised.

'They never are,' Pel agreed. 'When did she see this?'

'Unfortunately the day after the barn fire,' Cherif said. 'It

148

wasn't what Madame, the fat woman, saw – she telephoned earlier that morning. The man was seen running away shortly after lunch. The young woman was doing the washing up, gazing out of her kitchen window.'

'No, but she fell down the stairs to her death that night. Maybe she saw him arriving,' Pel suggested, 'the evening before, on the end of a gun.'

Aimedieu replaced the receiver. He looked puzzled. 'The bags at one time contained heroin,' he said. 'On the outside they showed traces of human excreta, faeces, and the writing on the door was of the same, human excreta. They say it's likely that it comes from a person of North African descent – they discovered traces of harissa, a red pepper paste, in it.'

'Naturally,' Pel said, smugly giving them the benefit of a sickly smile.

'Patron,' Aimedieu asked, 'how did you know?'

'*Rlla*!'

The city clocks chimed midday and as Pel was preparing himself in front of a small mirror for his luncheon engagement with Judge Casteou the door burst open. 'This is becoming an irritating habit,' he said to the excited journalist standing there. Pel continued trying to flatten a stray lock of hair that made him look permanently untidy but in the end he gave up; he didn't have much hair left and he decided to leave what there was to a peaceful retirement.

'Look, Pel,' Sarrazin said, 'habit or no habit, I'm getting a bit fed up with being your blasted messenger.' He banged a piece of paper down on the desk. 'At least let me know what the hell's going on.'

Pel strolled over to the desk and looked at the paper. 'Vlaxi's house is haunted,' he read. He calmly lifted the telephone. 'Nothing important,' he said to Sarrazin who was visibly seething. 'There's a letter here I want taken down to Fingerprints,' he said into the receiver. 'Come and collect it, would you? No urgency, now will do.'

'Aren't you at least going to have the place searched?' Sarrazin couldn't believe Pel was being so cool.

'I may. I'm having lunch with Judge Casteou, as a matter of fact. If the subject comes up I'll have a word.'

Cécile had come into the room and was making for the letter on the desk. 'Do you know what this means?' she asked.

'It means I'm going to be late for my lunch date if I don't get a move on. *Bon appétit*,' he said, and left them both mouthing swear words at his back.

As both the young Juge d'Instruction and Chief Inspector Pel had a more pressing engagement they enjoyed each other's company over a sandwich before setting off out of the city. They were back in their offices just before two o'clock. Pel came through the front door of the Hôtel de Police actually humming, which caused the desk sergeant to consider making an appointment with his doctor – he thought he was hallucinating. Debray was coming across the main hall with a bundle of photos he'd just extricated from his Identikit computer. He handed them to Pel, who glanced at them quickly, thanked him and hummed his way towards the stairs. Debray looked at the desk sergeant, who shrugged his shoulders. 'It won't last long,' he said.

It didn't.

Dr Cham was waiting patiently in Pel's office when he arrived. He stopped humming immediately.

'The autopsy on the cat, I presume,' he said seriously.

'It was poisoned.'

'Thought it would've been. Tell me more.'

'There were traces of cyanide. It came from the sack of dried cat-food.'

'Thought it would have. Her killer knew her eating habits.'

'The cat was male, Pel,' Cham pointed out, 'and it's quite normal for cats to eat cat-food.'

'I was referring to the fat woman's killer. I want a second autopsy done on her. I'm sure you know what you're looking for.'

'*Jésu, d'accord*, Patron, but when's the funeral?'

'Not until tomorrow afternoon, and it may have to be postponed. Before you ask, I have all the necessary papers to authorise such actions.'

*   *   *

'You did what?' Darcy shouted at him when Misset had explained what he'd done.

'Left them like a couple of lovebirds to eat their meal. I've been on my feet all day. I needed to eat too.'

'So why didn't you grab a sandwich at the bar and call in from there?'

'I had a sandwich for breakfast,' Misset replied sadly. 'I thought it was time for someone to replace me, if you still wanted the bloke followed.'

'You thought you'd had enough so you came back, you great oaf!' Darcy was finding it hard to control himself. Misset's brain had been so long in neutral he wondered seriously if he was still able to engage first gear in an emergency. He took a deep breath and hung on to his temper. 'So tell me about the man he's eating with.'

'Young, slim, medium-length dark hair, well sun-tanned, brown eyes, very well dressed and with quite a bit of ironmongery.'

'Ironmongery?'

'Heavy gold chain and St Christopher round his neck, gold bracelet, gold watch, couple of heavy gold rings. Oh, and he bites his fingernails.'

'How very interesting,' Darcy said wearily. 'He sounds like Pradier's type, both a bit flashy and covered in gold plate.'

'His car was a bit of all right, though,' Misset added thoughtfully.

Darcy sighed. 'Tell me about his car.'

'It was an Opel Calibra, bright red, a very nice piece of machinery.'

If Misset's brain wasn't working in top gear, Darcy's was: he knew exactly what that meant, and who Pradier was eating lunch with. He snatched up the phone. 'Who's left in the office? I need someone plus a car, immediately!'

As Darcy and Nosjean left the Hôtel de Police with a squeal of tyres, Cécile was rushing about looking for someone to tell. She found Pel. As usual he scowled. 'Sir, they've found Lucien. He's with Pradier in a restaurant.'

151

'That's nice.' Pel continued turning papers over on his desk. 'But don't you think you should go and see?'

Pel stopped and looked hard at the girl. There was an idea forming in his head which at first had seemed ridiculous, but recently he had begun to ask himself if it was as ridiculous as all that.

'Why?' he asked quietly.

For a moment she appeared not to know what to say and struggled to find a reason. 'Because, well, you've been looking for him for ages, because his parents live in Clavell and his mother was killed, because he's been seen talking secretively with the farmer who had the fire at Clavell, because that's where Vlaxi was found, because he's been deliberately elusive.'

Again Pel looked at her, the puzzles in his mind slowly sorting themselves out. 'You know an awful lot, young lady,' he said. 'A lot about things that I would have thought wouldn't normally have concerned you.'

Cécile said nothing but stood her ground.

'And you think that I should hurry along to the restaurant and talk to Lucien and Pradier?'

Cécile nodded.

'Urgent, is it?'

'Yes, it is,' she replied and for an awful moment Pel thought she was going to cry. He made his decision.

Pel went to the door and shouted down the corridor for Annie. 'Radio to Darcy and Nosjean, tell them to keep the two men in sight but not to approach them, I'm on my way. And tell Cherif I need a driver. I'll meet him downstairs two minutes ago. And keep an eye on this little minx. Don't let her out of your sight.'

Annie dashed off at her usual whirlwind speed, dragging a surprised but apparently pleased Cécile after her. Pel made for his desk drawer and his spare cigarettes. He had a feeling it might just be a longer day than he'd anticipated.

He was right.

16

Darcy had been round the back and gone in through the kitchens to take a look at Lucien and Pradier, to make sure they were still there. They'd reached the coffee stage and were busy ordering cognac as Darcy went back to Nosjean, who was waiting in the car a couple of places behind the shiny red Opel. They'd received Pel's message and knew better than to interfere before he arrived. They didn't have to wait long.

'They appear to be congratulating each other,' Darcy told him. 'According to the head waiter they ordered half a bottle of champagne towards the end of their meal.'

'Half a bottle? Lucien is careful with his money.'

'Or Pradier is careful with someone else's.'

'No one's careful with someone else's.'

'Cherif, go round the back and wait by the kitchen door,' Pel said. 'Nosjean, plant yourself by the main entrance. Darcy, come with me.'

They gave Cherif time to get down the side alley and arrive at the back door before Pel and Darcy went into the restaurant. Immediately they were greeted by the head waiter. He recognised Darcy as the police officer who had been asking questions five minutes previously. 'No trouble, I hope?' he asked.

'*Moi non plus,*' Pel replied, heading for the table that contained Lucien and Pradier.

As he approached, Pradier, who was sitting facing him, recognised him as the detective who had questioned him and a look of dismay crossed his face. Lucien noticed and turned to see Pel. After introductions were made Pel and Darcy were invited to join them for the *digestifs* and, without waiting for them to agree, two cognacs were ordered. Pel and Darcy took their seats and allowed a waiter to bustle about serving them before speaking. Lucien sat patiently with an ambiguous smile stitched to his face while Pradier fidgeted uncomfortably.

'So,' Lucien said at last, 'to what do we owe the great honour of being pursued by Monsieur Pel?'

'Who said you were being pursued?' Pel growled back.

'I was being pursued this morning – from farm to farm, it appears.' Lucien looked cocky; he'd outsmarted the police and was pleased with himself. 'And now I think you have pursued my colleague, Monsieur Pradier, to our lunch engagement.'

'Inspector Darcy was looking for you this morning, and yes, Pradier was followed.'

'May I ask why? Or should I inform my attorney to deal with this police harassment?'

'You are not being harassed,' Pel snapped. 'Your mother died in suspicious circumstances and I wanted to talk to you. It's now over a week and you still hadn't put in an appearance. As you quite obviously weren't going to come to us we've had to come to you. Pradier was picked up for handling stolen goods – he surpassed himself and on instructions from elsewhere tried to sell them back to the original owner. It was reasonable to believe he'd want to get his own back and that he might lead us to his source. That in any judge's books is not harassment, it's called a day in the life of a long-suffering policeman.' Pel took a deep breath. 'So cut the crap about attorneys.'

'Oh dear, oh dear, *il s'énerve*.' Lucien smiled smugly and lit a fat cigar he'd extricated from his jacket pocket. Pel disliked Lucien already – and he was far too young to smoke directors' cigars.

'No, I'm not getting all worked up,' Pel said calmly, 'but I'd like to get one or two things worked out. I think you may be able to help with my inquiries.'

'As they say in the movies.' Lucien puffed happily on the vulgar cigar, his young hand barely able to hold the thing. Darcy noticed Misset had been right about one thing, he bit his fingernails. Somehow it didn't go with the image of smoothness and confidence. There was something else hiding beneath the surface of carefully applied veneer; he wondered when it would show.

154

'Well . . .' From behind his barrel of tobacco Lucien studied the two policemen momentarily. 'I don't have the time right now. I have an important meeting, so if you'll excuse me . . .' Lucien attempted to rise from the table but Darcy beat him to it and, putting a hand firmly on his shoulder, gently pushed him back down into his chair.

'You'll have to find time, Lucien,' Pel told him. 'We've been looking for you for a long time and you are now going to put up with me for a few more minutes.'

'I shall put up with nothing at all,' Lucien shouted, attracting the attention of the other people in the restaurant. 'I call it police harassment. I have a reputation in this city and just because my poor dear mother fell to her death in her own home you're trying to make life difficult for me. Have you no pity?' Rumblings of police brutality could be heard round the edges of the room like a distant thunderstorm.

'Please don't give me the poor dear mother routine,' Pel said quietly. 'We know damn well you couldn't stand her and only went to see her if you had to – even then you did nothing but shout abuse at her.'

'So the neighbours have been telling tales, have they? How very interesting. I wonder what other little fairy stories they made up.'

Pel was sizzling silently. Lucien was one of the most obnoxious little squirts it had been his misfortune to meet, and he'd met a few in his time.

'If you want to hear a fairy story, Lucien,' he said, 'I can tell you a good one, but it doesn't have the obligatory happy ending. However, if you're sitting comfortably, and I see Darcy's persuaded you that you're not after all intending to go anywhere, I'll begin.'

Lucien feigned nonchalance and disinterest but the act wasn't working quite so well any more.

'Once upon a time,' Pel began in a patronising voice, 'there was a little girl who was clever at school and very pretty. But she had no parents and lived with her wicked old grandfather.'

Darcy was watching Pel as well as Pradier who was opposite him. Pradier was looking confused and Darcy wondered where Pel was leading, but one thing was sure: he was obviously

155

beginning to enjoy himself. He couldn't see Lucien's reaction, standing behind him, but he felt the man stiffen under his hands.

'Now, although the little girl's grandfather was a very wicked old man the little girl loved him and when he was sent to prison she started planning his rescue in the form of a very expensive appeal lawyer. Unfortunately, what she discovered was that Grandpa had been convicted of a crime of which this time he wasn't guilty; he'd been framed.'

'As they say in the movies.' Lucien was trying to make it all sound frivolous but his smugness was slipping and the cigar, Pel noticed, had been abandoned.

'The little girl was frightened; she'd trusted all the wrong people. She went into hiding. In the mean time the grandfather had heard that his little girl was keeping bad company, the very same that had put him behind bars, then that suddenly she'd disappeared off the scene completely. It worried him so much that he escaped from prison and asked a policeman for his help in finding her. She was very lonely and wanted to see her grandfather so she set off on a long journey to his hideout, because she knew all the time where he would have gone now he was free, but when she got there her grandfather was gone, all that was left was the bashed-in door and a few broken bottles. Now she was sure she knew who had taken him, the baddies who had framed him, so she scratched the leader's name in the fireplace and led the policeman to the hideout to find clues. But when she returned she discovered the leader of the baddies who had framed Grandpa had been for a six-month swim in a neighbour's pool so it couldn't have been him who had organised it all. It had to be her boyfriend, who'd been second-in-command of recent operations. The boyfriend she'd chosen in order to keep her up to date with what was going on. He'd killed the old boss of the baddies and sent him sailing in the swimming pool and was now busy boasting he would do the same to Grandpa if he didn't cough up the information about the hidden loot he wanted – because, you see, her boyfriend, the new boss of the baddies, didn't know he'd been bedding Laura Lebon, the granddaughter of the famous Poltergeist.'

156

Lucien had gone very pale. 'What a delightful little story,' he croaked, 'but I don't see how it concerns me.'

'I haven't finished,' Pel pointed out. 'The boyfriend, because he's not really an international crook, but a little business man with a little wife and a little house and apparently very little brain, didn't think big. When he captured the grandfather he had to hide him and, for lack of a better place, he eventually took him back to his own little village and put him in the original boss's house and tied him up in the cellar. It was the same night he set fire to the farmer's barn to frighten him because the farmer had been stealing little plastic bags of heroin from him. It was a nice little plan because while everyone was watching the fire, no one saw the famous criminal arrive in the square and be pushed into the big house. No one, that is, except the boyfriend's mother, who was a nosy old bat and too big to go outside and watch the fire, so she watched the baddies instead. And from her upstairs window she saw her little boy being a baddy. When she warned him to be a good boy, he was, as usual, foul to her, and she said she was going to tell the policeman. So to shut her up once and for all the son killed her.'

'I didn't kill her! It's a lie!' Lucien screamed.

'And now the massive mother is dead, and the big boss baddy is dead, all you've got to do is collect the loot and get rid of the Poltergeist. But I've got news for you, Lucien – he escaped. Pradier didn't tell you that, did he?'

Pradier at last opened his mouth. 'How do you know that?'

'While you were busy celebrating here a certain young judge and I paid a call on the house at Clavell,' Pel told him. 'Pradier didn't have the nerve to own up to that little problem, because he's not been looking after him the way you expected. He's been in police custody just recently.'

Lucien was white. His lips parted as he shot a look of disbelief at his partner Pradier, but Pel went on smoothly before he could speak. 'And there you were, happily convinced that shortly you'd be able to dispose of the Poltergeist and carry on bringing in illegal immigrants, stuffed with drugs, keeping them in the barn at the farm until they deposited their contraband into buckets, and you'd go on making a lot of money delivering

157

the drugs under the cover of your legitimate business, Produits Paysans. Vlaxi and the Poltergeist didn't like your cruelty to immigrants, did they? Do you know why, you fool? Didn't you bother to find out? Or didn't you care? Well, I'll tell you anyway – because they were immigrants too. Vlaxi said he was Spanish but he actually came from Algiers and the Poltergeist escaped from the Nazis at the beginning of the Second World War. They've both had fairly hair-raising experiences at the hands of bastards like you. At first Vlaxi was quite happy to help immigrants into France illegally, but when he found out about your drugs and how they got here he told his old friend the Poltergeist . . . That's why they wanted to stop your nasty little racket and why you had to get rid of them. It was convenient that the Poltergeist escaped, wasn't it? It gave you a chance to grab him and anything he was willing to give you to save his life, then murder him anyway, but what you didn't reckon with was Pradier's inefficiency, the Poltergeist's talent for becoming invisible, plus of course a very bright young woman leading the police all the time to your doorstep. You've been had, Lucien, which just goes to show how small-time you are.'

Lucien's shoulders had sunk; he looked beaten. They'd got him. Most of it had been guesswork and there were still pieces of the puzzle missing, particularly in terms of good hard evidence for the courts, but Pel had got it right nevertheless. The table fell silent for a moment, an audible pause. Pel and Darcy waited patiently for a reaction. Neither of them expected what happened next.

A frightened Pradier was watching Lucien across the table. Lucien was running a finger round the inside of his collar as if it had suddenly become too tight; perspiration had broken out on his forehead. Slowly he lowered his hand to his hip pocket for a handkerchief. He withdrew a Browning 7.65.

In a spring as light as a cat he had removed himself from in front of Darcy, who was now looking down the barrel of the gun. A woman at the next table screamed. Everyone in the restaurant turned to look. The clatter of cutlery on crockery stopped abruptly.

'Been had, have I? Small-time, am I?' he spat. 'We'll see, you bastard. With my bloody family I didn't get much chance. My

158

mother was always hanging round my neck – as a kid she wouldn't let me go out to play in case I got my new clothes dirty. She was mad, mad as a hatter, and my father too weak to do anything about her. My silly wife was to shut my mother's mouth and at least it diverted attention temporarily. If only she'd had children – God knows, I tried hard enough, but she couldn't even get that right, stupid bitch. I had to make something for myself. There were things I wanted. I wasn't going to just sit around and become a colourless citizen like my father. I was out to have what I wanted – more than I could get out of working with smelly peasants too. I met Vlaxi when he moved to Clavell. It was brilliant, everything I'd ever wanted to be, the chance to change my life. The chance to prove to everyone I was someone, someone important, someone to be respected, someone to listen to, and you, you *flic* pigs, you're not going to stop me now. Vlaxi, the potty little wog, tried to stop me and look what he got!' Lucien's distorted face showed hatred and greed. They could almost see the venom dripping from his mouth as he spoke.

'Now listen carefully,' he went on more quietly. 'I'm taking Pradier and I'm leaving this restaurant. You're not going to stop me, nor is anyone else. Do you understand?'

'We have men at both doors,' Pel pointed out.

'Let them try. I'll shoot the lot of them, just like Alain Delon in *Le Clan des Siciliens*.' He grabbed Pradier by the arm and made for the door. The other diners leapt from his path.

Nosjean had obviously been watching discreetly from the wide plate glass window. He appeared in the doorway, barring their exit to the street. He stood with his legs apart, his arms outstretched, pointing a police issue Magnum 357 straight at Lucien. There was only a moment's hesitation.

There were two loud reports, sending the already frightened inhabitants of the restaurant diving for the floor. Women screamed, the smell of cordite filled their nostrils, but Pel and Darcy noticed none of this.

It was over in a split second. Too late they realised what had happened; their colleague's feet lifted from the floor as if he'd been kicked by a mule, the look of surprise on Nosjean's face turned to agony, and he fell in a crumpled heap in the doorway. On the front of his shirt were two oozing red stains.

Lucien dragged at the unwilling Pradier. They stepped over the prostrate body of Nosjean and were away before Darcy or Pel had time to stop them. The door at the back of the restaurant flew open. Cherif appeared, gun in hand. He took one look at the scene and turned away.

'Jesus Christ!' Pel approached Nosjean. 'Call a bloody ambulance,' he shouted, but Cherif was already dialling.

Darcy stopped briefly by his colleague then leapt into the street. The squealing of tyres was heard as he took off in pursuit of the already disappearing red Calibra.

Having loosened Nosjean's collar and belt and placed his own jacket under his head, Pel left Cherif by his side and ran to the second police car parked outside. He took hold of the radio.

There was ice in his voice as he gave his instructions.

17

Pel called his team in. News had spread fast; they all knew what had happened. The doctor who'd arrived to tend Nosjean and had gone with him in the ambulance had looked grim. Mijo was told her husband had been shot. At the Hôtel de Police they waited to know if Nosjean was alive or dead. And they waited for news from Darcy. He'd taken off alone after Lucien and Pradier, and was presumably too occupied with chasing them through the busy streets and out into the country to dare take a hand from the steering wheel and radio in. So they waited. Downstairs phones rang, policemen and civilians bustled in and out of the main hall, but in the Sergeants' Room there was silence. Most of them stood. The Chief and Pel sat staring at the phone, waiting.

When the news finally came, Darcy sounded breathless.

'*Accouche, mon brave,*' Pel said gruffly. 'Where the hell are you?'

'Château de Charnet. Pradier must have brought Lucien back

160

here, thinking the château was big enough to hide them, or that they could escape by one of its famous secret passages, but he didn't count on the Baron and the Baroness. Although they've both taken a beating – I saw them briefly on one of the balconies. Apparently they're not co-operating.'

'Good,' Pel said.

'Not good,' came the reply. 'When they were sent on to the balcony, it was to inform me that there was a *voyage scolaire* in there. They're holding a group of ten schoolkids, aged between four and five years old, who were visiting the château with their teacher. Lucien and Pradier have rounded them up and are threatening to start wounding or killing if their demands are not met.'

Pel's heart skipped a beat: it was a situation he'd always dreaded and never had to face. Children held to ransom. Although he had no children of his own he was nevertheless very fond of them, finding them on the whole extraordinarily perceptive and surprisingly honest. Something went wrong in the system, he felt, to turn them into the twits most adults tended to be. He was also aware of the public feeling in France if a child were shot by terrorists, because that was what they must now consider Lucien and Pradier to be. The French as a nation loved children. Mother of God! How in hell was he to handle this one?

'I don't want to,' Pel said quietly to the Chief, 'but I believe it would be for the best to call in the boys from RAID. They're trained specially for this sort of thing. You'll have to inform the Préfet, who'll inform the Ministre de l'Intérieur, who's bound to call in the special unit. Tell them we're at the château and awaiting their arrival.'

The Chief breathed a sigh of relief. Pel had taken the exact decision he'd hoped for. The moment Darcy'd told them about the hostages he knew the situation was too important for action purely at local level; they needed the experts, and for once Pel agreed. It made life much simpler. Nobody liked interference from Paris, but this time it was necessary. He turned swiftly to another desk, snatching up the phone before Pel could change his mind.

'I'm on my way,' Pel told Darcy. 'Keep everything as calm as you can. Tell them we'll listen to their demands.'

As the room emptied, Pel noticed Cécile sliding out through the door in the shadow of big Bardolle. He took hold of her arm. 'And you, young lady,' he said, 'had better come with me.'

As de Troq' drove like Alain Prost through the Burgundian countryside with Annie and Cécile clinging to each other in the back seat, Pel grasped the dashboard with one hand while holding the car's telephone in the other. He rapped out orders regardless of being tossed about under his seat belt.

'I want a dozen men from Uniformed Branch. Tell Turgot where to send his men: every exit from the château's grounds must be covered, including cart tracks, plus more men inside the perimeter. The place must be sealed off, and tell him I want him personally on the scene immediately. Get the local gendarmes out, spaced around the small roads leading to the château. No one is to get within shouting distance of this little caper without a specific okay from me or the Chief. When the press turn up, and they will when they see all the activity at headquarters, they must be stopped at the gates. Tell Bardolle and Debray to close them and keep them closed from the moment we're inside. The press are to elect a representative and you are to allow that man, and only that one man, through. When the nationals arrive with the TV crews they are to be kept outside. Got that?'

As the huge main gates clanged shut behind his team, Pel left Annie in the car with Cécile while he gave his instructions. De Troq', knowing the château better than the rest of them, disappeared inside with Brochard, their guns drawn, to position themselves not far from where Lucien and Pradier were holding their hostages. Aimedieu, Pujol, Rigal, Misset and Cherif were sent round the sides and back to cover the rest of the building. Pel went to join Darcy. In the afternoon sunlight the château with its tall towers and glittering varnished roof looked magnificent and peaceful.

'What do we do now, Patron?'

'Wait,' Pel said. 'I've got the whole team out here, plus a few others. I've sent someone to pick up Lucien's wife and his father, they should be here soon. The Chief is on his way as soon as Paris has been satisfactorily informed. We mustn't rush things, I want to give the experts time to get here.'

'You don't think Lucien'll get nervous?'

'Yes, eventually. It'll be then that he'll send out a second message, or an ultimatum. Until that moment, we do nothing but wait. In the mean time, do we know where the party of schoolchildren are from?'

Darcy shook his head. 'Not yet, Patron, but they won't be expected back yet. No doubt a minibus'll arrive to collect them soon. The driver'll tell us where they're from.'

'The minibus must be allowed to come through to the outside of the gates. Bardolle is to let the driver through, on foot. Let everyone know.'

An hour crawled by. In the cars parked in the shade of the trees around the château the policemen smoked their cigarettes and bit their fingernails. Nothing happened. The Chief arrived and joined Pel and Darcy. 'Recherche Assistance Intervention Dissuasion', he said, 'are on their way. Since they were formed in 1985 after the Paris bombs they haven't failed. Let's hope they'll perform as well this time. They're well trained enough, our band of Superflics – I just hope they realise they're dealing with children hostages this time, not adults. They're an aggressive lot and I don't want this to be any more traumatic for those kids than it has to be, I made the point forcefully. They'll be here shortly so we'll have to wait and see what happens. Their commanding officer, Colonel Narbonne, gave strict instructions that we should do nothing but survey.'

'That's precisely what we are doing. What about the wife and the father?'

The Chief sighed. 'The wife had a *crise de nerfs*; her nerves were already on edge because her husband was back in town but hadn't come home and now she's under sedation. Her doctor informed me that there's little point in asking for her co-operation before tomorrow morning.' He sighed again. 'The father virtually refused to come. He said his son has always been headstrong and capricious, nothing he says will make any difference, it never has. He'll come if he really has to, but he doesn't see the point and doesn't want to. I told him not to go anywhere but to sit by the phone just in case – useless bloke, as weak as water. I expect he's sipping camomile tisane prepared with loving care by the cleaner. What a set-up.'

More than twenty-four police officers, some in cars, some hidden in the grounds, silently watched the sun change position in the sky and begin its dignified descent towards the horizon, gently lengthening the shadows and turning the roof a brilliant gold. De Troq' and Brochard patiently waited in the dark corridor, tensely holding their guns to their chests, outside the locked room where Lucien, Pradier and the hostages were. Still nothing, except that quite a few of them had run out of cigarettes. Pel, surprisingly, hadn't yet and was still showing a remarkable amount of patience.

Suddenly the glazed door to the balcony above them slammed open, a gun appeared and was fired twice above their heads to attract attention, then a neat young woman was pushed out into view. She regained her balance and stepped carefully to the balustrade. 'I am Mademoiselle Delmas, Instructrice at the Maternelle de l'Ecole de Longvic. I am responsible for the ten children being held inside this château. I am their teacher. They are hungry and frightened . . .' She paused. 'So am I.' She appeared to swallow hard, briefly looked over her shoulder from where she had come then continued. 'Please reassure us. Please send something for the children to eat and drink. Please indicate that you have heard me and that you will do as I have asked.'

Pel reached in through the car window for the loudspeaker. 'We have heard what you have said and will comply with your request as soon as possible. In the mean time can you give me any further information on the children? It's nearly four thirty – their parents must be informed.'

Before she had time to reply a further shot was fired and they understood she'd been told to get back inside.

'Well, at least we know now where the kids come from. Get someone over there to gather up the parents and bring them here.'

The car phone buzzed. 'The driver of the minibus has arrived to collect the children. He says they're from –'

Pel cut the message short. 'Send Debray back to the school

164

with the driver in his bus to explain and pick up the parents – make sure you get them all. A uniformed officer is to replace Debray on the gates. Turgot will arrange a police escort to and from the school. Get them back here as fast as possible but without any panic.' It was easier said than done, he knew. In the mean time a reception committee had to be established for them. Annie was replaced by a man in uniform to guard Cécile, and she and Didier Darras were told to get over to the gates and be ready to receive the parents when they arrived. Coffee and cognac was ordered for them, while cakes and orange juice were due to arrive for the children inside.

The minutes ticked by in silence. After the moment of high activity, the château and its grounds lapsed back into the peaceful fading afternoon sun. Pel screwed up his final finished pack of cigarettes and threw it into the car. He stared up at the high stone walls of the castle: he had a feeling in his guts about this one and for once it wasn't his suspected ulcer, it was worse, far worse.

The food and drink arrived, collected from the gate and transported to the parked police cars on large plastic trays. Annie claimed her part for the parents now due to arrive at any minute, at the same time thrusting a new *cartouche* of two hundred cigarettes into Darcy's hands along with a Fingerprints report she'd forgotten in the chaos, then she galloped away.

Pel read the report Darcy offered him. 'At last I know for certain who the damn girl is, not that it makes any difference now,' he said. 'Distribute the cigarettes as necessary, I don't want any jumpy policemen under my command.' Darcy handed his boss the first couple of packets and hurried off to greet the hysterical parents who were now spilling through the main gates.

The parents rapidly understood the situation and the need for calm; to Pel's surprise they listened to explanations and instructions given, then shut up. When Darcy returned everything had gone quiet again.

'Where the bloody hell are the men from RAID?' The Chief had finally lost his patience. 'We can't do nothing for ever.'

Pel reached for the loudspeaker. 'I'm going to let them have their grub – if nothing else, it will appear that we are

165

co-operating, and I can't think cakes and orange juice are going to change much except stop the kids bleating for tea.'

As he lifted the machine to his mouth, the main gates burst open to let five white Renault Espaces sweep in at full speed and come to a shrieking halt, chucking up grit and dust within a few feet of Pel and the Chief. A tall man leapt from the first vehicle. 'Put that down! There is to be no communication until I say so.'

RAID had arrived. Pel scowled at them, but lowered the loudspeaker. The commanding officer, towering over Pel, with a face that looked as if it had been chiselled from granite, introduced himself and asked for information.

He got it, brief and precise, Pel again emphasising that there were children being held as hostages.

'I'm aware of that,' Colonel Narbonne snapped. 'What were you doing when I arrived?'

'About to tell them tea is served.'

'Two minutes to get my men into position and we'll carry on. I'll give the signal.' He turned swiftly and went back to his vehicles in the settling dust. The first three emptied their black-hooded members of RAID on to the gravel driveway. Pel strained to hear the orders being given but it was impossible. Already he was wishing he hadn't asked for their help. From the look on the Chief's face he was thinking the same thing. Clothed in black from head to foot, Narbonne's men dispersed as told, disappearing in all directions. Within a matter of seconds five were seen silently padding across the roof; they crouched down barely visible just above the balcony where the schoolteacher had made her appearance.

'Now you see them, now you don't,' Pel said bitterly. 'Do you think the buggers can fly? They were up there mighty quick.'

Before the Chief had time to answer, the Colonel was back. 'Training, Chief Inspector, training,' he said coolly. 'My men are the élite.' He was carrying his own loudspeaker. 'Right,' he announced, 'tea-time.

'Your refreshments have arrived.' His voice carried clearly across the open space between them and the château. 'I shall be sending a man up with them. Be ready to open the door.'

The door to the balcony crashed open and Mademoiselle

166

Delmas was pushed out. She stumbled to the edge and called down. 'Please don't send anyone up.' She was obviously close to tears, which was hardly surprising. 'Don't send anyone up,' she repeated. 'If an approach is made to any of the doors of this room, they will shoot a child.' A cry was heard from where Annie was restraining the parents. Darcy looked briefly towards her; things were now only just under control in that corner of the grounds. The young woman on the balcony continued. 'I shall lower a container, you are to half fill it, so it can be easily seen that it contains nothing but food and drink, and I'll pull it up. Please,' she begged, 'do as I ask.'

The Colonel nodded to Darcy and one of his men, who made their way forward towards a log basket that was slowly coming down the side of the château on the end of a number of knotted curtain cords. They carefully placed some food and drink in the bottom and watched it climb back up to the balcony. As it arrived they saw the Baron and the Baroness, their faces badly bruised and streaked with blood, step forward to help the schoolteacher haul the basket over the parapet. Within a few moments the process was repeated. When the last basket was loaded and gone from sight, the two men retreated to the shadows of the trees where the cars were parked.

The Colonel was waiting with his next question. 'Who knows the internal layout of this place?' he asked briskly.

'De Troquereau.'

'Get him here.'

Pel's mind was whirring, and while de Troq' arrived and explained as best he could, drawing a rough sketch for Colonel Narbonne, he slipped away to temporarily relieve the policeman guarding Cécile, but all she told him was that she'd been on a guided tour of the castle when she was little and everyone knew of the secret passages, although their whereabouts were largely rumour. Pel could have read that in the guidebook.

As he was returning, the Baron appeared on the balcony. He no longer stooped, and in spite of his wounded face Pel was sure he could see new life in the old boy.

'I have an announcement to make,' he bellowed, 'on behalf of the bastards behind me. Are you listening?'

'We hear you,' the Colonel confirmed.

167

'Firstly, I am to tell you that any negotiations will be made through Chief Inspector Pel. They say, and I quote, they do not want to deal with a group of ponces leaping about like ballet dancers in black leotards with stockings over their heads.' Darcy smothered a smile; Colonel Narbonne shot a furious glance in Pel's direction. 'I must see Chief Inspector Pel before I continue,' the Baron de Charnet shouted.

Pel looked at the Colonel, who signalled for him to move forward. As he stepped into the now fading sunlight, the Baron continued. 'Ah, Pel, pleased to see you again. Now listen, they want someone called the Poltergeist. Do you know him?'

Pel shouted that he did.

'They want him, then they want one of those minibus things to take them under police escort to the airport where a plane is to be waiting with a crew and full tanks. If at any point on their journey to the plane they are hindered they will immediately start the executions. Have you got that?'

Pel indicated that he'd heard and understood, as had every-one else as far as the gates and beyond. The Baron's booming voice carried incredibly well in the otherwise silent twilight. Gasps of horror could be heard from the group of parents but it soon went quiet again as they waited for the next instalment.

'For the moment, sleeping bags must be sent up for the children. Mademoiselle Delmas is doing a marvellous job, they think it's a game, but once night falls even they will realise the game is over and start asking to go home. The strain is incredible, so if we can get them to sleep it would help. Pel,' he bellowed, 'for Christ's sake get cracking.'

Pel withdrew to the shadows to be greeted coldly by Colonel Narbonne. 'The Poltergeist,' he said, 'do you know where he is?'

'No.'

'I thought not – the whole of France is after him. But at least it gives us time to get organised. They're expecting to spend the night here, so we've got until dawn at least. Good.' He strode smartly back to his men and his vehicles to make plans.

'He might think it's good,' Pel growled. 'I think it's bloody awful.' He looked at Darcy. 'Ideas?'

'A call from the heart on the television for the Poltergeist to give himself up?' Darcy suggested lamely. 'I don't suppose he will for a minute even if we had found his granddaughter, which we haven't.'

To Darcy's surprise Pel didn't bite his head off. He withdrew a cigarette and placed it carefully between his lips; his lighter flared briefly then extinguished. Pel removed the unlit cigarette and threw it on the ground. 'Get the press representative over here', he said. 'I'll be back in a minute.'

Pel strolled towards the car where Cécile was seated and extricated the policeman guarding her. He slid in beside her.

'How are things, young Cécile? Going according to plan? Or perhaps you didn't expect this little hiccup.'

She stared at him.

'It's over, your little pantomime. Your grandfather escaped from Vlaxi's house, the place isn't haunted by the Poltergeist after all and he's on the run again, so you no longer need me to protect him.' Cécile was open-mouthed but speechless. 'That's what you've been doing, isn't it? First leading me to the men who sent him down to get them put away, so he was no longer in any danger after a successful appeal, then when they did get him, to help me find him and save his life. They want him pretty badly, don't they, my dear – apart from the hard cash he could supply them with, he knows enough about them to stop their little import business of drugs wrapped up in illegal immigrants and put them away forever. I'll say this for you, you've been pretty quick off the mark and very smart – but not smart enough. Cécile, or should I say Laura Lebon, cat burglar of the very rich to finance the lawyer for your grandfather, your time is up.'

Cécile looked astonished for a moment, then removed the long wig of auburn tresses, revealing her own spiky blonde hair. 'How did you know?'

'My informant, and it became quite obvious someone was feeding me information, had to be Laura Lebon to know where the Poltergeist had been hiding and what Lucien was up to, but she couldn't know what the police were planning or how to get them on the move unless she had an associate at headquarters. There was only one possibility and that was Misset, but as

169

I'd deliberately kept him hidden in Records until recently he would've had to have been very clever to feed Laura all the correct information.'

'And that man hasn't got a – '

'Yes,' Pel interrupted, 'I've already heard your opinion as to what he hasn't got in his head, so there had to be an alternative. There was only one, young Cécile, the criminologist who arrived every morning on her motor bike, a brand new trail bike worth 30,000 francs. That's one hell of a lot of motor bike for a student. Laura Lebon had left some good bike tracks through the vineyard to Grandfather's hideout. It took me a couple of minutes to work it out,' he said modestly, 'but I got there in the end.'

'I even changed the colour of my eyes, my height, my shape, everything.'

'And my wife runs a beauty salon. She had some very interesting things to say on the subject of coloured contact lenses, heels of shoes, aesthetic padding, I believe it's called, and so on. In fact, she told me anything's possible.'

'That's what gave me away?'

'There were too many coincidences too, it made me feel uneasy.'

'You don't believe in coincidences, do you?'

'Not in crime fighting,' Pel agreed. 'There's nearly always a reason.'

'There was one though.'

'The fat woman conveniently calling about her cat's being poisoned – and you deliberately put that through to me to draw my attention to Clavell.'

'That and the fact she saw something she wanted to tell you about. I still don't know what it was,' she admitted.

'Your grandfather arriving at the end of Lucien's gun,' Pel told her. 'She saw her son in the square brandishing a firearm and when he couldn't be found she threatened to tell us.'

'She was about as loyal as Lucien,' Cécile said bitterly. 'He killed Vlaxi.'

'Like mother, like son. How long had you been seeing him?' Pel asked.

'Long enough to know he was too hot for me to handle alone.

170

He boasted that Vlaxi was his partner – in fact, at first I thought he was Vlaxi. That's why I became his girl – I wanted him for sending my grandfather down. They were supposed to be friends.'

'I'm sure Vlaxi knew your grandfather would only stay behind bars as long as was convenient. I wouldn't be surprised if Vlaxi set the wheels in motion for his escape as soon as the prison door clanged shut. Those two went back a long way, as your planted photo proved.'

'It took that clot Misset long enough to find it.'

'It must have been a nasty surprise to find your grandfather gone from his hideout.'

'I went to reassure him, I knew he was worried about me. Then it was my turn to be worried when I found the door broken in and him gone.'

'Worried enough to send the address to Clouet, to get me galloping down there, and worried enough to go back through the vineyards on your wretched bike and scratch VLAXI in the soot, leaving a number of wonderfully clear fingerprints in your panic. That's what finally gave you away – they matched with the fingerprints I had taken from you at the Hôtel de Police.'

'Well, it's all academic now', she said, accepting the cigarette Pel offered and drawing on it deeply. 'Pradier, the errand boy, did lead you to Lucien in the end, as I'd hoped – even I didn't know where he was recently – but as a result poor Nosjean's in hospital and ten children are in danger, not to mention the other people inside.'

'You'd have been a lot more help if you'd come forward in the beginning and simply told me all.'

'And have you use me to recapture my grandfather? He's had two years behind bars – '

Pel interrupted; he had more important things on his mind. 'Right now I've got ten kids in grave danger and I need your help in freeing them. Lucien's demanding your grandfather, he wants to take him with them. Do you have any idea where he is?'

The girl shook her head.

'Would you be prepared to make an appearance on a news flash asking him to give himself up?'

'They'll kill him.'

171

'They could have when they had him under lock and key in Clavell. I don't think they're ready for that. I think they still want the loot he has hidden, and he hasn't told them where yet.' Pel wasn't at all sure he believed what he was saying but it was his only chance. From the expression on Cécile's face he knew she didn't believe him either.

'Yes, I'll do it, but . . .'

'Don't worry – when he's handed over, if he turns up, we'll be right behind him. You've seen the men from RAID; they know what they're doing, they're specifically trained for this sort of situation. And if necessary,' he added, 'I'll go with him myself.'

Sarrazin was waiting with Darcy when Pel finally returned some minutes later, but he went straight over to Colonel Narbonne. 'I want to try a television appeal for the Poltergeist to come forward. Do I have your permission, or shall I do it without?'

The Colonel glared at him. 'You have my permission as long as you and your men don't go anywhere near the château.'

'Agreed,' Pel said, 'but when you do want to go in, let me know. I may be able to help.'

'May I ask how?'

'I might just be able to lay my hands on someone with a knowledge of the inside of the château, a good knowledge. Someone who can lead them unseen and unheard right into the room.'

Narbonne grabbed Pel by the arm. 'Who? Where is he?'

'After the news flash.'

Narbonne half closed his eyes and studied the small Chief Inspector with suspicion. 'Bribery?'

'No,' Pel said, 'brains and good police work.'

The Colonel nearly managed to crack his face into half a smile. 'You're no fool, are you?' he said. 'Affirmative. I'll wait – we've got until dawn, after all.'

When Pel arrived back at his car he spoke briefly to Darcy and Sarrazin. The journalist's face lit up at the prospect of a scoop, then fell just as rapidly. 'By the way, we just called my colleague at the hospital,' he said. 'I'm afraid it's not looking good for Nosjean. He's alive, but it's touch and go.'

172

'Thanks for letting us know. Is Madame Nosjean, Mijo, there?'

'My colleague's holding her hand and feeding her courage from his hip flask.'

Cécile emerged from the car to be escorted through the trees to the television lorry that had been allowed through the gates. Sarrazin led her up the steps and gave her instructions. On Pel's orders the men from TF1 vacated their lorry except for the technicians needed to make the broadcast. They planned a recorded interview to be broadcast first on their channel and immediately afterwards on all the other channels. The interview was to be between Sarrazin and Laura Lebon, the granddaughter of the Poltergeist, in the presence of Pel. At first Cécile was too tense to make a useful or comprehensible statement but finally they got it right and came out into the coolness of the evening to breathe a moment before the interview was finally put on the air. As Pel dragged on his cigarette as if it would save the day he heard a quiet voice he recognised.

'Chief Inspector Pel, that won't be necessary,' it said. 'Tell them not to broadcast. I'm already here.'

Pel turned to see the Poltergeist half hidden in the shadows.

He looked about him quickly, glad no one was paying him any attention for once, before joining him. 'How the hell . . .'

The Poltergeist half smiled. 'I've been here ever since the story broke. I'd been following Lucien just so I'd know what he was up to, and so he wouldn't find me, ever since I got out of the smelly cellar they locked me in. Pel,' he said, 'I said I'd give myself up if you found my granddaughter safe and sound, so here I am.'

Pel was amazed: it was the first time in his long career a criminal had kept his word. 'But I'm not just here because of that,' the Poltergeist continued in a low voice. 'I'm here because I know the château like the back of my hand. Old de Charnet was pretty good at hiding my Resistance refugees during the war. The place is riddled with secret passages. Lucien should be behind bars and I'll do what it takes to put him there.'

Pel studied the man carefully. 'Your granddaughter knows

about the secret passages too; she's been pretty busy since you've been in prison. The château was one of the places she got into to whip a few priceless possessions to pay for your appeal.'

'The little minx!' The Poltergeist looked suitably shocked but there was pride and amusement in his voice. 'Point is,' he said, 'how do we use our knowledge?'

The broadcast was cancelled but Sarrazin was allowed the pleasure of announcing the latest on the situation to the millions of evening viewers. He did a straight interview with Pel and it came over on the television screens as very calm and professional.

Pel then went to talk to the parents, who were wilting in the background. They were astonishingly calm. Only one father seemed to be out of control and Annie soon got him behind a large tot of brandy and sitting in a nearby car to cool off. Pel explained the situation, that bedding had been sent up together with more food and drink. Personal cuddly toys and messages had also gone up in a final basket at the suggestion of one of the mothers. Seeing the teddy bears and fluffy rabbits make their ascent to the parapet and the hands of the schoolteacher made the policemen watching want to weep: the kids up there were no more than babies. Christ, Pel thought, we've got to get this right. Some of the parents were near breaking point but holding on bravely and listening tensely to every useless piece of information that was given them, which wasn't much and wasn't often.

It was past midnight as food arrived for them and the waiting police. The parents fell on it as if they were starved but Pel suspected it was simply the relief at having something to do. The men on duty attempted to eat, knowing it was going to be a long night, but after the first bite abandoned the attempt. They'd lost their appetites.

Pel's men were called in and replaced by Narbonne's men, and while Pel watched them arrive for a conference beyond the rapidly set up spotlights he saw the strain in every face. Even Misset looked exhausted, but didn't say a word.

The meeting between the Poltergeist and his granddaughter had discreetly taken place in a car well away from the crowds

174

and another meeting was taking place between Narbonne, the Chief and Pel. Narbonne was informed of the presence of the wanted man, of his, and his granddaughter's, knowledge of the château. His face momentarily brightened visibly.

'Thank God for that,' he said. 'I was preparing a dawn raid of smashing through the windows from the rooftop on the ends of ropes. Not a particularly pleasant way to wake up the youngsters in there.'

He lifted his hand-held radio and spoke in almost a whisper. 'All orders for "Batman" are cancelled,' he said. 'Stay in position and wait. Only move if they move. All units confirm.'

Two o'clock came and went; still the three men conferred. Although Pel's men had been relieved of duty, no one left. They stood under the trees and waited. The parents finally settled themselves against each other, not to sleep but to rest at least. Across France television sets were left on while their owners dozed on sofas waiting for news. There was none. No decisions had been taken, no orders given.

But they were close. Very close. And they were running out of time. Dawn was approaching; something had to happen then.

18

Standing watching the night losing its depth, Pel felt tired, tired and as grey as the coming dawn. During the final hours of darkness plans and preparations had been made; they believed every point had been covered, every footstep mapped out. It looked good. Good, if it all went according to their expectations, but if something went wrong – and miserably they knew damn well it was possible, for all Narbonne's confidence – it could end up as a horrible massacre. It didn't bear thinking about. Pel shook himself abruptly, like a dog leaving his basket; he stretched, ran his hands over his face and rubbed his eyes. His skin felt prickly with tiredness, his eyes full of sand and his mouth inevitably like the bottom of a dirty ashtray. He'd finally finished the last packet of cigarettes he'd been allotted and was almost grateful – he was sure his lungs were full of cinders. Narbonne was moving about silently to his right, checking and rechecking, the Poltergeist and his granddaughter were being briefed in a car by Darcy for the last time. Its doors stood open but he couldn't hear the voices. Behind him, all around him, his men were propped against the wheels of cars or tree trunks, dozing uncomfortably, shivering occasionally. Beyond the trees towards the entrance was the group of parents, huddled together in the minibus, supplied with blankets and sleeping at last now that exhaustion had won its battle with anxiety. In front of the main gates was the television lorry; beyond, various cars, press vans and a pile of people were strewn haphazardly like rag dolls as if someone had tossed them there. It was peaceful, silent. It was a nightmare.

The Chief stirred and rose as he approached. 'Time?' he asked. Pel nodded.

As a watery sun became visible on the horizon, tingeing the sky with pale streaks of pink, Narbonne gave his signal. Pel took a deep breath and moved out from under the trees. The Poltergeist walked beside him. They stopped in front of the balcony and looked up. One of Narbonne's men, still covered from head to foot in black, crouched alongside. As they came to a halt, he rose, brought his right arm back, his left foot off the ground, and threw a pebble the size of a ping pong ball into the air. It was accurate; they heard it clatter against the window pane beyond the balcony. He threw another, smaller this time, and another, until he was throwing nothing but a handful of gravel. Then he ran for cover, out of sight.

Pel looked round: by the gates nothing stirred. He knew various groups behind him were silently organising themselves and waiting their turn. Already there were twenty-three men in position. Dawn crept slowly into the sky.

The door to the balcony opened. Mademoiselle Delmas appeared, looking weary but wide awake.

They'd decided against loudspeakers so Pel cupped his hand round his mouth and shouted carefully to her, 'The children, are they all right?'

'They're still asleep.'

Pel breathed a sigh of relief. So far so good. 'The man they want,' he went on, 'the Poltergeist, he's here. Tell Lucien, please.'

She withdrew, to reappear a few moments later at gunpoint. Her hands were now tied behind her back as Pradier pushed her in front of him using her body as a shield. Pel didn't let his eyes wander to the five black silhouettes on the roof. He stared hard at Pradier. It was Lucien they wanted; he was the dangerous one, the one who would kill if necessary. He was also clever; he'd sent Pradier out in case it was a trap. Pradier wouldn't be attacked while Lucien was still inside with the youngsters. Even so Pradier advanced very little and Pel suspected he was no more than a vague shadow coming from under the eaves to the men on the roof. He stepped forward briefly, enough to see Pel and the Poltergeist, and withdrew again immediately.

At last, from somewhere beyond the balcony, they heard Lucien's voice. 'Okay, strip him and winch him up.'

Out of the corner of his eye Pel noticed movement to his left. Cécile was leading her group out round the side of the building to a cellar door.

He looked at the Poltergeist, who shrugged. 'He'd like to come by the inside staircase, clothed,' he shouted.

'You're joking, Pel,' Lucien's hard young voice shouted back. '*Demerdez-vous*, I want him winched up in his underpants. That way he won't be loaded down with guns, grenades, microphones or any other shit.'

'We'll need a moment to set up the winch. We'll also need one of you on the balcony to attach it.'

'No problem, it's the butler's turn.'

The second chance of getting them to the balustrade in clear view and vulnerable was gone. Lucien was careful and crafty; so far he hadn't shown himself once. There weren't going to get many more chances. It was looking painfully clear that they'd have to break into the room after all. Pel didn't want to; it was dangerous but looking more inevitable with every minute that ticked by.

The butler appeared, immaculate apart from his missing tie, received the weighted end of a rope thrown from the ground, passed it round the stonework and let it slip back to the ground.

With this Narbonne's man hoisted up the necessary equipment
to make the series of pulleys for winching a man up the side
of the château. With very few instructions, little time and no
noise, the butler busied himself with his task. Efficiently,
silently he worked alone, finally taking the end of a second
rope, tied to the first, and passing it through the pulleys. The
two ropes made their circuit and touched the ground with
both ends. The butler adjusted the contraption a last time and
withdrew. On the ground a harness was attached to the now
undressed Poltergeist, plus a further safety belt on the second
rope. Pel had to admire the man. He looked totally unperturbed
at being manhandled up the side of a small Burgundian castle
in nothing but his underpants. He even managed a lopsided
smile and a thumbs-up sign before the pulleys on the ground
started turning and the massive Bardolle hauled on the rope.
Not far away, Brochard, brought up on a farm and with
muscles to prove it, braced himself with a further man from
RAID gathering in the safety rope, just in case.

Cécile was also going up. She led her silent barefooted party
up the inside of the château. She carried no light although it
was still pitch black in the belly of the building, and the men
behind her carried only tiny matchbox-size torches. Getting in
had been easy. While all the entrances had been bolted, she'd
slipped through the same cellar window she'd used the night
she'd taken the Baron's antique guns. They'd already negotiated
the maze of cellars and the first flight of steps to the ground
floor, and were expecting to start up the main staircase. However, she bypassed it through the grand entrance hall, quietly
pushed open the tall doors to a drawing-room the size of a
municipal campsite and padded over to the fireplace. Five RAID
members, plus Darcy and de Troq', padded across the oak floor
behind her. Not a word was spoken. They'd gone over it a dozen
times; there was no need to speak. They might be overheard
– ancient buildings carried voices strangely, sometimes quite
clearly from room to room, whether by chance or design it
wasn't sure, but it was a risk no one wanted to take. She
moved a small tapestry-covered stool into the vast fireplace
and climbed on to it. Her fingers searched the side wall of the
inside of the chimney, causing lumps of soot to scatter into the

grate. She was sweating. It had to be there, she knew it was – of all the buildings her grandfather had spoken, this was the one that had fascinated her the most. She could have found her way round it blindfolded. She knew the ring-pull was there between the great stones, hidden in the loose sandy mortar, it had to be. Unless the present Baron had found the moving stone, hadn't understood and had cemented it up. Her upper lip was damp with perspiration. It had to be there.

It was. She slipped her finger through the ring and tugged sharply. On the other side of the wall a short rusty chain ending in a thick metal pin tightened and came out of its lock. She felt it give. As the metal pin fell away the balance of weight was no longer held rigid and with a gentle push she pivoted the moving stone on its axis. As her feet disappeared from sight the seven men behind her followed one by one through the side of the fireplace.

Inside the tiny chamber there was no light but they could hear Cécile already above them. Briefly their lamps were turned upwards before they too began climbing the twisting steep staircase. It was tiny and claustrophobic, built in the days when men were smaller. Slowly the men following Cécile twisted and turned and swept away the cobwebs that caught on their faces.

Pel saw the first rays of sunshine; a thin mist was curling in over the château grounds, giving everything a ghostly effect. He looked up towards the Poltergeist who was already over half-way through his journey. Bardolle's biceps were too good, he was lifting him too fast! He'd arrive too soon. Mother of God, isn't anyone keeping tabs on the time? It was all worked out to the second, why were they letting Bardolle haul on his ropes like an *abruti*? He didn't dare look at his watch, or say anything – it could give the game away. Lucien must be lurking somewhere, making sure they were doing what he wanted. The man beside Brochard had noticed a signal. He whispered urgently to Bardolle; it sounded like no more than an early morning breeze rustling the leaves on the trees. Bardolle stopped hauling, kicked the lock closed on the pulley and passed his forearm over his face and across his hair. Pel knew he wasn't tired, he was built like a carthorse and had just about the same strength and endurance, but it was a plausible play for time. When he took up his rope again the Poltergeist rose more slowly.

At the top of the tiny staircase, their hair matted with hundreds of years of cobwebs and dust, Cécile's party drew breath. They were faced with a T-junction. Cécile didn't hesitate before turning to the left and dropping on to her hands and knees. The men needed their lamps before following, crawling on all fours one behind the other. It was suffocating in the tunnel, they seemed to be breathing centuries-old stale air and dust, but still no one said a word. They passed by a small entrance to a room, its interior dimly lit by the dawn seeping through the two arrow-thin windows in the far wall. They caught a glimpse of some dust-covered furniture, although how it had got there was anybody's guess. Darcy, suffering now from housemaid's knee, suspected it was brought up in small pieces and constructed in the room. De Troq' directly behind him knew this to be so and also knew of a number of famous people throughout history who had spent some time hiding there. One duke had lived there for more than six months happily writing his memoirs, while the Revolution of 1789 was cooling off. He blinked hard, dismissed the past and crawled forward.

At last the tunnel opened out into a small chamber. Although there was still no room to stand, they stretched their legs out in front of them and sat for a moment. Cécile took one of the torches and shone the feeble beam on to the wall in front of her. There was the metal pin on its chain. She removed it and let it dangle gently against the wall. A very slight pressure allowed her to pivot another moving stone on its axis. A dim light crept round its side but they saw nothing; she'd allowed an opening of only a couple of centimetres.

What they heard however was what they'd expected.

Pel watched the Poltergeist reach the parapet and half climb, half scramble on to the balcony with the help of the butler. Then he disappeared.

180

This was the worst part.

Pel held his breath. So did the Chief. Surprisingly, so did Narbonne.

From their hiding place behind the fireplace they heard voices.

'At long last, we meet again.' It was Lucien. He was dangerously close.

Apparently the Poltergeist ignored him and was busy shaking hands with the Baron de Charnet and his wife.

'Good grief,' they heard the Baron say, 'it's young Blanc, after all these years! What on earth have you been up to all this time?'

It seemed incredible that in the face of possible death the Baron was as chatty and welcoming as he would have been serving aperitifs to the family at Christmas, but he and the Poltergeist had worked together, running an escape route for the Resistance through the château, and from what Darcy heard the reunion was a joyous one. He couldn't help admiring the old boy.

A sharp thud was heard as Lucien became bored with the pleasantries, his fist catching the Poltergeist's cheek and making him stagger.

'You don't look like the great criminal any more, standing there in your knickers. In fact you look the fool you really are.' Lucien again.

'Perhaps you're right.' The Poltergeist.

'I want you out on the balcony asking that shit Pel what's happening about the bus and the plane. I want it organised in the hour. Tell him.'

'May I ask for my clothes? I'm cold. If it was winter I could stand by the log fire.' The Baroness's eyes flickered; she looked briefly, searchingly, at the Poltergeist's face. The Baron didn't seem to be listening. But he took his wife's hand and shuffled towards the balcony window. They'd both understood the signal.

'No, you may not ask for your clothes.' Lucien laughed. 'Personally, I like the way you look.'

Cécile pushed open the moving stone to reveal the inside

of another enormous chimney. The fireplace was just a few feet below.

'I say, it looks like being a jolly fine day. Come and have a look, old chap.' The Baron was cuffed on the back of his head for his efforts, but it had brought Lucien across the room away from the fireplace. Pradier was slumped against the far wall wishing it was all over.

'Get out and give them the message.' Lucien pushed the Poltergeist forward.

He went out on to the balcony and called down. 'They want the bus and the aircraft within the hour.'

'The aircraft is ready and waiting,' Pel shouted back, 'and the bus is to be the children's school minibus. I'll have it brought forward now so they can see it.'

Two of Narbonne's men moved on to the ledge inside the chimney. The three remaining waited on the other side of the moving stone with Darcy and de Troq'.

The minibus was pushed forward into visibility and stopped beside Pel.

The Poltergeist disappeared from sight again.

From inside the chimney they could hear Lucien crowing from the other side of the room.

'See how easy it is, Pradier – they're doing everything I ask them. Look, down there. Look at Pel standing beside our transport. He doesn't look as if he's slept all night. I bet if I asked him he'd dance a jig for me.'

Pradier heaved himself to his feet and reluctantly went to look.

'I expect he would,' the Poltergeist said. 'He'd do anything to save these kids. You're a prize bastard.'

The green light!

Two RAID men dropped into the fireplace, took aim, fired.

From where Pel stood, his neck aching from staring upwards, he heard the two shots clearly. Two more shots followed. They weren't planned. What had gone wrong? Perspiration trickled down the back of his neck.

19

After the four shots they heard nothing. The noise had brought the parents to their feet suddenly wide awake, terrified their child had been murdered. The reporters rose and stared. Their cameras had been forgotten, but their brains strained to hear something more. The policemen leapt up, all eyes turned urgently towards the château. Everyone watched the balcony, waiting. Waiting for someone to say something. No one spoke. They didn't know the nightmare was over.

The Baroness quietly replaced the minute Gaulois pistol in the silver urn sitting on the mantelpiece. Now that her hands were untied she'd just wanted to be sure. As the other three men emerged from the chimney, closely followed by Darcy, de Troq' and Cécile, the children began stirring; the gunshots had woken them. They had to be removed as rapidly as possible before the traumatic sight of two dead men, each with a bullet straight through the centre of his head and another through the heart, imprinted itself in their young memories. Each adult scooped up a sleepy child and headed for the door before they could rub their eyes and see the collapsed bodies and the splashes of blood.

The whole operation had taken no more than half an hour. It was over before anyone had realised it had started.

The first child appeared in the arms of the Poltergeist two and a half minutes after the shots had been heard. Darcy and de Troq' followed, also carrying two diminutive shapes. They both gave the thumbs-up.

Now came the chaos.

The running parents, the squawking television men, the reporters – Holy Mother of God! The reports he was going to have to write! But Pel was past caring. He watched the children reunited with their parents. The tension and the worry, plus the sleepless night he'd endured, were making his eyes water. Good grief, someone might think he was being emotional!

Narbonne appeared in front of him. He took Pel's hand and shook it briskly. 'I think congratulations are in order. We did it.'

The Hôtel de Police was full of congratulations but Pel was having none of it. The children were all safe, Lucien and Pradier were dead, the Baron, Baroness and their butler had been discharged from hospital with minor cuts and bruises. The young exhausted schoolteacher was finally resting. It had already been announced that she would receive the Médaille de Mérite et de Courage. The Vice Squad on the coast were smiling and clearing up the Lucien connection to immigrant and drug trafficking. The Poltergeist was again behind bars. But, and this was making Pel's ulcer play up, his granddaughter had disappeared in a puff of smoke – plus Lucien's father had tried to commit suicide and was at that moment having his stomach pumped out. And Nosjean was still fighting for his life.

'Damn, blast and hellfire!' He hadn't even got a cigarette. 'Darcy, come with me!'

Darcy joined his boss as he strode towards the staircase. He didn't stop until he was neatly planted behind a large cold beer, leaning against the bar across the road. He was puffing aggressively on a newly purchased cigarette. Darcy couldn't help smiling; he looked like an old-fashioned steam engine.

'Bloody girl!' Pel exploded. 'How the hell did she slip away?'

'She'll be back,' Darcy reassured him, 'and at least you've still got the Poltergeist. What I can't understand is why he didn't disappear too.'

'Because he promised to give himself up once his granddaughter was safe.'

'And he kept his word?'

Pel nodded. 'He made no attempt to remove himself from my custody, and let's face it, in the happy confusion following the release of the kids he could easily have hidden up a tree or something.'

'Incredible.'

Pel took a well-deserved swig at his beer, draining his glass and beckoning for another. It was only half-past ten but he'd been on his feet since the day before and it felt like decades. The sun had burnt off the morning mist and was busy scorching the geraniums that had appeared in all the window boxes and along the terraces at the beginning of June. Pel sighed. Yesterday hadn't finished yet.

'What's the news on Lucien's suicidal father? Is he ready to interview yet?' he asked.

'Not quite, the hospital told us to leave him until this afternoon. It's not surprising that he couldn't take any more. His life is in ruins – mind you, it didn't look too hot before. However, permission has finally been given for his wife's funeral, and his one and only son will soon be going the same way. He has no grandchildren. I guess he just didn't want to go on. In the note that was found he said he couldn't tolerate the disgrace of the family.'

'Silly sod.'

'Silly sod is right,' Darcy agreed, 'because for the first time in ten years he was free. No ghastly wife, no foul son breathing down his neck, and he still has his lady friend.'

'And his guilt,' Pel said.

'His son's criminal career wasn't entirely his fault, although I agree he could've been less weak, but I don't think he had a clue what was going on.'

'No,' Pel sighed, 'but I'm still going to have to arrest him for the murder of his wife.'

'Him?'

'That's the bit I got wrong, Darcy. Tell me, how did he try and commit suicide? Shooting himself, hanging himself, slashing his wrists?'

'No, poison.'

'The same poison that killed a couple of cats and finally did for his wife. I'd like to bet Doc Minet will find traces of cyanide in what they pumped out of his stomach as they did at the second autopsy carried out on his wife.'

185

'How the hell –'

'It was the cats dying – seemed strange to poison cats in a small village. But it was possible, they could have been worrying the poultry of the neighbours, or scratched a child, you know the sort of thing. But after exhaustive questioning of the inhabitants of Clavell, no one had complained about the cats, although there were quite a few of them – everyone said that while it wasn't up to them to feed them they really didn't give a damn. Usual neighbourly attitude. There was only one person who fed them, Madame Lucien, the fat woman, and she wouldn't poison her cats knowingly. So it had to be unknowingly. I sent Aimedieu back to dig one up. It died of cyanide poisoning.'

'But why poison the cats?'

'That wasn't the aim,' Pel explained. 'The aim was to poison the fat woman. I thought it was her son because she'd seen him brandishing a gun in the square of Clavell, but in fact he didn't know, he was away at the time, so she only left an unpleasant message with his secretary. If you remember, when she died, amongst the ton of debris discovered in her stomach, Minet was surprised to discover a quantity of cat cookies. The woman's own doctor explained that her husband, so fed up with her obesity and constant eating, often hid everything edible in the house or refused to do the shopping for days. But her eating was an illness and he'd even seen her rifling the dustbin under the sink in an attempt to find something to stuff into her mouth. Her doctor wasn't in the least bit surprised to find she'd taken to eating with the cats. Lucien junior denied emphatically that he'd killed her, and when I thought about it afterwards it would have been unlikely he'd have known about her eating cat-food. Only her husband could have known that. When he discovered we'd dug up a cat no doubt he raced to the dustbin to find the sack of cyanide-laced cat-food gone too. It was then he realised we'd be back to arrest him eventually and decided on suicide. He managed to kill a couple of cats, but his wife was just sick. I found a box of rat poison in the garage when I went to Clavell with Judge Casteou to visit Vlaxi's house. We took a sample for analysis. The lab has now explained that it was old and the cyanide content had deteriorated; she could have consumed

300 milligrams, which would normally be a lethal dose, and not necessarily have died, particularly if she consumed a lot of liquid, and let's face it she consumed a lot of everything. I don't think her husband knew how much was necessary and she was taking in far too little to kill her, but over the space of a week or so the accumulated amount made her very ill, the large quantities of Valium she took every evening made her very dopey, and when she got up that night to be sick she stumbled and fell down the stairs, breaking her neck. It's my guess her husband was in the house at the time waiting for the inevitable to happen. His car was seen leaving around midnight, so he might even have pushed her, but he certainly left her dead or dying.'

'He said he was with the daily woman.'

'So they both lied – what's new about that? Unfortunately we don't know what time he arrived at her flat; he was always very discreet and no one noticed him. The point is, we now have good evidence that he attempted to murder his wife. I don't think it'll take much to make a weak man like him confess. He knew he'd been discovered the moment the cat-food was taken away and the funeral postponed for a second autopsy to be carried out.'

Pel had been right. With very little persuasion Lucien's father confessed everything, denying however all the time that he even gently pushed his wife down the stairs. He maintained throughout all the questioning that he had spent that evening and night with his mistress. His mistress naturally agreed and didn't waver from her story. Finally the neighbour had to admit she wasn't a hundred per cent sure she'd seen his car leave the village that night – it could have been someone else. Although it seemed unlikely. It looked as if the prosecuting counsel would have to accept 'not guilty' for murder and substitute the lesser charge of 'administering poison with the intent of injuring'. It was highly possible Lucien's father would walk out of the court into the arms of his ever faithful and patient mistress with only a suspended sentence and a large dose of stomach-ache after his feeble suicide attempt.

187

Darcy had been wrong. The Poltergeist's granddaughter didn't turn up again, but he didn't care. With his arm round the lovely Kate he was busy house-hunting and planning their future.

Nosjean remained in a coma for nearly a week and it was only when his wife, Mijo, announced to his silent face that she was pregnant that he finally groaned and cautiously opened his eyes.

The summer roared into the nineties all over France, schools closed, beaches opened, the holidays started. Even Pel treated himself and his wife to a long weekend in the Tarn, invited by Kate to her run-down château which was now being renovated by her parents, old friends of the Pels. It was a splendid weekend with plenty of good food and excellent wine. Darcy didn't talk shop once and when it was too hot to move the three couples sat happily in the shade while Kate's two boys galloped round the yard kicking up clouds of dust.

However, the morning of their departure, at the long table on the terrace, Darcy silently handed Pel a newspaper and waited for the fireworks.

Having woken to the golden early morning sunlight streaming through their half-open shutters, Darcy had made soft and glorious love to Kate before switching on the radio to find some romantic background music ideal for rolling over and doing it again. Instead he'd heard the news. Within moments he was dressed and heading for the car. Kate understood his sudden departure when he returned half an hour later with the newspaper.

They were going to have to spoil Pel's weekend peace. At breakfast everyone watched Pel; he was the only one who hadn't been informed.

'Yesterday evening,' he read, 'at a summer soirée of magic organised by a young social worker and her team of prison visitors, a band of seven magicians and clowns arrived at Fresnes prison. The seven, under very strict security, left two hours later having entertained 153 men in detention. Unfortunately, it was discovered at lights out that the famous Poltergeist was missing from his cell. It is believed he must have escaped with the entertainers. A spokesman for the prison said, 'We can't believe it. They and their equipment were thoroughly searched, twice.'

188

Pel didn't finish reading the article. He removed his spectacles from the scowl on his face and placed the newspaper on the table. 'They've done it again,' he said, startling everyone by letting a crooked smile emerge from the scowl. 'They've damn well done it again. That girl's got him out.' He sighed, checking the smile and salvaging the scowl. 'Life's going to be hell when we get back. Holy Mother of God, life's going to be hell.'